MIMICO

PRAISE FOR JEROME DOOLITTLE AND HIS LATEST TOM BETHANY MYSTERY, HEAD LOCK

"Doolittle's rich imagination and offbeat sense of humor, neatly blending wit and raunch, give this story considerable energy."

—*Publishers Weekly*

"Jerome Doolittle's taut writing is wired with explosive charges. . . . I look forward to a long and happy acquaintance with Tom Bethany."

—*Boston Globe*

"Doolittle fearlessly tramples on some risky ground. . . . You'll be cheering in the aisles. . . ."

—*West Coast Review of Books*

"Bethany makes a great hero. Another strong entry in an excellent, underappreciated series."

—*Booklist*

"Tom Bethany is the funniest thing to come down the Massachusetts Turnpike since Spenser."

—*Carl Hiaasen*

D0824264

PRAISE FOR JEROME DOOLITTLE'S PREVIOUS TOM BETHANY MYSTERIES

BEAR HUG

"Riveting—as full of tension as Christmas Eve shopping at Toys 'R' Us."
—*Washington Post Book World*

"A dandy finish, but the real pleasure is in savoring Doolittle's anger, at the whole S&L mess and all it symbolizes for him."
—*Los Angeles Times Book Review*

"*Bear Hug* is an exciting, tense tale, and Doolittle uses his flair for dialogue to let his supporting players paint pithy self-portraits. . . . It'll be a genuine pleasure to see him go to the mat again."
—*Orange County Register*

". . . Superb hard-boiled fare in every sense."
—*Booklist*

STRANGLE HOLD

"Jerome Doolittle goes for the gold in *Strangle Hold,* which wins in the . . . Tough Guy/Rough Justice Event. . . . The writing is hard-edged, sure and crackling. . . . [A] masterpiece."
—*Trenton Times*

Books by Jerome Doolittle

Body Scissors
Strangle Hold
Bear Hug
Head Lock

Published by POCKET BOOKS

JEROME DOOLITTLE

HEAD LOCK

A TOM BETHANY MYSTERY

POCKET BOOKS

New York   London   Toronto   Sydney   Tokyo   Singapore

This book is a work of fiction. Names, characters, places and
incidents are products of the author's imagination or are used
fictitiously. Any resemblance to actual events or locales or persons,
living or dead, is entirely coincidental.

POCKET BOOKS, a division of Simon & Schuster Inc.
1230 Avenue of the Americas, New York, NY 10020

Copyright © 1993 by Jerome Doolittle

ISBN: 0-671-74570-0

First Pocket Books paperback printing August 1994

10 9 8 7 6 5 4 3 2 1

POCKET and colophon are registered trademarks of
Simon & Schuster Inc.

Cover art by Dennis Ziemienski

Printed in the U.S.A.

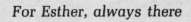

For Esther, always there

1

THAT PARTICULAR SPRING DAY, FOOLING AROUND in the library, I was interested in why good intentions so often wind up making things even worse than they were before. Consequently I was taking notes on a great reform called the Federal Election Campaign Act of 1971, which gave us political action committees. Before the act, it had been easy but illegal to buy members of Congress. After the great reform, it became legal and even easier.

I was working my way through the language of the bill and not, to tell the truth, very interested. It was too nice a day to be in Harvard's Widener Library.

How about my high school idol, Henry Wittenberg? What would the greatest amateur wrestler of all time be doing on a day like this? Henry Wittenberg would be doing isometric exercises, just as I used to do on spring days like this, bored like this, in the back row of high school classrooms.

So I locked my hands behind my head, filled my lungs, and pushed my head backward against the hands with increasing force for four seconds and with maximum force for six more seconds. At this point in the process my old physics teacher, Mr. Xavier Prum, out of Luxembourg by way of Hitler, looked up from his demonstrations one day and said, "Mr. Bethany, would you please be so good as to share with the class why your face is so round and red like a cherry?" Since it turned out I didn't have a clue, he used the occasion to explain certain principles of hydraulics to the group.

But now nobody else in the reference library seemed to care that my face was getting round and red like a cherry, so I took hold of the sides of my chair and inhaled to get ready for number two in Wittenberg's daily routine of isometrics for the busy office worker. Just then somebody squeaked.

One of the many dumb things about schools is that a lot of the time they have cork floors, like the one in the reference room of Widener. Cork floors are supposed to be silent, but they haven't worked out any better than the Federal Election Campaign Act. Somebody's rubber soles were squeaking my way, like sneakers on a gym floor. Mostly, we readers in Widener are too polite to look up when this happens. We stay hunched over the heavy oak tables, pretending we don't hear anything. We don't want to embarrass the squeaker. Next time, the squeaker may be us.

But I looked up once the noise was past me, and took off my reading glasses so I could rest my eyes by letting them roam around the room. The light from the high windows was slanting down steeply now, near noon. It disappeared into the brown cork floor and the quiet ranks of books bound in maroon and dark blue and black, leaving the enormous room somber no matter what was going on outside with the sun.

The other communicants, sitting still at the rows of refectory tables, mostly wore grays and browns and muted blues, as if it were still winter. There was only one patch of in-your-eye springtime color in that room, and I was it. I wore a sweater of bright yellow, the yellow of daffodils and forsythia. It was the type of loose sweater that Arnold Palmer wears in the ads, with billowing sleeves that almost hide the cuffs—the type of light sweater you wear in spring or on cool summer evenings. The sweater had been a good idea when I was walking through Harvard Yard to the library a couple of hours earlier. But now the blue of the sky through the windows made it look as if shirt-sleeve weather had come at last. Perfect weather for a slow stroll down to The Tasty for lunch.

The sun outside was as warm as it had looked from Widener's windows, warm enough so that I decided to walk over to the Harvard Union and buy a *Globe* at the student shop on the first floor. I took my paper over to the semicircular stone bench inside the John White Hallowell gate and skimmed through the pages quickly, paying just enough attention to be sure there was nothing worth clipping inside it. There wasn't. The economy was still in free fall, of course. The newspapers were very excited just then about free falls. Anything headed downward—SAT scores, voter confidence, the dollar— was in free fall. I released my *Boston Globe* into free fall, too, from a point just above the trash can next to the gate.

I tied my pretty yellow sweater around my waist. The buds on the lilacs along Quincy Street were fat and ready to pop. The grass was mostly brown still, but a little green showed if you looked hard enough. The Chessmaster was sitting at his usual table on the terrace outside the Au Bon Pain, now that it was warm enough again. The Chessmaster is a Harvard man who now takes on all comers for two bucks a game. As I watched he pondered his next move for about a second and a half, before making it and hitting the timer that started the countdown for his current victim. Inside The Tasty I took one of the stools near the window. It was worth keeping an eye on the street again, now that the sun had shucked the girls out of their winter clothes.

"Bethany, my man," said Joey Neary, turning a hamburger patty over on the grill so that the pink side would turn gray and match the other side. "How they hanging?"

In a bunch? Right one high?

"Not bad," I said.

"Your lady called."

"Hope?"

"You got more than one?"

"What did she want?"

"She said call her. I wrote it down." It was her home number in Washington. Funny she'd be at home, on a weekday. She took time off after each of her three babies was born, but apart from that she hadn't missed a day at work since graduating from law school.

I ordered a bowl of soup and a container of milk, something light so I wouldn't have weight on my stomach when I went over to Malkin later to work out with the Harvard wrestlers. I was a sort of unofficial and unpaid assistant to the coach, which gave me access to the gym and to workout partners. Once I had been good enough to make the Olympic team, but it turned out to be the year Carter boycotted the games. Sorry about that, as we used to say during the Southeast Asia War Games. Even at this late date, my ability and experience were enough to keep me ahead of most Harvard wrestlers. But it was getting tougher every year.

I had planned to go back to the library for an hour or so after lunch, but I decided the hell with it. I'd go back to my apartment, see what Hope wanted, and then listen to k.d. lang's new CD till it was time for practice. Ms. lang was already better than Patsy Cline, and still climbing.

My apartment is only a few steps from Harvard Yard,

on Ware Street. The name Tom Carpenter is on the mailbox downstairs, and on my lease, and on a full set of I.D.'s as well. My neighbors in the building think I'm some kind of consultant on something or other, who keeps to himself. Only a very few people know that there is no Tom Carpenter, and that the man who lives in the apartment with that name on the mailbox is actually Tom Bethany. My reasons for dropping out of the world's computer data base years ago were personal, and probably a little weird, and only a little illegal, and by now more and more irrelevant, unnecessary and outdated. But I still like the idea that strangers can't find the entrance to my den without making a considerable effort.

The air inside the apartment was overheated, and so I opened all the windows. What came in was a little cooler than a spring breeze, but it was still pleasant. Then I dialed Hope Edwards at her home number. Generally I call her at the Washington office of the American Civil Liberties Union, which she runs. That way I don't run the risk of her husband answering. He may know about our long-standing affair, but then again he may not. He may not care if he does know, but then again he may. Anyway, I seldom called Hope at home. She answered before the first ring was over.

"Hey," I said, "what's up?"

"Oh, Tom," she said, which told me right away it was something bad. Usually she calls me Bethany.

"What is it?" I said. "What's wrong?"

"I went to the doctor this morning, and ... Tom, I don't know how to say this ..."

"Jesus, Hope, what is it?"

"I'm pregnant."

I let loose with the first thing that jumped into my head: "Thank God."

"Thank God?"

"Sorry, I didn't mean it the way it sounded. I was thinking cancer or something."

"Oh."

"What do we do?" I asked.

"I need to talk to you about it. Can you come down?"

I recently got my hands on a lot of money, enough so that I can get by at my modest level for as long as they keep issuing Treasury notes. The Roaring Eighties are over at last, leaving behind them the looted shells of the insurance companies and the S&Ls and the corporations and the pension funds. So I took the money I stole from one of the looters and loaned it to the U.S. government with the understanding that the rest of you would pay me interest on it every year, without the slightest effort on my part. It may help to think of me, along with a whole bunch of rich Arabs and Japanese and Germans and Republicans, as the Mafia. Now think of the Internal Revenue Service as our enforcer, and of yourself as the shopkeeper who pays protection to us every April.

Bottom line, as we say down here on the bottom where your money winds up, I not only can live modestly these days without working, I can even splurge a little now and then. So I took a cab out to Logan Airport instead of the T, and I took a plane to Washington instead of driving nine hours or so in my new Subaru, new to me anyway, and instead of taking the Metro, I took another cab from National Airport to the Tabard Inn.

"I can give you your old room," said Edward Cohen, the owner.

I told him I didn't want my old room this time, but I didn't tell him why. The room I usually stay in was where it had happened, not six weeks ago, during a long lunch hour Hope had spent with me.

I had told Hope I'd probably be settled in by eight, and just at eight the phone rang.

"Hey," she said.

"Hey to you."

"So. Here you are. We are."

"Did I have a nice flight, you're supposed to say."

"Did you?"

"It was okay. Took off. Landed."

"All you can ask of a flight."

"All you can ask," I agreed. "When can I see you?"

"Tomorrow's supposed to be nice. I thought maybe if we took a walk."

We settled when and where, and that seemed to be all the business we had that could be done over the phone. "Well, then, that's that till tomorrow," Hope said, and paused a moment. "Bethany," she said, "I do, you know. I really do."

"Is there anybody with you?"

"No."

"Say it straight out, then."

"I love you."

"I love you, too. It'll be all right. Somehow."

I went to sleep wondering just how.

Hope had told me to meet her in Georgetown, by the towpath. I saw her standing beside the canal, looking at its dark water. She turned when I said hello. While I held her for a long moment we said nothing, and then we began to walk, still saying nothing. Hope was a little shorter than I was, but not much, so that we were able to walk hand in hand without the jerkiness that comes when your strides are too badly mismatched. Spring was two or three weeks further along here, so that the trees were pale green and all the new grass had come up. It should have been a nice walk.

We came to where a big mulberry tree leans out over the brown, slow water of the Potomac Canal. By then I had figured out that maybe she was keeping quiet because she was waiting for me to go first. So I told her how sometimes when I used to run along here, the path had been covered with blue-black splotches where people stepped on the ripe mulberries that fell. I told her about the carp that made little kissing sounds when they caught the mulberries as they fell in the water.

"I never heard of a fish eating fruit," Hope said.

"Well, these ones do," I said.

"Why are we talking about fish?" Hope asked.

"We're scared."

"We sure are. Let's sit down." So we sat down on the bank of the canal and stopped stalling.

"Well, it happened," Hope said. "I thought I was being careful but it happened. I'm sorry."

"It's just bad luck," I said. "You read about ninety-five percent effective, ninety-eight, whatever. You never figure you'll be in the other two percent."

"I've been in the two percent before. Steven."

Steven was her fifteen-year-old son, the youngest of her three.

"There's something I never asked you," I said. "A lot of things I never asked you, I guess."

"Ask it."

"Does Martin know about us?"

"He knows we're friends. Once or twice when I've mentioned seeing you, he's asked why I don't bring you around."

"Why don't you?"

"I thought I'd feel awkward. I thought you'd feel awkward."

"Do you think he'd care if he knew?"

"I honestly don't know. It's a funny position." Martin had discovered late in the day that his secret feelings for men weren't just a phase but were a permanent part of him. While he was pretending otherwise, though, he and Hope had married and had three children. He was a wonderful father; she was a wonderful mother; the

8

kids were wonderful kids. A wonderful family, except that he had been exclusively and discreetly homosexual for years.

"Up in Alaska, when I was screwing anything I could," I said, "I used to wish my wife *would* find somebody."

"I don't think it's quite the same, Tom. Probably you wanted out, didn't you, and you hoped she'd let you off the hook by making the first move?"

"Probably you're right. And the difference is that you don't want out, isn't that right? I've always assumed that, anyway."

We assumed a lot more about each other than we ever said. So far, what we assumed seemed to be right.

"No, I don't want out," Hope said. "You know the joke about the two ninety-five-year-olds who go in for a divorce? The judge asks them why now, after seventy-five years of marriage? 'Well, judge,' the husband says, 'we were waiting till the children died.' "

"Jesus, that's an awful joke."

"Exactly."

"So that means you don't want to have the baby?"

"Not if you're talking about divorce and remarriage."

"Wouldn't that be the only real way?"

"Not necessarily. Martin and I could raise the baby as his."

"Would he do that?"

"I don't know. Do you want me to ask him?"

"This is tough, isn't it?"

"It's tough, all right."

"What do you think, Hope? What do you want to do?"

"I'm a little old for a baby. Not really too old, but a little old."

"Do you want one, though?"

"Do you?"

"I left the baby I had. I don't know how good a father

I would be." I hadn't seen my daughter since the divorce. I send her birthday and Christmas presents, along with an awkward letter every month. They're nonletters, really, like the mimeographed year-end things that people send with their Christmas cards. She answers about one in three. Her real father is her stepfather, or so I hope.

"Does that mean you don't want a baby?" Hope asked.

"I'd want your baby. Our baby. I'm just scared, that's all. A lot of things about it are terrifying."

"I'm scared, too. Probably I should have just gone ahead and had an abortion. Not told you."

"I think I think it's good that you told me. I think I'm glad."

"I wanted you to have a say in it."

"Not really my say, is it? I'm not the one who's pregnant."

"I don't mean it wouldn't be my decision in the end. I just meant I wanted to see what you felt before I decided."

"I don't really know what I feel."

"Don't you? Don't you think we're sort of closing in on a decision here?"

"Are we?"

"Listen to us. You say you're scared and you're a lousy father. I say I'm scared, and I'm getting a little old for this kind of thing and my kids won't be dead for another sixty or seventy years. We're really not too enthusiastic about this pregnancy, are we?"

"Is that what you want to do, then?"

"Abortion? Yes. I was pretty sure before, and now I'm all the way sure. That's why I wanted you to come down. So I could see you, not just talk to you on the phone."

"What happens next?"

"I'll just make an appointment and get it done. No need for you to stay around."

"Is there a problem if I do stay around?"

"Naturally not."

"Then naturally I will."

A lifetime of scrounging and living poor builds up habits. I could afford to stay in the Tabard for a few days or a few weeks, but I didn't want to spend the money. So next morning I started calling around, and in the afternoon I moved to a little Georgetown house on Thirty-fourth Street. A friend of mine was keeping the keys for a dentist friend of his who was spending a month in Montego Bay. In his master bedroom the dentist turned out to have a water bed with flannel sheets, which was an odd combination even for Georgetown. I settled myself in his tiny, windowless guest bedroom instead.

Normally I would have wanted to show the water bed to Hope, and laugh about it with her, and maybe even give it a try to say we had. But the idea didn't sound funny just at the moment. I wondered if this kind of shadow would be between us from now on. I wondered what this abortion would do to us. I remembered the last time we had been together, the time that had led to all this.

I had been spending a couple of days in town, looking up some filings at the Securities and Exchange Commission for some investors. Their particular investment was in a congressman who hoped to be governor of California. One of his potential rivals had been a congressional liaison guy in Bush's White House. My job was to run down a rumor that the guy had stood to profit personally from his work on Bush's banking "reform" bill. Presumably they called it a reform bill because it repealed the last of the reforms that Roosevelt had put in to prevent another Great Depression. In any event, I couldn't find anything over at the SEC that proved the rumor.

"Actually, I'm not surprised," I told the man who had hired me. "Why would the bankers have to waste money paying off a guy on Bush's staff? It's like the British journalist."

"Fuck does that mean?" my investor said, so I recited him the old poem:

"You cannot hope to bribe or twist,
   Thank God, the British journalist,
   But seeing what the man will do
   Unbribed, there isn't reason to."

"Fuck does that mean?" my investor said again. The guy was a movie producer after all, not Ezra Pound.

"Means Wall Street didn't have to hire guys on Bush's staff. They got 'em for free."

That was in the late morning of my second day in Washington, when I talked to the rich producer. Lunch, a very long lunch, I spent in my room with Hope. We had gone straight to bed, because I was leaving the next morning and we didn't want to waste a minute of our time together. Hope hadn't even gone into the bathroom to, as they say, freshen up. Now that I thought about it, she seldom did. Now that I thought about it, I wondered what method she used, and why I never asked her. It could hardly have been the pill or an IUD, since her sex life was precisely as sporadic as mine. As far as I knew, that left a diaphragm. Hope had said she was being careful, so when had she put it in? Before leaving home? In the ladies room at the office? Was a diaphragm something a woman would carry around in her purse? Was it something you would insert in a ladies room? Weren't these all things that a person would know if he wasn't a complete oinker?

So I had a spell of feeling guilty because I hadn't been

more sensitive, more responsible, more this and that. I knew that the accident would have happened in exactly the same way if I had been a regular Kevin Costner kind of guy, in touch not only with my own feelings but also with the feelings of Native Americans, buffaloes, wolves, and the Great Spirit herself. Somehow this rational thought didn't help at all. It was no time for rational thought. It was time for confused, intertwined emotions about marriage, birth, parenthood, love, death, commitment, guilt; innocence, responsibility, and irresponsibility.

And about abortion itself. In the polls, most people say they think it's wrong, but you ought to be able to have one if you want to. Maybe this isn't entirely clear or entirely consistent, but then the issue is only an easy one to the simple-minded zealots on both extremes.

Try not to be simple-minded and the zealots on the right holler situational ethics, as if that were a bad word, and as if there were any other kind of ethics. Hope and I—mainly Hope—were in a nonsimple situation, and yet I was confident that abortion was the best of all the bad ways out of it. But I couldn't help asking myself what if, what if, what if . . .

And I knew Hope was asking, too. I wondered what it would do to us, all this imagining of a baby that would never be.

I microwaved a dinner for myself, while Hope was probably getting a proper meal ready for her double-parent nuclear family. Afterward I watched TV, hoping it would flatten my brain waves into nonthought. But it didn't. I thought of Hope sitting in her study, trying to work through the stuff she always brought home from the office in her briefcase. But failing. Thinking instead about tomorrow. What we had started in the Tabard Inn was going to end on a raised table with stirrups, in a clinic across the river in Arlington.

2

NEXT MORNING I WAS KEEPING AN EYE ON THE window so I could get to the door before Hope had to block traffic on the narrow Georgetown street. I got to the front door fast enough, so the BMW behind her hadn't even started to honk. Hope drove a Saab. I couldn't tell if it was ten years old or last year's model. All Saabs look alike to me, the way all Fords looked alike till they stopped making the Model A. To make room for me in the passenger seat, Hope had had to transfer a pile of teenage litter to the backseat. The car smelled of the kids' setter, Yankee. His tongue and nose had smudged the inside of both rear windows. Dog hair was all over. Normally I would have had fun with all this, but now I said nothing.

Hope headed down to M Street and over Key Bridge. The day was bright and sunny. I saw a couple of scullers on the river and wondered if they were from Hope's boat club. You can tell from the colors on the oar blades, but I didn't know what the Potomac Boat Club colors were, and didn't ask. She didn't offer anything about the day, or the boats. She drove.

14

We went through the ugly high rises near the bridge and headed out toward Glebe Road. "Did I tell you about this clinic?" Hope said at last. "I'm involved in some legal work for them. Well, not me personally. The ACLU. Interesting First Amendment issue. What's free speech, anyway? Picketing is clearly free speech, okay. But how about chaining yourself to the undercarriage of a doctor's car when he stops for coffee on the way to an abortion clinic?"

"No," I said.

"Clearly no, sure. But what about if you're also holding a steel sign that says Babykiller on Board and it's chained to your wrist?"

"Still no."

"That's what we're arguing, too."

"Hope?"

"Yes?"

"This doctor, is he any good?"

"She. Yes, she's good."

"Because you know her, or because you checked on her?"

"Actually I don't know her. I've checked."

"How long does it take?"

"Not much more than half an hour, they said. Then they have you rest for a while to make sure you're all right."

"There's anesthetic, I guess?"

"Local. It's supposed to be uncomfortable, not too much more. Try to stop worrying."

"I'm the one who's supposed to be saying that."

"But you're the one who's worrying," Hope said.

"Why aren't you?"

"I am, a little. But not too much. Tom, I've talked with dozens of women who have had abortions. This early in a pregnancy, the risk is pretty near zero."

"All right, I'll stop worrying. See, I'm not worrying anymore."

"You can worry a little."

I looked at her as she drove, looked at her perfect profile. I wanted to say how much I loved her because she was funny and brave, and soft and tough, and on and on.

"You have the perfect profile," I said. "To me, anyway. I think it's perfect."

Hope took her eyes off the road, and looked at me for a second and smiled. "Thank you," she said. When she looked back at the road she was still smiling, just slightly.

The smile went away when we turned the corner of the block where the clinic was. "Why are the police here?" she asked. An Arlington County cruiser sat next to a sign that read Commonwealth Surgicare, Inc. The building was a one-story brick building that had probably started out as a three- or four-bedroom split-level bungalow. It had been around since the fifties, to judge from the size of the shrubs and trees. Down here any crocuses had probably withered, but tulips and jonquils bloomed along the borders of the path leading into the clinic.

"Let me out while you go park," I said. "I'll ask the guy."

The Saab disappeared behind the clinic, where the old backyard had been turned into a parking lot; I went over to the cruiser. The cop just looked up at me without speaking, doing the best bored and indifferent Master-of-the-Universe impression he could handle from a sitting position.

"Hi," I said. "What's going on?"

"Just routine," he said.

"They got you guys out here every day, huh?"

"Not usually. You got business inside?"

"I'm with a patient, yes."

"Well, you can go on in," he said. "This is just routine."

Hope was coming back from the parking lot, and we went up the walk together past the bright tulips and jonquils. I should have worn my yellow Arnold Palmer sweater down to Washington, considering the weather. But considering everything else, I had brought a dark green one instead.

"What's the cop doing?" Hope asked.

"He said it's just routine, except usually they're not here."

Inside, stairs went down and up. We took the up stairs to what used to be a sort of landing-entry hall. Now it was a reception area, with a woman in a white nurse's uniform sitting at a desk. She looked at her appointments schedule and said, "Ms. Edwards?" Hope nodded. "If you and Mr. Edwards will have a seat, I'll tell Doctor you're here."

The receptionist disappeared and came back with a woman wearing a short white coat. The name tag on it said she was Myra McLarey, M.D. Dr. McLarey was not much more than five feet tall, sharp featured and very thin. She should have looked fragile, but she didn't.

"Ms. Edwards," she said, holding out her hand, "I can't tell you how grateful we are for the help you've given us." And her small, high voice should have sounded girlish, but it didn't. She shook Hope's hand and looked at me.

"Did you want to see me?" Dr. McLarey asked.

"This is a friend of mine," Hope said. "Tom Bethany."

"Oh, I'm sorry," the doctor said."I thought perhaps you were from the police. Good to meet you."

Her hand was small as a child's, but with the surprising strength that children can have. "Nice to meet you," I said. "There is a cop, outside, though, as a matter of fact. Is something going on?"

"Probably not. We heard rumors that people from the Life Force might be coming around today. I don't pay much attention. Nerve warfare is one of their little tricks.

Bomb threats, false rumors of demonstrations. Nine times out of ten nothing comes of it, but ever since they murdered Dr. Gunn, we notify the Arlington police as a matter of course."

"What's the Life Force?"

"You're not from around here, then?"

"No, Massachusetts."

"It's what the Pastor calls his antiabortion shock troops. You've heard of the Pastor? The Reverend Howard Orrin?"

"Oh, yeah, I've heard of the Pastor." Howard Orrin was a televangelist from Newport News. Orrin had announced his candidacy, on a platform of Christian white male supremacy, in the Republican primary for the Senate seat from Virginia that would be opening in the fall. Republican leaders in Richmond and in Washington hated him, of course, in the fraternal way Cain hated Abel. They didn't like to admit that his platform was built of the same material theirs was, except he had left the bark on his. The Pastor didn't care if the establishment Republicans hated him. He thrived on hate. It was what had made him the front-runner in the race up till now, according to all the polls.

"The Pastor has an antiabortion movement, too?" I asked.

"Very much so," Dr. McLarey said. "They've put on a number of fairly nasty demonstrations around the state. One was in Alexandria a couple of months ago. They've been in the papers here, but maybe they haven't attracted much attention nationally."

"Not in the *Boston Globe*, anyway," I said. "He calls it the Life Force, huh? Not a bad name, actually."

"A very good name," the doctor said. "Unfortunately, Howard Orrin is not at all stupid. Well, shall we get started, Ms. Edwards?"

"Hope, please."

"Hope, then. And I'm Myra. Come along with me."

"Want me to come?" I said to Hope.

"It isn't customary," the doctor said. "But I suppose . . ."

"I guess I'd rather you didn't," Hope said. "But I'm glad you asked."

"There's a waiting room," Dr. McLarey said. "That door on your right."

Hope and the doctor headed for the lower floor of the split-level, presumably where the surgery was. Or surgeries. The names of three doctors had been mounted on the wall as we came in. Maybe each one had separate operating rooms, or whatever they called them.

I had just entered the waiting room when I heard the front door of the clinic open. I waited for the other shoe to drop—the door to close—but there was no more noise. I glanced out. The girl standing in the doorway didn't seem to notice me. She was standing there looking at nothing, with the thousand-yard stare you sometimes saw in Vietnam. She was holding something in her arms, too closely for me to see what it was. The girl was dressed just like any other female kid in the mall or waiting for the school bus. She had on a short beige miniskirt, so tight you could see the lines of her panties. Her loose blouse was of some filmy fabric that showed the bra she barely needed. She had matched the hot pink blouse with hot pink shoes that looked like light, flimsy ballet slippers with bows on the toes. On her fingers, all her fingers, she wore lots of cheap rings. That was it. No socks, no stockings, no hat, no slip, and no sweater, although she had to have been chilly outdoors in her see-through blouse. But uniforms don't have to be comfortable; all they have to do is identify you as a member of your tribe. Better to be chilly than to be different. The girl looked about twelve to me, but was probably thirteen or fourteen. I figured this because the freshmen girls I see going in and out of the Harvard Union at mealtime look fifteen or sixteen to me, although most of them have got to be eighteen or nineteen.

"Close the door," said the receptionist. Her voice was matter-of-fact, not annoyed.

The girl looked down at whatever she was carrying, almost as if she were consulting it. Then she turned and shut the door behind her.

"Are you Kimberly Butler, honey?" the receptionist asked. The girl nodded.

"Well, would you step up here, Kimberly? The information I have on you isn't complete." Again the girl glanced downward in that odd way, and then obeyed. She sat in the chair the receptionist indicated, and answered the questions put to her. I could barely hear her small voice: "One one two nine Harmon Drive, Arlington. ZIP code? I don't know, really. My mom knows."

"It's all right. I can look it up. Phone number?"

"You're not going to call, are you?"

"It's just for our records."

"Because I'd die if they knew. Mom and my father."

"Everything is confidential, dear."

Once the receptionist had what she needed, she said, "It'll be a few minutes before Doctor is free. That's the waiting room, up there."

I stepped back from the door and sat down on one of the plastic-seated chairs along the wall. The girl came in and saw me, and went right out again. The thing in her arms was a stuffed animal with a blue ribbon around its neck. It looked like Tigger, in *Winnie the Pooh*.

"There's a man in there," I heard her say to the receptionist.

"He's just waiting for a patient."

"He makes us feel funny," the girl said. Why "us," I wondered. And I wondered who I reminded her of.

The receptionist's voice softened. "It's all right," she said. "You can sit here by me and wait. Didn't you come with anybody, dear?"

"Roy didn't come in, did he, Binkie?"

"Is he waiting in the car?"

"Roy went to the arcade. Roy's going to come back and pick Kim up afterwards, isn't he, Binkie? Why are you shaking your head? Don't shake your head, you bad thing."

A step or two slow, I realized she was talking to the world through her stuffed animal.

"Why don't you come with me, dear?" the receptionist said. "I want you to talk with one of our ladies. She's very nice. You'll like her."

I heard the two of them go off, and then the receptionist came back. Two more women came in, separately, and I heard the receptionist taking down their particulars before escorting them to the lower level. There was some abortion literature on the table in the waiting room, and so I was able to imagine what was happening to Hope. A tranquilizer injected into the arm. After that kicked in, the injection of the local anesthetic. "The patient normally feels no more than a pinprick," the brochure said. Right.

Table. Stirrups. Speculum. Dilation of cervix. "The physician carefully aspirates or scrapes the products of conception out of the uterus." Nice PR touch there: "products of conception."

The whole process was supposed to take "approximately a half hour under normal circumstances." It was more than a half hour now. It was thirty-four minutes. Had circumstances been not normal? Which was to say abnormal? What was wrong?

Dr. McLarey appeared at the door.

"What's the matter?" I said.

"Nothing at all. I just came by to let you know we're finished."

"Oh. Well. That's fine. That's great. Can I see her?"

"She's lying down resting. I'd rather give her fifteen or twenty minutes more to shake the wooziness."

"Oh, okay. Sure. But she's really all right?"

The doctor smiled, which totally transformed her thin,

severe little face. "She's perfectly fine and as healthy as a horse," she said. "What does she do, triathlons?"

"She rows."

"From her muscle tone, I'll bet she's good."

"She was first in her division at the Empire Games last year. In 1988, she placed third at the National Master's. I think that's what they call it, even for women."

"You don't row yourself?"

"No, I wrestle and run. Listen, Doctor, do you happen to know what's going on with a girl named Kimberly Butler?"

"Do you know her?"

"No, I just heard her come in. She's in trouble, that girl."

"Yes, she is."

"Did you . . . I mean . . ."

"Perform an abortion? No, she's too disturbed to undergo something like that. What she really needs is psychiatric help, but that's beyond the scope of what we do here. We've given her the name of a counselor, but she probably won't see him. She wouldn't be here without even her boyfriend if her lines of communication weren't totally down."

"Her boyfriend's at some goddamned arcade."

"She said he'd be back. I hope she's right. One of the nurses is sitting with the poor little creature downstairs."

Dr. McLarey said she'd take me to see Hope in twenty minutes or so, and I settled down to wait. But I was too jumpy and distracted to concentrate on the magazines in the waiting room—or even to sit down. I crossed over to the window, which opened onto the street side of the building. The curtains on it were made of some kind of spun glass material that let in the light, but you couldn't really see through them. I opened the curtains and looked out for a while at the street. Nobody came by, which was natural. The clinic was on a short dead-end

street with a little turning circle at the end of it. The
Arlington County cruiser was still parked out front.
From the way the cop's head drooped he could have
been dozing.

Two long black cars turned into the block, one right
after the other. At first I didn't understand what I was
seeing, and then I registered that they were two old
hearses. When I was wrestling and going to an occasional lecture at Iowa in the late 1970s, a couple of rich
fraternity kids used to take a hearse with a keg in it to
football games. It was about the same vintage as these
old Caddies out in the street.

One of them pulled into a driveway on the right, and
the other headed into the driveway directly opposite it,
on the left. Then they both backed straight out, until
their rear bumpers almost met in the middle of the
street. The whole thing had been precise and practiced
and very quickly done, although the drivers seemed un-
hurried. The six P's, as the dummy sergeants used to
say in the army. Prior Planning Prevents Piss-Poor
Performance.

The two hearses now formed a complete barrier across
the street and the sidewalks. Nothing could get past
without smashing through the hedges and shrubs and
low fences that bordered the yards on both sides of the
street. I understood that they meant to block off the
street, but I still couldn't imagine why.

The two drivers got out of their cars. One was dressed
as Death, with a skull mask and black, hooded robe; the
other wore a surgical mask and a surgical smock spotted
with red paint. Death pulled a blood-smeared scythe out
of the back and laid it on the ground. The two men put
signs saying Life Force on the inside of the front windows, locked their doors, and went to the rear of the
two hearses. Each of the men lay down on his back and
busied himself underneath the rear of his car. It only
took them a moment to free short lengths of tow chain

that must have been fastened out of sight to the under-carriages. One of the men produced a padlock, worked the hasp through the end links of the two chains, and locked them together. The two men then started to walk away, at first unchallenged. But the policeman finally came alive.

The cop got out of his car and waved at the disap-pearing men, presumably shouting at the same time, al-though I couldn't hear from inside. They made no effort to escape. They turned around calmly and began to walk back toward the officer. The three met by the roadblock made by the two hearses. I went to the waiting room door and got the receptionist's attention. "The Life Force people just barricaded the street with a couple of hearses," I called to her. She hurried to the front door, peeked out the small window in it, and ran downstairs.

Back at my own window, I saw that the cop had stood the two men beside his cruiser. The scythe lay on the ground beside Death as the cop busied himself on the radio. But he was already way behind the curve of the action. School busses, one after another, were appearing at the end of the block to unload passengers. Most of the busses had the names of churches or Sunday schools painted on the sides. The people aboard each bus got up as soon as it stopped moving, and then filed off effi-ciently, without haste and without delay. As soon as one bus was empty it disappeared and its place was taken by another. Six busses had already unloaded before I heard the first sirens of police reinforcements, and hun-dreds of demonstrators filled the street leading to the clinic. Not ten minutes had passed since the two hearses had shown up. It was an impressive example of what you'd probably think of as military precision, if you'd never been in the military.

"My God, where did they all pop up from?" said Dr. McLarey, behind me. The waiting room had the best view of the street, and a number of the clinic staffers were with the doctor. I told them how it had been carried out.

"This guy Orrin is good," I said when I was done. "Those two hearses would have blocked the street even if the cop had been on the ball. The guys wouldn't have had time to chain them together, maybe, but the barricade would have lasted till the busses got here. By then the street would have been so full of people that the wreckers couldn't get in to drag off the hearses. Now the clinic will be sealed off for hours. At least I guess that was the point of the hearses."

"Plus the symbolic value," Dr. McLarey said. "Look at that sign." Someone had just jammed a sign saying Funerals in Progress under the windshield wiper of one of the hearses. Another sign said If You Love Life, Pass It On.

A large woman wearing a light blue windbreaker with Life Force on the back was carrying a poster headlined America's Holocaust. The photo underneath showed a sort of doggie bed made from a rumpled American flag. A fetus was curled up on the red and white stripes. The blue part with the stars was above its head. The poster was like a Reagan photo op—it didn't make any sense, but it looked good.

Other demonstrators, many of them also wearing the Life Force jackets, carried signs saying Support Our Unborn Troops, Read My Lips, No More Abortions, Civil Rights for the Preborn, Let My People Grow, and Abortion the Ultimate Child Abuse. One placard showed a photo of "The Real Coat Hanger Victim," which turned out to be the cute little fetus from the pro-life billboards. The one that looks sort of like E.T. as a kid. Maybe Steven Spielberg didn't know what message he was sending by portraying his extraterrestrial as a cute preborn baby brother, but the antiabortion propagandists picked up on it fast enough.

"What's going to happen?" I asked the doctor.

"Nothing much till the TV gets here," she said. "Then they'll all start shouting and waving their signs around."

"When will that be?"

"Pretty soon. They notify the TV in advance."

"Is there any other way out of the parking lot?"

"Not by car. Nobody will be able to leave until the police haul those hearses out of there. Nor will any new patients be able to get in. That's the supposed point, of course. Disruption of the clinic's services."

"Slowing down the holocaust," I said.

"Ridiculous, isn't it?" Dr. McLarey said. "Except when you consider that absurdities like this have brought us the present Supreme Court. Without these media frenzies, I doubt if either Reagan or Bush would have ever given the abortion issue a second thought."

We watched in silence for a minute. The situation didn't seem menacing, but what did I know? So I asked. "There have been bombings," the doctor said, "but they couldn't very well set off a bomb while their own people are here. It's nothing more than harassment, pure and simple. We just have to wait it out."

"I'd better tell Hope what's going on. Is it okay to see her now?"

"I'll take you down."

Hope was sitting in a small room with two other women. On some irrational level I guess I expected her to look different, since I was surprised when she looked exactly the same. Same clothes she had come in, no signs of strain or pain or pallor. The three women had been talking when we came in. A low table in front of them held a plate of cookies, paper cups, and pitchers of fruit juice. They could have been three neighbors, taking a midmorning break in somebody's kitchen.

I would have kissed her, but we don't do that in front of people. "Feel okay?" I asked.

"Not bad, really. I was a little woozy before, but it's going away."

"We're going to be here a while. Demonstrators have closed the clinic down."

"We heard. We were just talking about it."

"There's a ringside seat in the waiting room upstairs if you want to watch," I said, and looked at the doctor. "If that's all right?"

"If she feels up to it, it's fine."

When we got back upstairs, the scene had changed. A couple of dozen police reinforcements had arrived, and so had many more demonstrators. Two wreckers sat one behind the other at the entrance to the street, come to drag the hearses off. But the drivers were just idling their engines, waiting for the crowd to let the vehicles through.

Among the newcomers was a fleshy man with a bullhorn. He wore one of the blue Life Force jackets, too. I recognized him from his pictures in the papers as the Reverend Howard Orrin. The Pastor held the bullhorn down at his side while he listened to a woman in police uniform, with captain's bars on her epaulets. He was nodding as she talked. When she was done he raised the bullhorn, and his amplified voice filled the neighborhood:

"I HAVE JUST ENJOYED A MOST FRIENDLY EX-CHANGE OF VIEWS WITH THIS FINE YOUNG LADY. CAPTAIN PARKINSON REPRESENTS THE POLICE POWER OF THE STATE, AND I HAVE TOLD HER WE WILL NOT RESIST THAT AUTHORITY. I MUST ORDER YOU TO GIVE WAY, THEN, AND LET THE WRECKERS THROUGH SO THAT THE MURDERS OC-CURRING INSIDE THIS ABORTUARY MAY CON-TINUE. REGRETFULLY THAT IS MY ORDER TO YOU, MY FRIENDS. WHETHER YOU FOLLOW THAT ORDER OR THE ORDERS OF GOD IS UP TO YOU."

"The Pastor is much too cute to actually go to jail himself," Dr. McLarey said. "He has his flunkies do that for him. Watch what happens."

The driver of the first tow truck revved his motor, let the clutch out, and edged forward a couple of inches. No one moved. One woman, who had been standing right up against the bumper, pretended that the truck had pushed her over and fell backward onto the ground. The engine went back to an idle and the driver sat there with his hands on the wheel. He was just a tow truck driver. He hadn't signed up for duty on any Highway of Death.

Captain Parkinson gestured to a sergeant carrying a bullhorn of his own, and he handed it to her. "CLEAR THE ROAD OR YOU'LL BE ARRESTED FOR OB-STRUCTING A PUBLIC WAY," her voice boomed. "I'LL COUNT TO THREE. ONE. TWO. THREE." No one moved.

"ALL RIGHT, GET THAT WOMAN OUT OF THERE." Two policemen grabbed the woman on the ground by the arms and dragged her off, forcing their way through the crowd. Captain Parkinson went through the count-down again. This time the people in the front rank moved on the count of three, sort of. Each person moved back one tiny step, and then another, for a total of per-haps two inches.

"Baby steps," Dr. McLarey explained. "They did it in Wichita. The idea is that the police won't arrest them as long as they're complying with orders, no matter how slowly."

The captain gestured to the driver of the first tow truck, and he eased forward into the couple of inches that had opened up. "We should be out of here by Satur-day," I said.

"Oh, things will speed up soon," Dr. McLarey said. "I know Captain Parkinson pretty well. She thinks we're murderers just as much as the Pastor does. But what she hates worse than murder is a challenge to her authority. She's a cop first and a pro-lifer second. See if I'm not right."

Captain Parkinson hung in there for a little while, though. She went through a half-dozen more count-downs, and the wreckers advanced perhaps a foot. But that was all the baby stepping she could put up with.

"ALL RIGHT," she hollered to her troops, "START CLEARING 'EM OUT!"

She was just in time for the television crews. Their trucks were nowhere in sight; presumably they hadn't been able to get through the jam of police cruisers, paddy wagons, ambulances, and empty busses. But a half-dozen different teams were entering the street, with minicams on the shoulders of the cameramen. Where tow trucks couldn't make their way, the TV people weren't having a bit of trouble. The demonstrators made a path for the honored guests.

The Pastor and many of his troops wore their Life Force windbreakers. Many of the police wore wind-breakers, too, with Police on the back. A few in both groups wore baseball-type caps in the colors of their par-ticular gang. I wondered if the people of any other coun-try were as pathetically desperate as we are to join teams and advertise our membership in them. Maybe the Japanese.

The TV teams went right to work with the other two teams to put on a good show for the only team that really mattered, the consumers at home who would be watching the six o'clock news. The TV performers fo-cused on the police performers as they ordered the anti-abortion performers to give way, and as the antiabortion performers went limp instead. Life Force was document-ing the show, too. A man wearing one of the light blue windbreakers was taking pictures with a motor-driven Nikon. Two more cameras were slung around his neck, and a heavy bag hung from one shoulder. Big-time gear.

At first the police tried to be as polite as you can be when you're dragging somebody off to a paddy wagon. But the crowd was screaming Communist and Judas and murderer at the officers. Although the demonstrators actually being removed didn't resist, they did holler out, as if they were being tortured to death. It was all pretty tough for authoritarian personalities to take.

After a while, sure enough, the antiabortion performers succeeded in goading the cops into taking up the role being assigned to them. Then the screams became much more convincing, as the police helped out with come-along holds that produced actual pain. Some of those being dragged off were women, who cried out more loudly and contorted their faces better than the men did. The cameramen rewarded this behavior by paying special attention to the ladies, which in turn caused the neglected male sufferers to shout louder in hopes of equal airtime. It was a professional performance from all concerned, and very smoothly done.

But it took a while.

3

OUR APPOINTMENT AT THE CLINIC HAD BEEN FOR nine-thirty, and it was noon before the wreckers had managed to haul away the hearses. The waiting room, with its view of the stage outside, had become the command post of the clinic. Dr. McLarey and the two other doctors, both men, ducked out to the receptionist's phone now and then to make calls. Most of the patients were watching TV in the lounge downstairs, sheltered from the noise outside. But Hope had stayed with me and the staff in the upstairs waiting room.

"This is a tough day to be a civil rights supporter," she had earlier said to Dr. McLarey. "My faith in the First Amendment is being pushed to the limit."

"But not past it?" the doctor asked.

"Not quite."

Now Hope was looking out the window while the doctors discussed whether the demonstrators would come back the following day.

"Captain Parkinson is coming to the door," Hope reported. The doctors went to the entrance hall to meet

JEROME DOOLITTLE

the policewoman while Hope and I listened from the top of the stairs.

"We have the street secured," the captain told Dr. McLarey. "Reverend Orrin agreed to tell his people to stay on the sidewalks and not obstruct the roadway."

"Earlier he told them to obey your orders, too," the doctor pointed out. "But I got the strong impression that his fingers were crossed. Do you believe him now?"

"Put it this way, Doctor. I believe now we have control. You can resume your business."

"We've shifted our remaining patients for the day to other facilities."

"Whatever. All I'm saying is that we have reestablished order, Doctor. Anybody that wants to come in or leave, they can."

"What do you say?" I said to Hope when the captain had gone. "Feel like going, or would you rather wait a while?"

"No, let's go."

"How many patients are waiting to leave?" I asked Dr. McLarey.

"Four others."

"So with ours that makes five vehicles altogether."

"Only four, actually. The Butler girl came alone."

"We'll take her," I said. Kimberly Butler was the shattered kid who talked to the world through her stuffed animal, Binkie.

"Will you? That would be wonderful."

"I was thinking it might be better if we all went out together," I said. "Kind of in a convoy."

The parking lot behind the building was out of sight of the demonstrators, so we were able to form up unobserved. Two of the patients had come with women friends or relatives, and one was with a man. I put the car driven by the man at the end of our little column, and myself at the head, and told everyone to shut the windows, lock the doors, keep moving, and keep it

32

closed up. Hope was in the backseat, holding Kimberly's hand. I reached back and punched down the door locks. Then I hollered to everyone to warm up the motors a little. I didn't want anybody stalling. After a few moments I waved my little convoy forward.

The real noise started as soon as the demonstrators saw us coming out from behind the clinic. There had been chanting and shouting and hymns all along, but the mob had had no one to focus on. Now it had us.

It was the most frightening thing I ever faced, by far, to be the object of hatred pouring out of hundreds of strangers. The signs were bobbing up and down, and waving, and then they were hitting on the hood and top of the car. Our car was out on the street, but moving at a crawl. The mob blocked my view on all sides. The car lurched, as if the mob had started to rock it, and then my progress stopped. I gave the gas pedal a nudge, to push forward whatever was stopping me, but the motor just raced slightly. It took me an instant to realize that six or eight men had taken hold of the front bumper and lifted the wheels clear of the ground. They were facing me, their mouths big holes in their faces as they screamed. A cameraman was crushed against my front fender, filming the men as they screamed. But why wasn't the car moving when I gunned it?

Front wheel drive, I thought at last. And next, not a thought but a rush of idiot rage—I'll show the pricks! I jammed gas to the Saab and the powerful engine roared crazily, and the front wheels were doing sixty in the air. On too much of a high to think, I rolled down my window, stuck my head out, and shouted, "Let's see how long you can hold it up, you cocksuckers!"

Too late, I saw that hands were on the window beside me, holding it open. I scrabbled with my own hand for the crank, and turned it but nothing gave, and I yanked viciously, with all my force. It snapped. I saw my hand turn red where the sharp stub had sliced my palm. No pain, not yet. Still in the flood of adrenaline, I grabbed one of the hands on the window frame and felt its thumb break. The hand disappeared and another one took its place, holding a crucifix.

The voices were shouting something in at us, and now the sound sorted itself out in my head into words. "You killed me, mommy," over and over again. I felt smooth coldness as something was forced past me and into the backseat, where Hope and the girl were, I heard glass breaking. I smelled something sharp and chemical.

"Go on, get out of here," a voice shouted urgently. It was a huge cop, hollering over his shoulder as he pushed people away from my door. Other cops were at the front of the car, clubs rising and falling as they hit the men who had been holding the Saab in the air. Behind them, well back from the danger, I saw the large, soft face of the Reverend Howard Orrin. The Pastor was smiling his work to see. He was standing in the middle of a bed of tulips and jonquils, all mashed flat.

I was back in control now, or closer than I had been. I was in shape to function, just bleeding from the cut in my palm. Hope and the girl were safe in the backseat, as far as I could tell from a glance in the rearview mirror. My foot had slipped from the gas during the attack, and the engine had stalled. But it started right up again. I let the clutch out slowly, pushing the struggling demonstrators hard enough so that they moved out of my way. Once I had room I speeded up, not much but enough so that I couldn't stop in time to keep from hitting anyone who didn't jump. Once I took the corner at the end of the block, the last of the Life Force troops were behind us.

I glanced at the rearview mirror and saw Kimberly Butler. She held Binkie to her face, hiding her eyes completely. The stuffed animal seemed to be making a mewing noise with every breath. Hope was leaning across the girl, doing something. When the rush of air came, I

realized she had been opening the window behind me.
I heard the crank as she lowered the other.

"What's the smell?" I asked.

"Formaldehyde. You better stop, Tom."

I pulled over and turned around. A wrinkled fetus no
bigger than a curled-up squirrel lay on the girl's lap. The
fetus was the color of modeling clay. It was cradled in
a curved piece of broken glass from the jar that had held
it. Other shards of glass lay on the seat beside her and
on the floor.

"Good Christ," I said. "Don't move."

"Don't worry, she can't," Hope said. "She's too
scared."

I found a road map in the glove compartment, got out,
opened the rear door, and tried to lift the terrible thing
off the girl's lap without her noticing. I didn't have to
worry, as Hope had said. Kimberly was paralyzed, all
systems shut down in self-protection. Just as well. My
hand was bleeding on the glass and on the fetus and on
the map. Somehow I managed to keep it off the girl's
clothes, but the seats, the door handles, and the steering
wheel—everything I had touched was smeared with red.

I put the fetus, wrapped in its road map, on the floor
in front of the passenger seat. I picked up all the glass
I could find, and wrapped that in another map. It was
slow and careful work, which was a good thing. My own
system needed to slow down. Once I had gathered up
the glass so that movement was safe again, Hope took
the girl into her arms and rocked her.

"Honey, it's over now," she said. "It's all taken care
of. Everything is all right." Everything wasn't all right,
of course, but the soft sounds and the motion began to
work after a while. "Honey, move your dolly and let me
look at you," Hope said, and the girl obediently lowered
her stuffed animal. "Oh, aren't you a pretty girl. Here's
a hankie, now wipe your eyes and tell us where you
live."

"I DON'T WANT TO GO HOME," Kimberly said, terrified all over again. "YOU CAN'T MAKE ME.'"

"Nobody's going to make you, honey."

Slowly, in the midst of the formaldehyde smell and the smears of blood and the fresh memory of terror, Hope brought the girl back into some sort of focus. She wanted to see Roy, her friend. Roy would know what to do. He was waiting at an arcade. She knew where the arcade was. She would show us.

The arcade was in a small, failing shopping center off Columbia Pike. It had a pet store on one side of it and a frame shop on the other. I parked on purpose near a big plastic trash can with a swinging door hung from its top. I dropped my two parcels into it, the broken glass and the little gray fetus.

Whole huge slabs of American life have somehow passed me by, for instance MTV and the Miss America Pageant and the Academy Awards and the entire game of baseball. I've never watched any of them, except for the time it took to change channels. I had never been in an arcade before, either. A couple of adults, chronologically speaking, were sitting at a table drinking coffee from a vending machine. One of them wore a Spiderman T-shirt. The other was still wearing his high school sweatshirt. Neither of them paid any attention to me, so I went over to one of the video games. It was showing a promo about the hero, Magnum Cox, Former Champion Street Fighter, Now Mayor of Metro City. His Daughter, Jessica, Has Just Been Kidnapped, and the deal was that I could help get her back if I fed the machine enough quarters. From the looks of it, though, Mayor Magnum was twice the man I was. Let him get his own daughter back.

Only two kids were in the arcade, so finding the boy was no problem. I called out, "Roy?" and beckoned at the one who looked up from his video game. He came up to me, frightened. He was sort of awkward, and sort of clumsy. He wore glasses. He looked like the kind of kid who would know all about Narnia, or Commodore 64s, or both. Normally the kind of kid I'd find some promise in.

"Enjoy your game?" I said. Normally wasn't now. This kid I didn't like.

"It's okay," he said. "Is something wrong? Are you from the clinic?"

"I'm from your girlfriend, Kimberly. Remember her? The one you dumped off for an abortion?"

"I went back for her twice, but the police told me to keep moving. I was just going again."

"Why didn't you go in with her, kid?"

"She didn't want me to."

"So what? Didn't you feel like you sort of had a hand in it?"

"No, not really."

I took him by the wrist and squeezed, not full strength but hard enough so he'd know he couldn't get away. "What the hell do you mean, 'not really'?"

He looked at me, confused. "Well, I just gave her the money from the savings bonds my grandfather gave me for college."

I dropped his hand. "To pay for the abortion, you mean?"

"That's right."

"But you're not the father?"

"We were just friends, from drama club."

"Jesus, I'm sorry, Roy. Let's start over, huh?"

I told him what had happened, and I gave him my temporary phone number at the dentist's house in Georgetown. I got his name, Roy Shipley, and his phone number. Just before I took him out to the parking lot to turn Kimberly over to him, I said, "One more thing, Roy. Did she tell you who it is? The father?"

"I'm not supposed to say who he is."

"Who told you not to say?"

"Kimberly."

"But she told you?"

"Yes."

It was no time to ask her, now with the girl still in shock, and it didn't really matter anyway. "Well, let's go out to her," I said, "and you give me a call if there's anything we can do for her. Anything at all, you just call me."

Kimberly didn't rush to the boy when she got out of the car, didn't even look at him. He put his hand on her shoulder, but she acted as if it wasn't there, so he took it off. She followed him to his old wreck of a Pacer, mottled with patches of primer, and got in without a word.

My particular block in Cambridge isn't wired for cable, so shadows from nearby buildings ruin my picture. But the dentist in Georgetown got terrific reception on his TV. In fact the colors seemed even brighter than in life.

My green sweater was right there on the evening news, looking much less drab than I thought it was. And there was the blue of the Life Force windbreakers, and the darker blue of the police uniforms. And the blood showed brilliantly red against the end-of-winter whiteness of my hand.

At least my face didn't show as I shouted a deleted expletive through the car window. But Hope and Kimberly Butler, through the window, were full-face on the screen and perfectly recognizable. You couldn't make out what was in the jar, just that a man had shoved something good-sized into the backseat. If it had been a football game they would have showed you what it was. They would have slo-moed it, or even freeze-framed it. But apparently they didn't do that for fetuses, not even on the six o'clock news.

As soon as the next news item came on I zapped off

the set with the remote and just sat there, waiting for
the call. It would come right away if she was watching
alone, and somewhat later if her husband was watching
the news with her. They'd have things to talk over. The
phone rang twenty-six minutes after I had turned the set
off.

"How did it go?" I said when I heard Hope's voice.

"Not so bad."

"Kids see it?"

"Oh, sure. Naturally."

"What did you tell them?"

"Lied, of course. They know the ACLU has repre-
sented the clinics."

"Won't work with Martin, though."

"No."

"He there with you?"

"Right here."

"And it's okay?"

"Not so bad. But I think you should come out after
supper. Would you?"

"Of course I will. Maybe it's even a good thing."

"Maybe. Who knows? We'll work it through,
somehow."

They lived in a large brick house painted white, almost a mansion, really, that sat in the woods on a winding road north of Massachusetts Avenue, out past the
British Embassy. It was the sort of house you can afford
if you have two Washington lawyers in the family, particularly if one of them is Martin Edwards. Hope makes
enough running the Washington office of the ACLU to
put her in the top 5 percent of Americans, I imagine.
But Martin is one of those Washington lawyers who are
paid so much that it makes you wonder if Danny Quayle
wasn't right about the profession. In the abstract, my
view would be that Martin ought to be taxed into bank-
ruptcy and put to work roofing houses or building cars.
But in actual fact, I've always kind of liked him, what

little I've seen of him. Of course we had always stayed entirely on the surface with each other, and he might turn out to be very different underneath. I had never really wanted to find out. Now I'd have to.

Martin Edwards and Hope had gone through Georgetown Law School together. Like Cheney and Gingrich and Buchanan and Stockman and the rest of the war wimps, he wasn't from the draftable classes. Unlike them, Martin wasn't a lying hypocrite, then or now. He had spoken out against the Vietnam War back at the time; later he had also spoken out against the war wimps' pathetic little weenie-wavers in Lebanon, Grenada, Libya, Nicaragua, Panama, and the Persian Gulf. And he had done it publicly every time, signing his name to ads, marching in demonstrations, writing letters to the *Post*. It wasn't in the same category as lying down on the train tracks or standing up to Bull Connor's police dogs, maybe, but it couldn't have scored him many points with his fellow partners down at Skaggs Philpott and Templeman. It was behavior that you might even call, in a corporate lawyer, courageous.

Martin came to the door when I knocked. He had always been polite and friendly to me, although at the same time slightly remote and amused. And he seemed that way now. "Something to drink?" he said to me. "No? You're sure? Hope? No? Well, I'll get myself a little bourbon, then. You two can be the designated drivers."

Did that mean something? That Hope and I were together, and he was out of the club? That we two were sober and respectable, and he was a dissolute drunk? What the hell was the matter with me. It was just chatter.

Martin came back with his drink and sat down. A tall, lean man with the kind of sharp-featured good looks that would age well, like Gregory Peck's or Clint Eastwood's. I wondered if I looked as calm and easy inside my skin as he did.

"Well," he said after he had tasted his bourbon, "I imagine we've all worked out problems that were a lot tougher than this one. Maybe we won't even have a problem at all, once we look at things together. From what Hope tells me, we have a lot of concerns in common."

"Speaking of which," I said, "where are the kids?"

"In their rooms doing their homework," Martin said. "At least Paul and Steven theoretically are." Their two sons were students at Sidwell Friends.

"They don't know about this?"

"They know you and I were on TV," Hope said. "They knew the ACLU is involved with the whole abortion clinic mess over there. They've always known you and I are friends. They didn't ask why you were along on this particular business call. I doubt if the truth even occurred to them. Children have trouble imagining that their parents have sex lives."

I never had any trouble. When he was drunk, my father often didn't bother to close the bedroom door. We'd stand outside and giggle. It was different for the Edwards children, though. Their parents slept in separate bedrooms and in fact didn't have any sex lives. Not at home, anyway. Martin's longtime lover was a married congressman from Illinois, Hope had told me. The congressman's wife lived back in Illinois while he kept a bachelor apartment in an anonymous high rise in Rosslyn, just across the river from Georgetown.

"Well, we do have sex lives, don't we?" I said. "Did you know all along, Martin?"

"Pretty much. I thought when Hope came back from the Carter campaign that she had found somebody. I was glad, actually. She seemed happier. Then when she introduced me to you at that reception in Blair House during the transition, seeing you together, I knew who it was."

"You never said anything to her, though?"

"It was a pretty tricky situation, wasn't it? I wanted her to be happy, but I didn't want to lose the kids. Or lose her, either. Probably that doesn't make sense to you, or does it?"

"Sure it does. I wouldn't want to lose her myself."

"I didn't want to lose either of you, either," Hope said. "I was afraid if I left Martin for you, I'd wind up losing you both."

I didn't want to go into why she thought that. Secretly it was the same thing I was afraid of, that the job I had done of gluing myself together over all these years would come unstuck under the pressure of real life. I had built myself a sheltered environment, and I wasn't sure I could survive outside it.

"And so all three of us went on the best way we could, didn't we?" Martin said. "Maybe it wasn't such a bad way after all."

"We sort of grew into each other's empty spaces," Hope said.

We sat there silent for a while after that. Martin finished his drink, and shook his glass a little so that the ice cubes ran around the inside of it.

"Well, now we know," he said at last. "Officially."

"Like the sixties," Hope said. "Let it all hang out."

"Which was idiotic, of course." Martin was the one who said it, but I believed it, too.

"Mostly," Hope said. "Maybe not now. Here."

"I hope," I said.

"Don't we all," Martin said. "Well, I think I'll get myself a refill. How about something for you folks?"

"Why not?" Hope and I said, exactly at the same time. In the instant we were looking at each other, wondering whether to laugh or be embarrassed, the phone rang. Martin moved to get it, but there was only the single ring. "One of the kids picked up," he said and continued on toward the bar instead. He had opened a beer for me and was mixing white wine with soda for Hope when their daughter appeared on the stair landing. Lisa was a sensible girl, a cello- and soccer-playing junior at Smith who was home on spring break. Standing on the stairs, Lisa hadn't said anything about the call yet. But Hope picked up some signal or vibration that I missed.

"What's wrong, honey?" she said.

"I don't know," her daughter said. "Somebody weird on the phone."

"What did he say?"

"She. She sounded just regular, that was the funny thing. She asked was I aware I was a murderer, but completely normal, you know? Just a question. I was so surprised I didn't say anything, and then she said all about murder and hell everlasting and I hung up."

"Oh, my God," Hope said.

"They thought I was you, didn't they, Mom?"

Before Hope could come up with something to say, Lisa went on: "I didn't figure that out till I hung up. That's funny, isn't it? She must have thought you were at that place because you were . . . well, a patient, you know? Instead of a lawyer."

"Yes, I guess she did," Hope said.

"But how did she know who you were?" the girl asked. "It wasn't on TV who you were, you or Mr. Bethany, either." Hope's children had met me now and then over the years, but not often enough to call me Tom.

I remembered the Life Force guy taking pictures of our little convoy. "They must have run the license plate numbers this afternoon at motor vehicles." I said. "Once they had the name, all they had to do is look you up in the phone book."

The phone rang again. Hope beat Martin to it, and listened for a moment. "I feel terribly sorry for you," she said gently, and hung up. I couldn't have handled the gentleness. It rang again immediately. This time Hope listened in silence, and then hung up. "You want to shake them, the poor women," she said. "You want to say wake up and smell the coffee, dear. Let the men do their own dirty work."

"Maybe we should get an unlisted number, Mom," Lisa said.

"I don't like unlisted numbers," Hope said. The phone rang again.

"We've got to do something, Mom."

Hope took the phone off the hook and let it sit on the table while we talked about what to do. Martin came up with the basic idea of a message on the answering machine, but his ideas for messages were too logical and lawyerly. Hope came up with the best suggestion. By the time I left, the machine was rigged the way she wanted it.

4

*N*EXT MORNING MY OWN PHONE RANG AS I WAS
getting myself breakfast. I figured it was probably for the
dentist, who seemed to be a popular guy to judge by the
calls I had been fielding for him. It was a young-sound-
ing voice instead, asking for me. "Mr. Carpenter,
please," he said. I use the Carpenter name a lot when
there's no good reason not to. The fewer people who
know me as Tom Bethany, the more comfortable I feel.

"Mr. Carpenter? Listen, it's Roy Shipley. From yesterday? She's dead."

Something stopped in me for an instant when he said
that, till I connected Roy's name with the kid in the
arcade. "Kimberly is?" I said. If I sounded the way I felt,
I sounded relieved that it wasn't Hope.

"She killed herself, Mr. Carpenter," he said. "She
jumped off the Calvert Street Bridge. Oh, my God, it's
so awful. All the way down while you're falling, you
must . . ."

"Okay, Roy," I said. "Okay, easy. Go slow. How do
you know she's dead?"

45

"Her mother just called me and said I killed her."

"Why did she think that?"

"They saw Kimberly on TV in the back of your car. Her mother and father did."

"Why would they call you, though? You weren't on TV."

"Kimberly must have told them who took her to the clinic. They must have made her tell. They thought I took her to the bridge, too."

"But you didn't, huh? What happened?"

"I don't know, except Mrs. Butler says she's dead."

"How are you holding up, Roy?"

"I feel awful. I feel like it's my fault, like I should have done something."

"Okay, fair enough. That's the way a good person would naturally feel. Just remember it's a bullshit feeling, though. Believe me on that. It's normal for a friend to feel guilty when something like this happens, but at the same time it's bullshit, because you didn't do anything, and nothing you did could have made any difference. You can't see that just yet, but after a while you will."

"Yes, sir."

"What are you going to do today? Have you got any friends you could have over or something?"

"Not really. I was going to go to school, that's all."

"All right, go. Just get through it the best way you can. Can you talk about stuff like this to your mom and dad?"

"My dad lives in Oregon. My mom left for work before Mrs. Butler called."

"Can you talk to her, though? Your mom?"

"I guess so."

"Will you do it, then?"

"I can try."

"Try then. Even if it's hard. Because when stuff like

this happens, you've got to talk about it to somebody. So will you? Promise?"

"I promise to try."

After he hung up I thought about the boy, walking stunned through school. I thought about the girl, thinking what you always think about jumpers, the same thing the boy had been thinking. That she was conscious all the way down. I saw a woman once after she jumped six stories onto a paved parking lot. She had landed on her back. She lay perfectly calm, as if asleep, except that her head was in a pool of dark red blood.

I called Hope's house to tell her what had happened to the girl who hid in terror behind her stuffed animal. I got Hope's recorded voice saying, "You have reached the J. Danforth Quayle Museum and Library. We're sorry we can't come to the phone right now, but please leave a brief message at the beep and we'll get back to you as quickly as we can."

The message wasn't as amusing as it had seemed the night before. Probably it hadn't been amusing then, either, but you did what you could.

At the beep I said, "Hope, pick up if you're in." But she didn't pick up.

So I called J. Wadsworth Fails IV instead.

Years ago J. Wadsworth Fails IV answered our classified ad and moved into the grad student group slum I shared in Allston, across the river from Cambridge. He had a lot of things not going for him. For instance, Fails wore blue tennis shoes with white soles. And he wore bow ties all the time. He wore one of two sports jackets all the time, too, a yellow linen one in the summer and a Harris tweed one the color of dogshit in the winter. Summer and winter both, he wore khaki pants with cuffs. And on top of all that, you had the name he went by.

"What does the *J* stand for?" I asked him a couple days after he moved in.

"For Jay," he said. "*J-A-Y.*"

"*J?*" I said. "*A? Y?*"

"Ah, no doubt you are wondering why I use only the initial. Why not, for example, just call myself Jay, like the eponymous bird, and let it go at that? The answer, Thomas—may I call you Thomas?—is that calling myself Jay Fails would suggest that I am a regular guy, and I am not a regular guy. I was raised with great care and at great expense to be an asshole, and I am, consequently, an asshole."

"For some reason I feel like I just got stuffed," I said. "Hell, yes, you can call me Thomas."

So we were friends from then on, and Jay was a lot of help to me in my schooling. He got books for me out of the Harvard library system, and he helped me pick the right lecture courses to sneak into. In fact, I stole pretty nearly the same education from Harvard that Jay paid for, except that at the end he got a doctorate in sociology. He also got a job, his first job ever. It was as a general assignment reporter for the *Quincy Patriot Ledger*, where his doctorate turned out to be as handy as an extra appendix.

The thing that broke him loose from Quincy was his accent. The *Patriot Ledger* tapped him to do a radio feed from their city room, a few extra bucks each week for reading the paper's upcoming local news over one of the Boston radio stations. Those plummy, patrician tones coming out of a place like Quincy caught the attention of somebody at Channel 4, and next thing you know you had that bow tie and those jackets on the tube giving you the hot skinny from the city room of the *Patriot Ledger*, and pretty soon after that Jay was gone from the Quincy paper and on the staff of the *Globe*. And now he was chief of their Washington bureau.

"Thomas!" he said when I phoned the bureau. "How

are you? How's Hope?" He was one of the few people
who knew about us. He had been present at the creation,
during Carter's 1980 campaign. In fact he was the cre-
ator, in a way, since he was the one who introduced us.

"We're good."

"She, at any rate, looked terrific on TV. Were you the
driver? I couldn't quite see, although I naturally thought
of you when I heard one of the demonstrators had a
broken thumb."

"Yeah, I heard that, too. A broken thumb."

"I do worry about the judgment thing, though,
Thomas. When you accompany a lady to an abortion
clinic, you have to consider how it looks to the world
at large. Looks very bad, Thomas. Looks as if you two
didn't know where babies come from."

Good. He would never joke about it if the thought had
even crossed his mind that Hope was there on anything
but ACLU business.

"One place they come from is this Life Force outfit,"
I said. "You couldn't see it on the TV, but they threw a
pickled fetus into the backseat with Hope and a little
pregnant girl we were giving a lift to. Bottle broke in the
kid's lap."

"Nice."

"That kid's parents saw her on TV, Jay. TV that was
there because this Pastor asshole called them up. The
parents must have crawled all over the poor girl afterward, and last night she jumped off the Calvert Street
Bridge."

"Really? I didn't notice anything in the Post. Do you
have her name?"

"I'll trade you."

"For what? We can get it from the cops."

"Trade me anyway. All I want is a look at whatever
clips you've got on the Pastor. I'm getting to where I
really don't like him."

"Actually, Susan Freedman has a pretty good collection on the good Reverend. Susan is one of my reporters. She thinks the guy is going someplace politically, so she's done a couple of background interviews with him."

"Okay, the girl's name was Kimberly Butler. She lived out in Reston, at one one two nine Harmon Drive." Remembering things is one of my tricks. I even remembered the phone number Kimberly had given the clinic receptionist, and I passed that along to Fails, too.

"I suppose she died too late for the *Post*," Fails said. "Either that or they don't know about the girl's connection with the demonstration. That she just had an abortion."

"That's the thing. She didn't have an abortion."

"What was she there for, then?"

"For an abortion, but she was so disturbed they sent her home."

"Disturbed by the demonstration?"

"Actually, she was ninety percent around the bend when she walked into the clinic. She flipped out totally when these Life Force assholes showed up."

"Flipped out how?"

"She'd only talk to you through a stuffed animal named Binkie. The woman that runs the place told the kid to go on home until she got it together a little more."

"Presumably she was there without her parents' knowledge?"

"Right. She had a friend from high school drop her off. Her parents didn't know she was pregnant till this Pastor guy put her on TV. Okay if I come over right now and talk to your reporter?"

"Sure. I'll ask her to pull her files."

I walked from Georgetown to the *Globe*'s bureau, on Pennsylvania Avenue just west of the White House. It was the kind of day that made you want to walk—warm and bright with now and then just a breath of a breeze.

I started out wearing my sweater, but before I had gone a block I tied it around my waist instead.

Jay's colleague, Susan Freedman, turned out to be a thin, active-looking woman with her curly, reddish blond hair sticking out Afro-style. She wore a short leather skirt and black tights that showed off her good legs. A loose black cotton cardigan hung halfway to her knees, covering all but the last inch or so of her skirt. Around her neck was a Moroccan necklace made out of old silver coins and lumps of amber the size of Ping-Pong balls. She had on yellow headphones, which she politely took off and hung around her neck on top of the amber when Jay introduced us.

"So you're interested in my old buddy, the Pastor," she said. "The Reverend Howard Orrin. He's all in here."

Freedman flopped an eleven-by-fourteen manila envelope on a vacant desk. It was fat with magazine and newspaper clippings, and wire service copy, and black-and-white glossies with photo service captions on the back.

"Well, you're in good hands," Jay said, turning to go. "Treat Susan right and maybe she'll let you listen to her Sting tapes."

"Up yours, too, Fails," she called after him. "Jay is totally a musical peasant. Listens to Brahms."

"Jay says you keep special track of the Pastor," I said.

"Not just him. All Nazis. I want to know when they're coming to get me, so I can beat 'em to the border. That's what did in most of my mother's family, back in the thirties. They didn't keep track."

"Antiabortionists are Nazis?"

"Sure they are. Hitler banned abortion practically first thing. In 1943 the French Nazis guillotined a woman for abortion."

"I didn't know that."

"You could look it up."

"And that makes Orrin a Nazi, huh?"

"Shit, yes. Skinheads, Klansmen, Al Sharpton, fundamentalists, all of them are. Guys like Helms, Buchanan, Reagan? To me, they're all anti-Semites, and to me that's a Nazi."

"Reagan's an anti-Semite? He spent half his life in the movie industry."

"Exactly. So how come he never happened to run across a single Jew he figured was smart enough to come to Washington with him?"

"Well, Weinberger—"

"Weinberger's an *Episcopalian!* I mean, give me a break! The only Jew Reagan gave a good job to was Charles Z. Wick at USIA, which is subcabinet, and it's an agency nobody gives a shit about anyway. And even Wick only got the job because he played piano at Reagan's parties and his wife was buddies with Nancy. Besides, the pathetic son of a bitch was born Charlie Zwick and changed his name. What does that tell you? Tells you he's an anti-Semite himself, like any Republican Jew. Same thing if you're in Likud. Look at Begin and Shamir."

"They changed their names?"

"No, they're anti-Semites. Look at it from the Palestinian point of view. Arabs are Semites, aren't they? Am I right or wrong on this?"

I was getting it all sorted out. Freedman used Nazi and anti-Semite to mean any kind of bully; if they weren't precisely anti-Semitic at the moment, they would be if they ever thought about it. And if there weren't any Jews handy right now, these potential Nazis would pick on a black or an Arab or anybody else who was smaller. Like, in Howard Orrin's case, women.

"So you're not saying that Orrin is actually a member of the American Nazi Party?" I asked. "Just that he's got the right stuff?"

"Hey, maybe I'm not being fair to the guy. Could be,

huh? So let me tell you a story, you decide. First time I was introduced to the Pastor, he said, 'Pardon me for asking, young lady, but would you by any chance be chewish?' So for one thing I'm saying, What is this 'young lady' shit?, since I hate to admit it but I'm only a few years younger than him. Then I start to wonder, Well, what about it, am I chewish or not? What does that mean down there where he comes from, to be chewish? And I really, literally, don't understand what he's talking about until he says, 'Of course Our Lord was chewish.'

"So maybe you're right. Maybe I *am* being unfair. How could the guy be an anti-Semitic Nazi pig when his best friend is a chew?"

Freedman left to go back to her personal version of Nazi hunting, and I slid the contents of the Orrin file out onto the desk. It was mostly press clippings, so of course you couldn't count on it too much. But you could find little bits of truth stuck in here and there, like oats in horse manure.

Years ago I read about a public opinion analyst who had a good idea. Presumably it wasn't a money-making idea, since I never heard of him again. But that doesn't mean he wasn't right. The idea was that as long as you knew what you were doing, the newspapers were full of stuff that you could count on absolutely. For instance, suppose *The New York Times* tells you the Minnesota Twins beat the Boston Red Sox 4–0 yesterday in Fenway Park. Investigation will prove that there are teams of that name, that they played each other in exactly that ball park on the date mentioned, and that the score was four-zip with the Twins on the long end of the tally. The newspapers are full of solid information like that. Senate roll call votes, the prices in ads, criminal charges brought, civil suits filed, verdicts rendered, sentences imposed, verbatim texts of speeches, stock market quotations. This kind of stuff you can count on, even act on.

But everything else is poetry, not science. You read it for amusement, not information.

Amusement, under this public opinion expert's definition, included most of what runs as news. Everything people had been told about, or hoped, or thought, or thought they thought, or said, or said they said, or said other people said, or said what they thought other people meant when the other people said it, and so on. Stick to the box scores, then, and forget whatever *The Times* tells you the manager said about Roger Clements being off his game because of trouble at home, and yatata, yatata.

So the public opinion analyst's good idea was to mine the papers for only what was practically certain to be true, and skip the rest. If a public opinion poll shows that four out of five Americans care deeply about the environment, for instance, don't even bother to read past the headline. But if the paper says voters in Springfield turned down a ten-million-dollar bond issue for a new sewage treatment plant by a two-to-one margin, log it in as hard data. That way you won't be confused or surprised when all those greens go out every four years and vote for the candidate from a party that hasn't nominated an environmentalist for president since Theodore Roosevelt.

If you go through newspaper stories in this way, you can reduce a fat envelope of clippings down to just a few lines—but the little bit you're left with is liable to be true. For instance I figured Howard Orrin was probably born in Wythe County, Virginia, on August 17 of 1946, since he looked about the right age and there'd be no point in lying about it. I believed that he went to public schools in Wytheville, too, although I'd want to check a little further on whether he was really an "honor student." I was on the honor roll at my high school back in Port Henry, New York, but it was a wrestling Roll of Honor that used to hang in a back corridor off the gym.

I was reasonably confident that Orrin had gone on to a community college in Roanoke, and from there to the Bethel Bible Institute in Frankfort, Kentucky. I was willing to bet he had graduated from it, too, just the way his résumé said. I was also willing to bet that if an orangutan came up with the tuition, it too could knuckle-walk out of Bethel Bible Institute with a diploma.

The young theologian then moved from Kentucky to Newport News, where he became assistant pastor of a small church. Being a superpatriot of draft age like Dan Quayle, Orrin joined the Virginia National Guard as a second lieutenant in the Chaplains Corps. By now, more than twenty years later, he was a colonel. Some of his staff even called him that. You had to assume he didn't mind.

He had married Merribeth Collins, the young organist in his first church. After two years they left to set up their own shop, the Church of Our Redeemer Risen, in a failed neighborhood movie theater. The Pastor struggled along for a few years, getting by, but just barely to hear him tell it.

Then the Lord stepped in, working for the moment through the agency of a time salesman for a local TV station. The salesman explained to Howard Orrin that all those preachers on TV didn't get there because of popular demand. They got there because they bought time from the station, just the same as Kellogg's Cornflakes did and Miller's, the Champagne of Bottled Beers. All those Sunday-morning sermons were really just long commercials, in cheap time slots that most advertisers didn't want. The only hitch was that you had to pay for the time up front.

No problem. The Pastor just renounced all his worldly goods to the bank in the form of second mortgages on his house and his church, and became an electronic beggar.

It worked out real well. Before long he was hustling for handouts on more than a hundred stations throughout the country. And soon he was able to build a new church that resembled Mount Vernon, only much bigger and made out of glass. The pillars were a wonder. Nobody in Newport News or anyplace else had ever seen glass pillars that looked like steeples. In front of the altar was a twenty-two-foot-long baptismal font set into the floor. It was supposed to be in the exact shape of the Sea of Galilee.

And in 1984, most wonderfully of all, the Pastor had caused to rise up, just north of Virginia Beach, a biblical theme park named Lordland.

"Ever been there?" said Freedman, who had walked over and found me looking at the stuff on Lordland.

"I've been pretty tied up," I said.

"Go. Take my word for it, you'll love it. They got this ride called Pilgrim's Progress."

"You're shitting me, of course."

"No, man. You start out in the Slough of Despond. The Pastor does a voice-over on tape. He has to tell the boobs what *slough* and *despond* mean, on account of a lot of you goyim have pretty limited vocabularies."

"Is that right? I've got to say, Susan, that strikes me as kind of anti-Gentile."

"No, it's just the facts. You guys don't do as well as we do on your SATs. You could look it up." As far as I knew she was right, so I let it go. What the hell, the Koreans and the Chinese probably do even better than the Jews. The important thing is to know your place.

"Tell me about Orrin," I said. "What sort of a guy is he?"

"Look at him," the reporter said, gesturing at one of the glossies in my pile. "The face says it all."

It was a roundish face with plump cheeks and the beginning of a double chin. The Pastor wore big, gold-rimmed glasses that suggested the World War II aviator style without actually going quite that far. The lenses were untinted, for one thing. I couldn't see any bifocal line. Since he was getting into bifocal age, that probably meant he had paid extra for the new kind where the line doesn't show. Why not? He was in show business, after all, which you could tell by the blow-dried hair that swooped down over his forehead, every strand in its carefully casual, razor-cut place. Nobody except politicians and actors wore their hair like that anymore, but of course Orrin qualified on both counts. The tops of his ears were fashionably covered with feathered wings of hair, but the bottoms stuck out on either side of his face in little knobs. He would have earlobes drooping pretty nearly down to his collar in a few years. Ever since Lyndon Johnson, I've figured a man with those hound-dog earlobes is going to lie to you even when he doesn't need to.

"You talking about the earlobes now?" I asked Freedman. "Or the blow job on his hair?"

"I'm talking about that little cupid's bow mouth."

"Not so little."

"Well, no. Kind of a medium-size cupid's bow mouth. Probably you had a chemistry teacher in high school with that kind of a mouth."

"Civics teacher, actually."

"What kind of a guy was he?"

"A nasty shit."

"See? You can tell by the mouth."

And the Windsor knot in the tie and the slightly over-sized cross in the lapel of his three-piece suit. The suit looked light gray in the black-and-white photo, but my guess was that it was powder blue in real life. Or possibly fawn-colored. The fabric was smooth and wrinkle free, what they call a blend. This means it's part plastic, better than straight wool. The first car I bought, I asked the salesman if the seats were leather. Better than leather, he said. This here is Naugahyde.

"How come there's no pictures of the little woman?" I asked Freedman.

"There is." She picked a shot out of the pile that showed the Pastor on what looked like a high school auditorium stage, orating under a sign saying, Pro-Choice Is Pro-Murder. Freedman pointed to a woman sitting in the row of chairs behind Howard Orrin. Howard filled a vest up tight, but Merribeth's clothes hung loose on her. She was the sort of woman that other women say would be attractive if only she'd fix herself up. She looked up at the Pastor as he talked, but with her head a little bowed and her shoulders a little hunched. It was short of a cringe, but it was definitely self-effacing. You got the impression she felt she needed permission to worship her man. Merribeth probably went through life murmuring "Excuse me" and smiling vaguely at strangers.

"They have any kids?" I asked Freedman.

"Two adopted boys, one preschool, the other first or second grade maybe. They're timid like their mother. He calls them little hellions. They sort of hide behind his legs and look embarrassed."

"I don't see them in any of the pictures. He doesn't campaign with them, huh?"

"Mostly they're back in Newport News with their mother. He's up here saving fetuses and getting on TV."

"He lives here?"

"For the moment, yeah. His campaign headquarters are here. He lives out on Williamsburg Boulevard, in a house that belongs to the rich widow of a big Washington furrier."

"I see."

"No, you don't. She retired down in Florida. She lets the Pastor live there because she's a big pro-lifer."

"Why does he want to be up here, though, politically? I thought the Washington suburbs looked like Sodom and Gomorrah to the rest of Virginia."

"To some extent. But the demographics are different since the Byrd machine days. The two big population centers are the Tidewater and the D.C. suburbs. Orrin's church is in the Tidewater, so he's already got a base there. By living in Arlington, he gets a base here, too. But the big reason for being here is access to free media. The Washington stations give you the best statewide market penetration. That's the point of this antiabortion bullshit, to get free time on Channel Four."

"He's not sincere about it?"

"Oh, he probably is. It's part of the larger control issue, isn't it? In sorrow thou shalt bring forth children, and thy husband shall rule over thee. It's right there in the Bible, plain as day. Penis Power."

I glanced at Orrin's picture again, him at the microphone and his uninspiring wife seated behind him. He didn't look like that much of an Old Testament patriarchal stud, but then neither does Mrs. Terry's little boy, Randall.

"Is he going to make it to the Senate?" I asked Freedman.

"Could be," the reporter said. "He's a hell of a speaker, if you like that style of speaking, and he's got unlimited funds from his ministry."

"He can't use that money, can he?"

"Not legally or openly, no. But you take a guy who's a paid staffer for Life Force or the Pastor's church, what's to stop him from doing a little moonlighting on his own time for the campaign? And nobody can track Orrin's money anyway. Millions of dollars pour into the mail room at Redeemer Risen every month, in small checks, and sometimes in cash, too. Where does it come from? Where does it go? Only the Pastor knows, and he ain't telling."

"So he's got a real chance?"

"Why not? He's a TV star. He's had his own show longer than Reagan did. And you've got the theme park factor, too. Reagan never even had his own theme park, unless you count California. Sure the Pastor's got a chance. Maybe he can go all the way.''

"President Orrin.''

"These old eyes have seen weirder shit than that, and recently, too. At least this actor isn't stupid.''

"He doesn't say anything very smart, at least not in these clippings.''

"When you're hustling the people he's hustling, it's smart to sound dumb. But there's no flies on Orrin, particularly where money and politics are concerned.''

"Is he smart enough to keep his fly closed?'' I asked. "A lot of these Christers seem to have trouble that way.''

"Him too.''

"Tell me about it.''

"Nothing to tell. Him too, that's all. Hey, a girl knows.''

"He hit on you, did he?''

"Nothing you could take to court, but sure he hit on me. Taking my elbow when he showed me to my chair. Holding my hand too long when he said good-bye. Telling me how much he liked my sweater.''

"One of those perverts that likes sweaters, huh? You're not cutting the guy a whole lot of slack here.''

"He didn't give a shit about my sweater. The point was I didn't have anything under it and you could tell it, know what I mean?''

"Yeah, I know. I'm kind of an expert on that myself. Most guys are.''

"Most of them don't look at your chest and ask if it's a little too chilly for you in here.''

"Okay, he was hitting on you.''

"Damn right he was. Next he would have told me about the pubic hair in his Coke.''

Once I had all I needed from Susan Freedman and her files, I walked over to Jay Fails's office and asked him out to lunch. As I had hoped, he took me to lunch instead, on the *Boston Globe*'s money.

"Good tip on that girl jumper," Jay said once we had ordered.

"You checked it out already?"

"Susan did."

"Oh, yeah? I never thought to ask her. What did she find out?"

"Not much more than you told me. But she's going out this afternoon to chase pictures."

"What does that mean?"

"Con pictures out of the family. Junior high graduation shot or something."

"Isn't that going a little far? It's not even a Boston story."

"Susan wanted to run it down anyway, so we'll have our own art on file, and a few quotes from the parents."

"How come?"

"Same reason she's done all this work on Orrin already. She thinks he's going to make it to the Senate, and she wants to be ready to swarm all over him when he gets big enough to be a national story."

"She's really fond of the guy, huh?"

"Well, that's the thing about good investigative reporters," Fails said. "They're world-class haters."

"I'll never understand that type of person," I said. "I always figure there's some good in everybody."

"Of course you do," said Fails. "That's the first thing people notice about you."

5

I SPENT THE AFTERNOON GOING THROUGH THE PE-
riodical files in the D.C. public library, adding details to
the picture of the Pastor that Susan Freedman had given
me. All along, I was thinking of Life Force's siege of
the Arlington clinic, and of the pudgy figure carrying a
bullhorn. Producer-director of his own campaign commercials, with Hope and little Kimberly and myself making unpaid guest appearances. Himself safe on the
sidelines while his unwitting or unwilling actors went
to jail, or onto television stripped naked of their privacy.
I kept seeing the young face of Kimberly Butler, blank
with shock as the little gray fetus lay in her lap in its
nest of broken glass. I wondered if she had jumped with
her Binkie, or if she had left the stuffed animal on the
Calvert Street Bridge far above.

After the library closed, I went back to the dentist's
house in Georgetown, watched "MacNeil/Lehrer" on the
dentist's cable TV, microwaved supper in his oven, and
called Hope on his phone.

I called five or six times before I started counting, and

five more times after. Each time the line was busy. It seemed likely that the line was jammed with nut calls, or that Hope and Martin had left the phone off the hook. I rang the number I had taken from the boy, Roy Shipley, and got him on the first ring.

"Mr. Carpenter!" he said. "I was just getting ready to call you again. I've been calling you for a while, but it was always busy."

"So was the number I was calling," I said. "What's up?"

"They think I did it."

"Whoa, back up. Who thinks you did what?"

"The Butlers think that me and Kimberly . . . that we . . . that I was . . . ."

"That you got her pregnant?"

"Well, yeah, and I didn't."

"I know. You told me you didn't."

"I told them, too. Mr. Butler. When he called. But he didn't believe me."

"Naturally not. He's an asshole."

"You know him?"

"Kimberly wouldn't have thrown herself off the bridge if he hadn't acted like an asshole to her after he saw her on the news."

While he chewed on that, I thought about the nasty fix the boy was in for having helped out a terrified girl. No good deed goes unpunished.

"You told me you knew who the real father was," I said. "Why don't you just tell Mr. Butler that?"

"I can't. I promised."

"I think we better talk, Roy."

Since we both knew the arcade on Columbia Pike, we met in the frozen yogurt shop two doors down from it. "How's the Everything Special?" I asked him. It was at the top of the menu for five dollars, billed as a Pigout Delight.

"I've never had it," the boy said. "Too expensive."

"Bring us two Everything Specials," I told the high school kid behind the counter, who had nodded at Roy when we came in. The kid turned to get our order, and we grabbed a table. "Friend of yours?" I asked.

"He's in my class, but I don't know his name. I don't know too many kids."

"How do you like school?"

"It's okay, I guess."

"Sucks, huh? Is it hard?"

"Not too."

"How are your grades?"

"Okay."

"How okay?"

"Pretty okay, I guess."

"Honor roll okay?"

"Well, yeah."

"Where are you in your class?"

"Third or something like that, but that's just because I hand in all the stuff. Plenty of kids are smarter than me, but they blow it off. I don't blame them. It's pretty boring."

"Well, shit, grades aren't everything. Remember Danny? Those kids could grow up to be Vice President."

Our order was ready, and we dug away at the huge peaks of swirled frozen yogurt for a while. The Brits have a disgusting kind of kids' candy called gobstoppers. The Everything Special stopped your gob, all right. Strawberries, banana slices, crushed nuts, M&Ms, and maraschino cherries oozed down the flanks in landslides of chocolate and butterscotch. We ate in silence and ate and ate, until our plates were clean.

"You know who else was on the honor roll in high school?" I said. "I know because I've been looking him up. The Pastor."

"What pastor?"

"The Reverend Howard Orrin. Didn't you see him on TV? Outside the clinic with the bullhorn?"

"Oh, right."

"What if he had stayed home minding his business that day? Where do you think Kimberly would be now?"

He had been too busy loading guilt on himself to think about where else it might belong. It took him a moment to think through what would have happened if Kimberly's abortion had gone off as planned and he had been able to pick her up afterward as scheduled.

"She'd be alive, I guess."

"Something to keep in mind, isn't it?"

Roy nodded.

"Let me ask you something else, Roy. This guy that got Kimberly pregnant, what if he had kept his dick in his pants? Where would she be today?"

"Same thing. Alive."

"Did she want to keep his name secret so he wouldn't get in trouble?"

"Mostly she was worried about her own self getting in trouble. I guess her dad is real strict. She figured if she complained about the guy to the school it would have got back to her dad."

"Complained to the school? Was this some punk in your school that raped her?"

"Nothing like that, no."

"Who was it, then?"

"I told her I wouldn't tell."

"Think about the situation, Roy. She'd be alive today if this guy had stood by her."

"You mean like married her?"

"That would be one way."

"He's married already. That was the whole problem."

"Roy, Kimberly's gotten into all the trouble with her parents that she's going to. It's too late to protect her by keeping the guy's name out of it."

"Still, it was a promise."

"But the reason for the promise is gone. Gone the minute her folks saw her coming out of the clinic on TV."

"I guess."

"So Kimberly isn't really the point anymore. Other girls are, girls down the line. Listen, how old was Kimberly?"

"Just fourteen. She skipped a grade."

"She didn't even look that."

"Well, yeah, she did look kind of young for her age."

"Okay, fourteen. If this guy is married, he's probably a grown man. Ever see him?"

"I've seen him lots. He's a grown man."

"So, see, he's not just some high school kid dipping his wick in girls his own age. He's a predator. With those guys, it's like a habit only worse. Like an incurable disease. He'll keep on messing up more kids till somebody stops him."

Roy thought it over, but not for long. After a moment he said, "Okay, it was Mr. Pearsall."

William Pearsall turned out to be an English teacher at the high school, and the drama coach. Last fall the drama club had put on *Ten Little Indians*, not starring Kimberly Butler or Roy Shipley. "Kimberly went to the tryouts, but she didn't have enough nerve to stand up and read," Roy said. "Anyway, she looks too young. Mr. Pearsall made her props manager."

"Did you try out?"

"I was the sound man. We had sound effects coming from different parts of the auditorium. It was kind of cool. Whenever there's a pep rally at school, anything like that, that's what I do. The audio."

"Are you a ham, too?"

"Yeah, I am." He knew I meant ham radio, not ham actor. "How did you know?"

"Just guessed." The really smart kids in my high school were all into things like model trains or airplanes, sci-fi, hi-fi, ham radio. School bored them. The ones who got good grades did it like Roy, with their left hands. Most didn't even put in that much effort. A surprising number of them dropped out. One of them was the smartest kid in my class, who wound up running a secondhand shop in Glens Falls. On weekends he dresses up in armor and reenacts medieval combats. In a better world he would have been tapped to become a teacher, and then turned loose in some high school to unpetrify young minds, and then made principal. But it isn't a better world, and most high school principals are ex-coaches.

"Did Pearsall coach anything except drama?" I asked.

"The ski club, that's all. They take day trips to West Virginia when it's cold enough to make snow. Only it's real expensive, with the lift tickets and the equipment and stuff."

"What kind of a teacher is he?"

"He's okay. Plenty of kids think he's like some kind of a star or something."

"Not you?"

"I guess I used to, before all this. It seemed like he took a real interest in kids."

"You got that right. How old a guy is he?"

"He's got kids of his own but he's not a real old guy," Roy said. "Like you? Middle-aged?"

"How old are the kids?"

"Just little kids. In grade school still." Late thirties, most likely, or early forties.

"Tell me about Pearsall and Kimberly."

Most of the kids in the drama club thought the teacher was really cool, it turned out. The way he carried his cable-knit sweater swung over one shoulder. The way he talked about Woody and Dustin and Susan, who was Susan Sarandon and he knew her from summer stock before anybody ever heard of her. The way he wore his tie, with one end just looped over the other. The men teachers had to wear ties, but there was nothing in the regulations about how they had to be tied.

He had made a big thing out of finding period props

for the play, which was supposed to be in England in the old days, maybe fifty years ago or something. "God is in the details," Pearsall would say. So he worked closely with Kimberly Butler, but still they couldn't come up with just the right kind of bric-a-brac and pictures and furniture, not locally anyway. For the good stuff, it turned out you had to go way down around Warrenton, and scout the secondhand stores and antique dealers for things you could get cheap. Or, better yet, talk the shopkeepers into lending props to you in return for a mention in the program.

"I'm surprised her father let her go on long drives alone with this guy," I said.

"He told Mr. Butler that he was taking the assistant props manager along, too. The assistant props manager was Tommy Antrim, only he lived in the south part of the county, so they would pick him up on the way, supposedly. Only really Tommy was never even invited."

"Kimberly told you this?"

"Later, yeah."

"Were you pretty close friends?"

"Not at first. Just to say hello."

"You didn't go out with her?"

"No."

"Ever ask her out?"

"Oh, no."

"Did you want to?"

"I wanted to but I didn't want to, you know? Probably she would have said no."

"Why?"

"She was too pretty."

She had been pretty, all right, with a frail and vulnerable Sondra Locke kind of a look. Appealing, in the way a lamb appeals to a wolf.

"Did she go out with other guys?"

"She didn't want to get her dad mad."

"How did she come to tell you what was going on with Mr. Pearsall, Roy?"

From loneliness, fear, and desperation, it turned out. One afternoon Roy Shipley had been backstage trying to figure out some wiring problem when Kimberly came into what she thought was the empty auditorium. At first he only heard her, making choking noises that he didn't understand. Once she got up on the stage, looking for a private place, Roy could see her for the first time. He realized that the noises were sobs. When she spotted him and put her hand to her mouth, startled, he asked her what was wrong.

"She just stood there for a minute and then she started to like blubber some stuff I couldn't make out, and then she was saying, Roy, help me, listen, Roy, can you really, really keep a secret, I've got to talk to somebody. She was saying all stuff like that . . ."

Then she sat down on the floor beside him, where he had been working on some wiring. All in a rush of words, she unloaded on him the burden she had been carrying. Pearsall, on their trips to the country, had told Kimberly she had real talent, but that it was trapped inside her. He had sensed it right away during the try-outs, but only because he had a background in the theater. The problem now was to set that God-given talent free, to unlock it from within the prison she had made for it inside her body. The first step would be to liberate her body itself, to learn to be at ease with it, to explore its marvelous potential.

And so on.

By the second trip he was liberating her body in a motel room on the Warrenton bypass. But when an accident somehow happened, it turned out Pearsall wasn't really so anxious to explore her body's full potential. There was his wife, after all, who was uninspiring and unimaginative and in every way inferior to Kimberly herself, but who was still the mother of his children, and who would surely get custody of them in a divorce, and then how could his salary stretch to cover alimony, child support, and the new household that he desperately wanted to set up with Kimberly, once she finished her schooling? And that right there, her schooling, would be another problem, for a teenage mother. So would the narrow minds on the school board, for him.

All in all, the best answer would be to go somewhere and get rid of this little difficulty, which raised still another problem. Any other time, he could borrow the money from his mother in Florida, only the thing was she wasn't in Florida right now, she was on a round-the-world cruise for the next six weeks, and would there be any chance that Kimberly herself, just on a temporary basis of course . . .

There was no chance, on her ten-dollar weekly allowance. Until, at a point when she was desperate to tell her troubles to a friendly human being, she practically literally ran into Roy backstage. Roy, sitting on the floor doing something with wires. Roy, as it turned out, with the savings bonds his grandfather had given him for college.

"I killed her," Roy said. "If I hadn't given her the money for the clinic, she'd be alive today."

"Kid, I've done lots worse than that," I said. "I happened to be in Washington the same day Reagan was shot. I could have grabbed the gun from that Hinckley asshole and Ronzo would have been a one-term president and later on two hundred thousand poor bastards would have never died in Iraq."

"I don't get it."

"Well, Reagan was way down in the polls back then on account of the recession, and the only thing that saved his ass was getting shot and becoming a hero. Otherwise Cuomo would have knocked him off in '84 and Bush would have never been president."

"I guess I still don't get it."

"What I'm saying is you don't want to carry things too far. I didn't kill those Iraqis, Bush did. You didn't kill Kimberly, either. If anybody did, it was Pearsall and the Pastor and her parents. They were her enemies. You were her friend."

The boy looked a little more cheerful. At least I hoped he was. I moved my spoon around in the puddle of butterscotch and chocolate and melted frozen yogurt, and thought about things.

"Look, Roy," I said at last. "Maybe we can do something about this Pearsall guy. You think you could help me on that?"

"Sure."

"I need to know his schedule, where he'll be at certain times, when he shows up to work, where he parks, things like that."

"I can find out easy."

"You know where he lives, in case he isn't in the book?"

"No, but I have a friend who could look it up. He's like a student aide in the assistant principal's office."

"Okay, fine. Now, look, Roy, there's something I should straighten out with you if we're going to be working together. I told you the name Carpenter but actually it's Bethany, Tom Bethany. I sometimes use Carpenter, that's all."

"Why?"

"I'm just kind of a nut on privacy. I don't see that it's most people's business what my name is, where I live. If I want them to know, I'll tell them."

I stuck my hand across the table. "Tom Bethany," I said, and we shook. "Now we've met for real."

"Pleased to meet you, Mr. Bethany."

"Just Tom," I said. "I'm only Mr. Bethany to doctors, nurses, and assholes that try to sell me stuff over the phone."

"Tom," the boy said. I liked it that he sounded awkward, trying out a middle-aged guy's first name. A good kid, but I knew that already. What other kind of kid would raid his college nest egg to buy an abortion for someone he hardly knew? And all of a sudden the awful thought struck me that I was no better than Pearsall in one important respect.

"Out of curiosity, Roy," I said, "how much does the clinic charge for an abortion?"

"Two hundred and fifty, only she needed five hundred because she wanted them to put her out. She was terrified of pain."

Hope wasn't. She had just had the local, so it would have been two-fifty.

Shit. At least I could have offered. Of course it was just an oversight that I hadn't. I was upset, thinking about other things, it never happened to occur to me, that's all. And of course none of that made me any less of a jerk. Shit, again.

Roy drove me in his junker to a cabstand a few blocks away, and himself went on home. Time to bite the bullet. I told the cabbie to drive me over to the District, to Hope's house. I had to straighten this business out face-to-face, and I didn't look forward to it, not a bit. She would be understanding, and not worried, and not mad at me, probably even really not. Which naturally would make me feel worse, not better. It's tough being in love with somebody who's nicer than you.

"You want to go Key Bridge or Memorial?" the driver asked.

"Which is faster?"

"This time of day? Probably Memorial."

"Take Key. I'm a little early."

It was a mistake, stalling.

6

I HAD THE DRIVER STOP AS SOON AS THE EDWARDS house came into view and I saw what was going on. Cars were parked all along both sides of the narrow street, nearly blocking passage. Twenty or thirty Life Force demonstrators were picketing with signs.

The family's two cars were in the driveway and the lights were on inside the house, but nobody showed at the windows. The downstairs windows, in fact, had the shades drawn. Hope and Martin didn't want the demonstrators to look in at them, or the children to look out at the demonstrators either, I guessed. I told the driver to pull over and cut the lights.

Most of the signs were the same as the ones outside the clinic, but a few were personalized. One read God's Law, not the ACLU's. Another said Satan's Lawyer Lives Here. I was hoping very hard to see the Reverend Howard Orrin, but he was nowhere in sight.

As I watched, a car passed and let off a couple of people in front of the house before its driver went off down the street to park. The newcomers went up to a very large young man who was standing a little apart from the marchers. He took two signs from a pile leaning against a tree and gave them to the pair, a man and a woman. Then the two went off to join the picket line.

I wouldn't have recognized the young man except for the splinted and bandaged thumb that stood out white in the gloom. I suspected I had broken that thumb during the demonstration outside the clinic. It had felt like a large thumb, on a large hand, but that was all I remembered of the owner. You don't remember faces when the adrenaline is pumping. And the TV cameras had only picked up part of my face. Still, the big man might remember me, but it was pretty dark and I'd have to take the chance.

"You got a radio?" I said to the cab driver. He kind of cocked his head, as if he hadn't heard me, which he probably hadn't. A scratched and dirty old plastic shield, by now more translucent than transparent, protected him from his passengers. I tipped open the little drawer you put the money through, and asked again. His voice came back at me saying, Yes, he did have a radio. "I need to talk to one of those guys," I said to the driver. "When I bring him back, think you could turn the radio on real high?"

"How come?" the voice from the drawer said.

I put a twenty in the drawer. The driver put the twenty in his shirt pocket. "Hey, you got it," came back at me from the drawer.

The only thing I had by way of a disguise was my reading glasses, so I put them on and got out of the cab. I walked toward the large young man with the bullhorn, as if I had important business with him.

"The Pastor wants to see you," I said when I had got close to him, and a little to his rear.

"Huh?" the young man said, turning. Now that I was next to him, I could see that he was four or five inches taller than my own five eleven, and probably weighed

HEAD LOCK

230 to my 180. But size counts for a whole lot less than
speed and skill in my particular sport. My volunteer
work with the Harvard wrestling squad gives me access
to workout partners of all sizes. Even the hippos in the
unlimited weight class don't give me much trouble yet,
although they seem to get tougher every year.

"Come on," I said to the big guy. "The Pastor's in the
cab. He doesn't want anybody to see him."

We were a couple of car lengths down the road before
he got to wondering and stopped. When I turned back
to urge him on, he took a good look at me. "I've never
seen you around the office before," the big kid said. It
might come to him that he had seen me through the
window of a car, though, and I didn't want to wait till
it did.

One of the big things you need to do in wrestling is
establish what we call hand control, which generally
involves moving against the other man's thumbs. In this
case one of those thumbs was broken, and so of course
that was the one I went for. Just grabbing it was enough.
He took in air hard and fast. I didn't want to squeeze
hard, and didn't have to. I knew he wouldn't try to move
or pull it away.

"Don't," he said. "It's broken."

"No shit."

"It's supposed to be immobilized."

"I'm going to immobilize your fucking thumb into that
cab," I said. "If I was you, I'd come along."

He came along. I heard Loretta Lynn through the
closed windows of the cab when we were still ten yards
away. I got in the backseat first, still holding on to the
splinted thumb, and drew him in behind me. I told him
to close the door, and he did. He had had time now to
figure out how to act. A man's gotta do what a man's
gotta do.

"Let go of my thumb," he said, loud so I could hear
him over the music.

75

"Why?"

"You wouldn't be so tough if my thumb wasn't busted."

"Sure I would."

"Let it go, then."

"Okay."

He looked with surprise at the hand I had just freed, and in that instant I went for his good hand. From the size of those hands, I knew he had real strength. Always look at the hands. But even the strongest hands are like the jaws of an alligator. Practically all the strength goes toward the closing of them, and practically none toward opening. I had his good hand in front of me, the back of it facing me, as if he were shaking his fist in my face. Both my hands were locked around his and I had isolated his index finger and was forcing it toward the heel of his hand. It would need a little more pressure before the knuckle gave way, but I knew it had to hurt like hell already. The cords were standing out on his big neck and his mouth was half open with the lips pulled back in a grimace that showed his gums, but he made no sound loud enough to hear over the music.

"Get out your wallet," I said.

He shook his head stubbornly, and then his whole body jerked when I bore down a little more on the finger I had trapped.

"Get it out or I squeeze till the knuckle breaks and then I go down the line to the next one."

The bandaged thumb on his free hand was no use, of course, but with two fingers he managed to fish the wallet out of his hip pocket. He probably didn't know that pickpockets also used two fingers to fish out wallets, and that they called the hip pocket the sucker pocket. If he had known, he wouldn't have kept his wallet there.

"Put it on the seat." He put it on the seat and I let up a little on the pressure. Positive reinforcement.

"What's your name?"

76

"Joel. Joel Hamilton."

"Well, Joel, open your door a little."

He opened it, and the dome light went on.

"Now hold your driver's license up where I can see it." He worked a Virginia license out of the wallet with his fingers, and held it up till I told him to put it down. Then I had him pull the rest of the stuff out of his billfold and spread it out on the seat. The only thing that looked interesting was a snapshot, and I made him hold that up, too.

"Your kid brothers?" He nodded. "Names?"

"Seth and Webster." Seth looked to be about ten, and Webster two or three years older.

"What's your mother's name?"

"Pam."

"Father?"

"Mark." The father was fat, but neither parent was particularly tall. Joel hadn't gotten his size from either of them.

"All right, Joel, shake all the other stuff out of your wallet onto the seat."

When he had done it, I pawed through things until I had absorbed the information on them. "You're a big boy, Joel, aren't you?" I said. "Play football?"

"Rugby."

"Club or George Mason?" He had a student card from George Mason University in his wallet.

"George Mason."

"Tough game, Joel."

"Spawn of Satan," the big kid said. No one had ever called me that before. Probably I haven't been running with the right crowd.

I put pressure back on his knuckle joint and he stiffened but didn't cry out. He was suffering for the Lord.

"Listen, you poor fucking idiot," I said. "What you're in now isn't a game. Your name is Joel James Hamilton and you live at six six one four Laurel Parkway, Springfield, Virginia, and you're a senior on leave from George Mason University. Your father's name is Mark and your mother's name is Pam, and your kid brothers are Webster and Seth. By tomorrow I'll know where your father works and where your brothers go to school. You following me, Joel?"

He nodded.

"What I do is I hurt people."

So I hurt him again, just short of breaking his finger. He screamed, but not as loud as Loretta Lynn.

"It's not a fucking rugby game with me, Joel. It's business. Now you get out of this car and you tell all your asshole friends to go home, it's over. I'm coming back in fifteen minutes and if I find so much as a sign lying on the ground, I don't say a word. I just go home and I get a good night's sleep and I go to work tomorrow. Doing my business."

He just looked at me.

"You still following me?"

He nodded.

"Get out."

I threw his wallet and papers out after him, and hollered through the fare drawer for the driver to move it. When I looked back, Hamilton was collecting his money and I.D. from the ground with his good hand.

I paid the driver off once we got to Massachusetts Avenue and walked slowly back down into the park. A stream ran along the winding road that led to Hope's house, and I found a log beside it to sit on while I waited. After ten minutes or so, enough time for the demonstrators to clear out if they were going to, I set out for the house again. Just before I got there a mobile unit from Channel 4 pulled up from the other direction, and a couple of men got out. No one else was around, and there was no sign that anybody had been. The house was still lit, and the downstairs shades still drawn. When I came up the men had checked the house number against a slip of paper one of them carried, and were standing around looking puzzled.

"This your house?" one of them said to me.

"No, I'm just visiting them."

"You know anything about a demonstration here?"

"Demonstration? What kind of a demonstration? This is a private house."

"Life Force. The antiabortion people."

"Maybe you got the wrong address."

"This is the address they called in."

"Got to be a joke, then."

They went back inside their mobile unit, probably to radio back to base. Airhead One calling Airhead Two. This is Airhead Two, come in, Airhead One. I went up and knocked on the front door. Martin opened it, looking pissed off for a second until he saw who it was.

"I thought you were the TV people," he said.

"They're taking off," I said. "They thought there was a demonstration here. I told them they probably had the wrong address." And the mobile unit, sure enough, was pulling away from the curb.

"They had the right address," Martin said. I was inside now, and saw Hope sitting with her kids. Lisa smiled at me. The two boys, Paul and Steven, said hello but didn't smile. They both seemed tense.

"There was a demonstration," Martin said, "but they just left."

"I know. I was here earlier."

"You saw them?" Hope said.

"Oh, yeah. Why didn't you call the cops, or didn't they come yet?"

"We didn't see any reason to call them," Hope said. "The demonstrators weren't violent. They weren't trespassing. They had a right to be there."

"Constitutionally speaking?" I said. "Freedom of assembly? Freedom of speech?"

"Well, yes," Hope said. "Sure."

"I gave a little speech to one of them," I said. "The big guy, the one with his thumb in a splint. I remembered him from before, outside the clinic. Remembered his thumb anyway."

"You guys better go on upstairs," Hope said.

"Oh, Mom," Lisa said, but she got up. The boys said nothing. They got up, too, and all three went up the stairs.

"You convinced him to leave? How?"

"I just took him out to the cab that brought me and I talked with him. Freely. Freedom of speech. Then he decided to send everybody home."

"Some talk," Martin said. "What did you say?"

"All I said was if he didn't go home I would come around where he lives and have little talks with mom and dad and maybe even his kid brothers."

"You wouldn't have done that," Hope said. I was glad she hadn't made it a question.

"No, but he didn't know that."

"He would have known it if I had been the one talking to him," Martin said.

"You weren't the one who broke his thumb outside the clinic."

I didn't add that Martin wouldn't have been entirely ready to break another one of the kid's fingers, too, whereas I was and the kid knew it. Already the situation was uneasy enough for Martin. He had stayed inside the house with his frightened family, doing the right thing from the constitutional point of view, while I was outside being Shane. There would probably be room in heaven for both of us, but I didn't want to raise that issue right at the moment. All I wanted to do was change the subject.

The phone rang and did the job for me. Neither of them made a move to answer, and it rang again. "We're letting the machine screen calls," Hope said. Her voice came from the machine. It wasn't the Dan Quayle Museum message anymore, just an all-business recording that said to start talking at the beep. A woman did.

"Outside the clinic the Lord revealed to me that you bore the mark I knew it when you smote the servants of the Lord with Satan's F word you should be put down like a sick bitch and die with a needle in your brain the way my Fluffy did you're worse than a bitch let me tell you missus or miz or whatever you call yourself you lezzie because Fluffy was only a dog and Fluffy was worth ten of you the smoke of torment rises forever by raining down sulfur of his wrath the name of Antichrist is 666—"

She had been talking at top speed to get it all in, but the click of the machine cut her off in midstride.

"You used Satan's F word at the clinic?" I said to Hope.

"I'm pretty sure not. Did you?"

"I could have. Sometimes I do."

That's what you can do when something scary happens. You can joke. But it was still scary, the crazy woman rushing to get as much craziness as she could onto the tape.

"She's the one who's sick, sick, sick," Martin said.

"She was saying 666, the number," I said. "That's the name of Antichrist."

"How would you know?" Hope asked.

"I've been reading up. The Antichrist is already putting his mark on things. That's what bar codes are. You must have had a bar code on your forehead yesterday."

"Are you serious?" Martin asked.

"Oh, yeah. That's what some of these freaks call bar code. The 666 System."

"My God."

"Been many of these calls?" I asked.

"All day, probably," Hope said. "But the tape is a loop. It only holds so many messages."

"This particular one has called at least three times," Martin said.

"The kids been listening?" I asked.

"Lisa got the first call," Martin said. "Yesterday when you were here, remember? So yeah, they've been listening. We figured it was best to deal with it out in the open and talk about it."

I looked at them both. "It," I said. "By 'it,' you mean the harassment their mom is getting because she was at an abortion clinic giving them legal counsel?"

"Right," Martin said.

I nodded. The nod meant good. Good that the kids didn't know what mom was really doing at the clinic.

Time to move away from domestic matters altogether, and onto the safer ground of the law. "What legal counsel could you have given to the clinic, anyway?" I asked. "Realistically, what can the law do to keep demonstrators from closing down a clinic?"

"Well," said Hope, "let's consider the rights of the demonstrators for a minute instead of our own. Imagine that they're antiwar protesters in the sixties. How would you want the police to handle them?"

And so on for the next half hour. At the end, I had confirmed what I already suspected from my research at the *Globe* and in the public library. As long as the protestors were willing to be dragged off to jail over and over again, there wasn't much the law could or would do to save the clinics and their clients from crippling harassment.

To make the point, the phone kept ringing. Hope had it beside her. She would listen to just enough of the message to learn that it was another accusation of mass murder coming her way, and then turn the volume down to zero till the machine clicked.

The real solution wasn't to turn the calls off, though. It was to turn the callers off. At last an idea came to me.

"I guess I'll go back to the dentist's house and turn in," I said. "Tomorrow I'll head on home to Cambridge."

"So soon?" Hope said.

"I guess I'll turn in, too," said Martin. "Read in bed a while. Always nice to see you, Tom."

I suspected he wanted to give us a chance to say good-bye, which I thought was a very decent, thoughtful thing for him to do. Even brave. Brave isn't scaring a big, dumb kid in the back of a taxicab. Brave is hanging in there day after day, changing diapers and going to the kids' games and paying off the mortgage and generally putting your own dreams and desires on hold. The real hero in *Shane* wasn't Alan Ladd. It was Van Heflin.

"Do you really have to go so soon?" Hope asked when her husband had disappeared upstairs to his separate bedroom.

"Only for a few days," I said. "I have some things to arrange."

"What kind of things?"

"Just things."

"Well, be careful. I don't know why I say that."

"When you know I won't?"

"Yes."

"Actually I will. Well, you never know how things will work out, but what I have in mind is pretty careful."

"What seems like careful to you anyway."

"Well, sure. I'm me."

"I know. Don't I know. I knew going in."

"Hope?"

She looked at me, waiting.

"I want to pay for the clinic."

"Oh, for God's sake, Bethany."

"Half, anyway."

"You know why I went to law school?"

"Come on. Half."

"So I could have my own money to spend."

I didn't think that was so funny, and she saw I didn't.

She didn't care. She was smiling, and then laughing. After a minute I started smiling, too.

"Can I call you a cab?" Hope said.

"Sure."

"Gotcha. You're a cab."

So everything was all right and now the hurt place was all gone. And she did call me a cab, and it came, and on the way down to Georgetown I kept turning it over and over in my head, how lucky I was to have somebody who loved me even though she knew me all the way through. A year ago, she would have known to let me pay all of it. That was because a year ago I didn't have money to spare. Now that I could afford it, the best way for her to deal with my guilt and sense of obligation was to treat the whole thing as meaningless between a couple of Rockefellers like us. As unimportant as who winds up with the lunch tab. No, let me pick up this abortion, Bethany. You can get the next one.

I didn't feel tricked and manipulated, because I knew she hadn't tried to trick or manipulate me. Nobody is quick and clever enough to figure out winning tactics in midmatch. That only comes from experience and instinct, and maybe instinct is just another word for character. The liar deceives people without thought, naturally, when he speaks. The bully naturally hurts and frightens people when he speaks. And neither does the kind person think about being kind. She just naturally draws out pain with her words, and heals.

7

NEXT MORNING I HAD A COUPLE OF ERRANDS TO run before catching a late shuttle back to Boston. One of them was at the *Globe* bureau, where I wanted to talk to Susan Freedman about her visit to Kimberly's parents.

"The father let me look at the pictures, but he wouldn't let me take them," she said. "He said everybody saw her picture on TV already, and I couldn't argue with that."

"What was he like?" I said. "A Nazi?"

"Not with me. With me he was very polite, kind of intimidated even. Mousy, practically."

"Lot of guys like that," I said. "They eat shit all day at the office, then they go back home and make the family eat it."

"I think you've got him figured about right, actually," Susan said. "Here's this totally insignificant guy, and his wife and his daughter—there's a kid sister, about eight—anyway, they're both hanging on every word he says. Ready to hop to it if there's anything daddy needs. It was weird. I don't know what it was like, maybe like watching the boss poodle, down at the poodle kennel or something."

"A Nazi poodle."

"Sure. Poodles got to have Nazis, too."

"But he didn't really seem like the kind of prick that his daughter would jump off a bridge to get away from?"

"He didn't act like that with me, certainly. The only hint was the effect he had on the wife and the kid. Actually, I think I could even have gotten those pictures out of him if I had felt like pushing a little bit harder. As it is, I got pictures of her anyway, only they're from the cops. Not exactly studio shots."

I slid a half-dozen photos out of the envelope she passed me, and spread them out on the table. "The cops give these things to the papers?" I asked.

"Normally they don't," Susan said. "My connection at homicide knows we won't run it, though."

"Jesus, I hope not." The eight-by-ten glossies were of Kimberly Butler's death scene. Her head had broken open when she landed. "If you're not going to run them, why get them?" I asked.

"Like the old Cole Porter line. To keep my love alive."

Jay Fails had said Susan was a good hater, and so she was.

"Mind if I keep a couple of these?" I said.

"What for?"

"I want to keep my love alive, too." I was a pretty good hater, too. Since I couldn't seem to shake the habit, about all I could do was try to make sure I hated the right people. No doubt Susan tried to do that, too. No doubt we all do.

"These should help," she said, handing me an overall shot and one of the worst close-ups. "Particularly since you met the girl. Jesus, in these shots she looks about twelve."

"That's what she looked like when she was alive, too," I said. "Any problem if I show these to the Pastor?"

"Just don't tell him where you got them."

When she left to get back to her job, I went through my little collection of phony cards. I had made up a whole pile of cards over the past year or so, fooling around with my laser printer and my scanner. The only time I had actually used one of the cards, it was an early effort that identified me as a reporter for the *Boston Globe*. I used it in Houston, where they don't know the *Globe* from *Pravda*. This time, for three or four different reasons, my fake *Globe* credentials would be a bad choice. On the other hand, the card that said I was a roving editor for the *Reader's Digest* would probably work just fine. If you want to talk family values, the *Reader's Digest* opens a lot of doors.

"Oh, hi," I said to the person who answered the phone at the Reverend Howard Orrin's Arlington headquarters. "This is Tom Carpenter. I'm a roving editor for the *Reader's Digest*, and I was wondering if your boss was in . . . Oh, okay. Listen, tell him I called, will you? I'm in town for the day and I'd like to get together with him for a few minutes sometime. I'll call back. Fine, thanks very much."

The voice on the phone had said that the Pastor was expected back from a taping session any minute. So I went out and called a cab and headed for Arlington.

Headquarters of the Orrin for Senate campaign were in a small shopping center not too far from the rich widow's Williamsburg Boulevard house where the Pastor lived. I paid the fare and gave the driver twenty bucks more to wait for me. I didn't want to stay long. I just wanted to get to know Orrin a little, so as to get a feel for how he might react to certain stimuli I had in mind for him later on.

Inside, I was explaining myself to the volunteer at the reception desk when the Pastor himself came in, followed by a couple of young aides. I started explaining myself to the candidate himself instead of to the volunteer. Sure enough, the magic of the *Reader's Digest* name got me right into his office, where he picked up the phone and ordered his calls held till further notice.

I told him I was doing a story on leaders of America's religious renaissance, with special reference to the sanctity of preborn life.

"The Reverend Howard Orrin isn't the story," said the Reverend Howard Orrin, as if he had said it many times before. "Life Force with its thousands of dedicated Christian soldiers is not the story. No, the story is twenty-five million dead children and almost as many hideously exploited women . . ."

I scribbled notes as he went on giving his answers to the questions I had dreamed up on the ride over. Now and then I stopped and asked him if he wanted to smooth out some quote that might sound a little awkward verbatim. I figured this was probably the way a real roving editor for the *Reader's Digest* would handle a leader in the fight for family values.

One of my probing questions was, "So, Reverend, tell me what got you interested in abortion anyway?"

"If I had to tell you in just two words why I'm pro-life, you know what those two words would be?"

"What?"

"My own two adopted sons. I look at those two little hellions, my rainbows of light, and I ask myself what if their poor, brave mothers had said when those little bits of preborn innocent human life were growing inside them, what if they had said, Well, I'm sorry as all get-out but I just don't think just now it would be *conveee-nient.*" He gave it the Church Lady's pronunciation. "After all, I have my bridge club and my lunches with the ladies and I just don't think I could manage it. Or I have my *career.* Terribly sorry, God, but I'm afraid my *career* is so much more important than a little soul for Jesus."

I smiled encouragingly and kept on scribbling, although the written word wasn't really up to the job. How could you get it across on paper that the Pastor had somehow made "my career" sound like "gonorrhea"?

"Let me tell you something else, Tom," the Reverend said, "and your readers will appreciate this. The whole pro-life thing isn't just good Christianity, either. It's good economics, too. Now these *liberals*"—and he somehow got liberals to sound like gonorrhea, too—"these *liberals* holler that the answer is contraception. Holler that there's too many people in America already.

"Well, I've got news for those negative cynics. We don't have *enough* people in America! Any honest economist who's ever studied the Social Security system in this country will tell you that by the year 2020 we won't have enough workers to support the retirees we're going to have. And they talk about planned parenthood! Planned poverty is more like it! For our senior citizens in their golden years!"

After twenty minutes or so I got tired of taking down foolishness and pulled my two photographs out of their manila envelope. "The way I work," I said, "I always talk to people on both sides of an issue . . ."

"There's only one side," the Pastor said. "God's side."

"They say you've got to give the devil his due, though."

"Not when the issue is the sanctity of human life."

"Personally I'm with you on that," I said. "Let me put it this way, though. Our policy at the *Digest* is always to give the appearance of fairness. You follow what I mean?"

I figured winking was going too far, but I raised my eyebrows a little. The Pastor nodded back. We were serious, grown men. We understood each other.

I handed the two photos to him, and he stopped smiling.

"What is this?" he asked.

"A girl named Kimberly Butler."

Orrin showed no reaction to the name. The Washington papers hadn't yet made a connection between Kimberly and the Life Force demonstration. They would, of course, once Susan Freedman's story came out in Boston.

"What happened to her?" the Pastor asked.

"She jumped off the Calvert Street Bridge. See that thing lying beside her? That's what she jumped with. It's a stuffed animal she called Binkie."

"These are awful pictures. How did they ever get disclosed into the public milieu?"

"I got them from the girl's parents. A free-lance photographer took them, one of those vultures that runs around all night listening to the police radio. He sold them to her parents."

"I don't understand. Why would the parents want such a thing?"

"It's a racket. The papers won't run pictures that horrible, and the photographer knows it, but the relatives don't. So he offers to sell the pictures to the family to keep them out of the paper."

"Why did you want them? Certainly the *Reader's Digest* would never run a foul, foul stack of stench like that."

"Well, of course not. But the parents insisted I should take them. I guess I sort of led them on, if you want to know the truth. As a journalist, you sometimes have to use the good cop, bad cop routine. Kind of act sympathetic and try to get inside the defenses of the person you're interviewing."

"I still don't understand why they gave you these pictures."

"The thing of it is, they made me promise to show them to you. Now remember it's not me talking here, it's them, okay? The parents. Anyway, they've got the idea in their head that you killed their daughter."

"Me! The girl's a total stranger to me."

"She was in one of the cars that your people stopped the other day at the clinic."

"Poor thing. We try to help those troubled girls, but so often we fail."

"Try to help them how?"

"Various ways. If a girl has actually gone through the preliminaries and shown up at the abortuary, about all you can do is offer sidewalk counseling."

"What does that involve?"

"Oh, pointing out that the fetus is a person, that abortion is murder—"

"Because the father said what was actually done, somebody threw a pickled fetus into the girl's lap. And that triggered a total emotional breakdown."

"Anything that happened like that would have to be a total accident. Any person that would throw a tiny corpse into a young girl's lap, that person, it seems to me, could be a psychopathic sex fiend or a pervert—"

"So it didn't happen?"

"I'm used to it, Tom. I'll never like it, but I'm used to it. I have been pilloried constantly with scurrilous allegations of this nature—garbage, trash that they've siphoned out of the sewers against me—"

"So it didn't happen?" I tried again.

"Tom, I would be outraged if such alleged conduct occurred directed to this young woman."

"So it could have happened?"

"Anything *could* have happened, in the heat of a demonstration. With hundreds of people around, police, press, infiltrators trying to discredit the movement. It's an old trick, asking someone to prove something didn't happen. You can't prove a negative."

"Of course not."

"But I tell you what I *can* say. I can say we would never condone behavior such as these people describe, and it is certainly not what we mean by sidewalk counseling. I doubt very strongly that any such action was

ever done by any person officially connected with Life
Force. We're all Jesus people."

"This fellow Butler, the father, he showed me the
fetus."

"He showed you *a* fetus, you mean."

"I guess that's right. You're saying that maybe he got
hold of a fetus somewhere, and used it to trick me?"

"Things like that have been done, I regret to say. I just
don't know the man. But let me tell you something,
Tom, I've had wide experience with these cases. Look
at it from the father's point of view. He agrees to an
abortion for his daughter. Maybe even insists on it. She
has the abortion, and she feels immediate grief over having killed her baby. It's a very, very common reaction,
believe me. Almost universal, particularly when the girl
is fortunate enough to come from a loving Christian
household. In her grief, she tragically kills herself. Who
is the father going to blame? What lengths is that man
going to go to, to keep that awful burden of guilt from
falling on himself? He killed a living baby. He killed his
own grandchild."

"Not in this case."

"Oh, it was a baby, all right, even in the first weeks.
I've got some photographs, too, Tom. Tiny, fully formed
toes. Little features . . ."

"I meant her father didn't kill anything. The baby died
when the girl did."

"I don't—"

"They wouldn't give the girl an abortion at the clinic.
They thought she was too disturbed."

"And naturally so, I might add. It's the biggest disturb-
ance in all creation, God struggling with Satan."

"Her family said she seemed a little withdrawn, which
was more or less normal for her, until her father turned
on the evening news and saw her coming out of that
clinic. It was the first the parents knew about her being
pregnant. There was a big blowup and she ran out of

the house and drove off somewhere and next thing she's dead."

"And the poor father blames me for that? Tom, I'm just a country preacher and I don't know much about a lot of things. But I'm an expert on morals and ethics, and I don't for a minute mean situational ethics, either. I mean the kind of ethics you find right here in this little book, which contains everything mankind needs to know about real ethics."

He had produced a pocket-size New Testament from his coat pocket and was waving it like a flag. One of the wire service photos in Susan Freedman's collection showed him doing the same thing.

"And I can tell you something from this holy book, Tom, and I wish I could sit down with this poor girl's father and tell him the exact same thing. There is sin here, but the sin is not mine. I'm not the one who went to a mass-production murder factory to deliver my own baby up to the butchers. The daughter this man raised is the one who did that. For a moment's thrill, the daughter he raised went out and got pregnant. To avoid the consequences that Our Lord God attached to that pathetic little thrill, she was willing to murder. I'm sorry for that poor man, for his pain and for his loss of a daughter, but I don't see how I fit into the picture, in no way, shape or form."

"I don't either, Reverend, but let me play devil's advocate here for a minute. The girl is pregnant. Her father doesn't know it. She goes for an abortion. The demonstrators terrify her so much that the clinic's doctors tell her to come back another day. On the way out, her picture gets on TV. She's shamed in front of her family and everybody she knows, and a few million other people. She runs away from home and jumps off a bridge. The father figures if it hadn't been for you, she would have had her abortion and wouldn't have jumped. So in his mind you killed his daughter. How do you answer him?"

"I answer that he killed his own daughter and his own unborn grandchild by not guiding her onto the path of righteousness."

"Exactly what I think," I told the Pastor. "The father drove her to it." With his palms up, Orrin shrugged his shoulders slightly, as if to say, What are we going to do with these poor sinners?

"Except I'm not sure the unborn grandchild was at a stage where it could be killed yet," I went on. "I mean, there's possible argument on that one. On the other hand the girl was definitely a living person, right up till she hit. No possible argument there. So I figure the father certainly killed the girl. And so did you."

"What?" Orrin said. He was surprised, but I had jerked him around so suddenly that he wasn't yet mad.

"If the father hadn't been a stupid self-righteous prick, she wouldn't be dead. And if you hadn't put her on TV like another stupid, self-righteous prick, she wouldn't be dead. So you both killed her."

"I think you'd better show me some identification from the *Reader's Digest,* mister."

"You don't think I've got some?"

"Let's see it."

"Well, I do. Only it's phony."

"I don't doubt it. Just exactly who are you, anyway, mister?"

I didn't answer. Instead I reached for the phone on his desk and disconnected it. That somebody would invade Orrin's own actual desk was so far outside his experience that he just sat there. By that time I had the dead phone in my hand, and it was a little late to protest. But he tried anyway.

"Listen, you put that back! Just who do you think you are?"

"You listen, you sorry sack of shit," I said.

I stepped quickly to the door and turned the lock. The phone was still in my hand, so I put it on a little table by the door and came back. I went around the desk to his side of it, so that I would be right inside his den. And when he tried to get up, I pushed him back down. He sat back down and stayed put.

Most adults, particularly adults in authority, are never, absolutely never, physically controlled by another person. They don't know how to react to something so unprecedented that it is, for them, literally unthinkable. Howard Orrin just sat there, looking up at me looking down on him.

"You have any idea who lives in that neighborhood your Gestapo was fucking around in last night before I chased them off?" I said. "It's people that could buy your whole goddamned amusement park and cathedral out of pocket change. Me and my service, those people pay us to keep the scumbags away from where they live."

"You're with a security service?" the Pastor said. It didn't sound like I was his idea of a rent-a-cop, not that I cared. The idea wasn't to convince him. The idea was just to steer him away from making a connection between Hope and me. "You could say that, Howie," I said. I figured Howard Orrin had probably hated being called Howie when he was a kid.

"When they hired me all the houses had alarm systems and shit. They still got the systems, but mostly they don't bother to turn them on. That's because most scumbags except you know enough to keep out. Let me tell you a story about why. Four years ago we caught this jungle bunny inside this one house, I won't tell you who lives there but you'd know his name from the papers, and at first my guys said let's just waste the fucker and dump him in Rock Creek Park.

"I told them, Look, why waste the asshole? Why not let's use him for advertising? So instead of killing the

fucker, we just cut one of his hands off and my guys
kick him out of the car in front of the dump where he
lives. Then they go down to the corner where there's
this bar full of his buddies, and one of my guys opens
the door and tosses the hand in. It's in this plastic bag,
so I guess it took them a while to flash on what it was.
By then my guys are gone."

"I never saw that in the paper," Howard Orrin said.

"Naturally you never saw it in the paper. You weren't
reading the right paper. Back then you were reading the
paper down in Newport News, asshole. Which is where
you live at one three six Hampton Heights with your
wife, Merribeth Collins, and your fucking rainbows of
life. Howard junior, and Christopher."

"What is it you want?" the Pastor asked, sounding
very shaky. Once he had time to think things over, he
wasn't likely to believe I was president of the neighborhood crimewatch. But that wasn't the point. The point
was for him to believe that a madman was on his case.
And his family's.

"I never want to see your people around my people
anymore, Howie. Never. Not fucking ever. I don't even
want no more shit with the phone calls, starting from
when I walk out of here."

"The demonstration at the Edwards residence was basically over already when you arrived last night," he
said. "We didn't have any plans to repeat it. I'll do what
I can about any phone calls, but you have to understand
that Life Force doesn't operate that way. I'm not saying
some of our members may not be making some of the
calls, whatever calls it is you're referring to, but I promise you that phone calls of that nature are not Life Force
policy. I'm like the general who sends out the orders to
the troops. I can't control it if one goes bad. I can't be
held responsible."

Before he could register what was happening I had
reached across his desk, grabbing his big, drooping ears,

and hauled him to his feet by them, so fast he didn't have time to squeal.

"The fuck you can't be held responsible" I said, right up close to his face. "I'm doing it."

On the way out of campaign headquarters, I picked up a handful of literature from a volunteer's desk for something to read in the cab to the airport. Most of it turned out to be rich man's propaganda about law and order for the lower classes (club Rodney King), welfare reform (starve Rodney King), quotas (don't hire Rodney King), raise tariffs (higher prices), raise competitiveness (lower wages), the sanctity of human life (make the bitches pay for their fun), tough on crime (fry human life), strengthen national defenses (bomb human life). One brochure sounded interesting, so I set it aside. The others I poked down behind the seat where cabbies hide seat belts from the passengers.

That got me to thinking about why the hell the seat belts were never out where you could get them.

"Hey, what's going on back there," the cabbie said after a while.

"No problem," I said. "I'm just getting myself a seat belt."

"You got the whole seat practically on the floor."

"You know the reason for that? The reason is because you don't bother to take thirty seconds every morning to make sure the belts are out where they should be."

"Nobody uses the belts in a fucking cab."

"Nobody can find the belts in a fucking cab, is why."

"Jesus, some guys."

By the time I was belted in we were just coming up on the National Airport turnoff. But it had turned out to be worth the effort anyway. I found seventy-three cents under the seat. I paid the driver off, and waited for my change.

"How about you promise me something?" I said when he had given it to me.

"Huh?"

"Promise me you'll check the seat belts every morning."

"Listen, I don't tell you your business, you don't tell me mine."

"Well, fuck it then," I said. "At least I tried to do it." I turned toward the door of the terminal.

"Hey, how about my tip?" the driver called, so I turned around again.

"That's what I tried to do."

"Huh?"

"To give you a tip."

"Listen, buddy . . ."

And so I listened, couldn't help it, until the terminal doors hissed shut and cut off his shouting. He wasn't serious anyway, or he would have got out of the cab and come after me.

On my way to the shuttle departure area, I stopped to make a phone call to the 800 number on the one brochure of the Pastor's that I had kept. I gave a credit card number to the woman who answered, and she promised that my order would go out the same day. I signed up to pay an extra four dollars for overnight delivery, to speed things up even more.

8

AT THE TASTY THE CUSTOMER COULD BE CONFIdent that practically nothing was prepared on the premises. Butter came in pats on little pieces of stiff paper, jelly was sealed in plastic, hamburgers were stacked in cartons with wax paper between each one, soup was in little cans, for hot chocolate you dumped powder from a foil envelope into warm water, iced tea was powdered, milk and juice came in cartons. But one thing that came onto the premises in its original form was eggs.

"Two over light," I told Joe Neary, the counterman. "And Wonder Bread toasted on one side only."

"How about you stop busting my balls, Bethany? The Ritz-Carlton is up the street."

"This is all I can afford. Listen, does the toast come with a little tiny dab of butter and grape jelly?"

"Actually you got an option there. You can get apple jelly, too."

"Surprise me."

"You want a surprise, here's one." Joey brought a red, white, and blue Federal Express package out from under

99

the counter. The business community shows more contempt for Old Glory than all the flag burners ever born. "I didn't order nothing," Joey said, "so this got to be for you."

I closed out all my credit cards years ago, so as to help me drop out of America's computerized data base. Whenever I want to buy something by mail I use Joey's card number and pay him cash. My car is also in his name, in return for letting him use it on any weekends I don't need the thing.

"What's in the package?" Joey asked.

"Videotapes."

"Snuff flicks?"

"Worse. Sermons."

Back home, I loaded two hours worth of the Pastor's televised sermons into the VCR and settled down in the La-Z-Boy recliner. My original idea in ordering the tapes had been that they, too, would help to keep my love alive. And actually the sermons were anti-American and anti-Christ, all right, but on top of that they were kind of interesting.

The Reverend Howard Orrin preached in an immense church with walls painted sky blue. There was so much glass in those walls, and in the vaulted ceiling, too, that the effect was almost like being inside a huge crystal aquarium. To his right was a giant TV screen the size of the ones that hang over a boxing ring. This one showed the Pastor slugging it out with Satan in real time. To Orrin's left sat the choir, known as the Daughters of Christ, in robes of robin's egg blue with white cuffs and dickeys. They sang now and then, but their real role was to look at the Pastor with stunned adoration as he preached, twenty or so pretty teenagers pouring love and submission out of their eyes. What it was really about was incest, of course. Just the way it was on the "Lawrence Welk" show, with all those newly nubile young things dancing at arms' length with men old enough to be their fathers or even grandfathers.

Orrin's voice was smarmy and oleaginous and entirely false, but I knew better than to think his flock would be put off by that. I knew better because of Reagan. Everyone kept writing that he was the Great Communicator because he was a skilled actor. The truth was that his performances went over so well not because he was a good actor, but because he was a bad one. Go see his movies.

A good actor—a Michael Moriarty or a Dustin Hoffman—would do sincerity by sounding like a real person actually being sincere. And nine out of ten television viewers would think Moriarty or Hoffman sounded insincere. After a lifetime of listening to thousands of no-talents on the tube and on the screen, people have got to where they believe that true sincerity sounds like a ham doing sincerity badly.

Same way with Howard Orrin. When the Pastor slathered on holiness or concern or all-encompassing love in a way that would make any sensible citizen blow his lunch, it just made his listeners take out their checkbooks. The glittering cathedral all around him proved that.

But I had never watched guys like Orrin for any longer than I had watched MTV, which was just long enough to punch the remote. So I was curious to find out what the Pastor's flock was getting for its money.

It turned out to be even more depressing than I thought. In two hours of Orrin's best efforts, the only theological message was Jesus loves me, this I know, 'cause the Bible tells me so. You didn't have to be good for Jesus to love you. All you had to do was two things. You had to accept Jesus Christ as your personal savior, and you had to send in your check or money order to his local rep, Howard Orrin. Then Jesus would love you so much he would give you money and health and happiness, and invite you to stay in his own lovely, tastefully appointed home when you died.

Orrin said this over and over again for two hours, and he was wonderful at the job. It was like watching a vacuum cleaner salesman sell a machine sight unseen for cash down and delivery after the customer's death. The Pastor's voice went down to a whisper and up to a shout. Now he was on his knees and now he was leaping into the air. One minute he threatened, the next he cooed with love. And always he was closing, closing, closing.

Missions abroad . . . work of the church . . . study guide . . . minimum contribution . . . cassette tape . . . defray the costs . . . listener-supported television ministry . . . your help now. Tomorrow will be too late. Jesus needs you now, now, now.

There was some hellfire, but not too much. Most of the message was that Jesus would make you rich and cure what ailed you and solve any other little problems you might have in the here and now.

Was it possible that people were dumb enough to believe this nonsense? What was really going on? What were the suckers really buying with their money?

Eventually I began to see, or thought I saw, that they were buying a friend. You couldn't lie down on a couch in Jesus' office, true enough, but then he didn't charge two hundred bucks an hour, either. And Howard Orrin's Jesus seemed to be considerably less demanding than a psychiatrist. To judge by the Pastor's sermons, Jesus wouldn't just sit there and listen stone-faced, or maybe even chew you out when you told him about the rotten things you had been up to. In fact you didn't even have to tell him. Jesus would love you right back if you just loved him. With this Jesus, you didn't have to fool around with any of that Sermon on the Mount liberal crap. This Jesus was as insecure as an unpopular third grader. All you had to do for him to love you was smile at him, and he'd follow you around for the rest of the year.

Back when I was stealing an education from Harvard by sneaking into lectures and using J. Fails's library card, I once sat down and read the New Testament to see what all the commotion was about. What struck me at the time was how much like a modern-day cult the whole movement was while Jesus was alive. You left your family and your whole identity behind. You gave up all your worldly goods—to the cult, or so I suspected. From then on you spent all your time in the equivalent of airports and bus stations, begging for money and converts.

But there was more religion to this particular cult than there seemed to be to the Moonies or the Scientologists or the Hare Krishnas. The Jesus of the New Testament didn't just want you to suck up or knuckle under to him so you could get a better deal in both this world and the next one. He also wanted you to give your neighbor a better deal in this world. He wanted you to love one another, and not throw stones at whores, and forgive your enemies, and turn the other cheek. And he went on and on about greed, just like the Reaganauts did. Only Jesus was against it.

But this whole idea of brotherly love and good works seemed to have dropped completely out of the Christianity preached by the Orrins and the Falwells and the Bakkers and the Robertsons and the Swaggarts and all their smaller electronic wannabes. Did they just skip over the hard parts in their book? To some extent, maybe. But they couldn't all be theological illiterates.

I've arranged my life so that I have nothing better to do than to look for the answers to questions like this as they occur to me. My main tool for this is the Harvard faculty I.D. card that I get each year from some grad student section leader willing to tell the university he lost his. I pay him the replacement fee plus fifty bucks, and we're both happy. So now I took my faculty I.D. and my questions about the Electronic Church to the divinity school library.

I figured that an afternoon would do the job, but one thing leads to another in libraries. It was three days before I was done rooting around in predestination, Calvinism, free will, Mormonism, the religious revivals of the 1820s, millenarianism, Jehovah's Witnesses, and the rest of the weird American stew that in our time produces specimens like Howard Orrin.

Once I had put together a sound theological rationalization for what I was going to do anyway, on the fourth day I moved into the second phase of my master plan for the Pastor. I set out for a massage parlor called Personal Leisure World, on Lowell Parkway.

It was a fine spring day for a walk, a yellow sweater day, but it was also four or five miles out there. So I drove instead but took along my running shorts and shoes. The Fresh Pond reservoir was on the way back, with its running path along the banks. Once I dislocated a man's shoulder at Fresh Pond, so this whole area had special memories for me. So did Personal Leisure World itself, which was in a low-rent shopping center that looked just as filthy and neglected as on the August day when I first saw it. Maybe even more so now, with the winter's collection of litter unfrozen not so long ago but not yet rotted or scattered.

The massage parlor looked about the same, too: part of the second floor of a small shopping center built in the fifties. It was over a drugstore, and the entrance was through an unmarked glass door that seemed to lead nowhere. There was a small sign in the entryway, and a big one up on the second floor where you could see it from the street if you were paying close attention. But word of mouth was what they counted on, not walk-in trade.

Memories inside Personal Leisure World, too. The same shelf with the same photo album holding Polaroids of what looked like the same girls but probably weren't. The big change was in Wanda Vollmer, the manager.

"Hey, champ," she said when she spotted me through the window in the wall that let her keep an eye on things from her tiny office. "What brings you by?"

Coming out of the office, her step had the bounce that means strength and energy to spare. "Jesus, Wanda, you look terrific," I said, meaning it. She had lost weight since I last saw her, and looked easily ten years younger.

"Exercise," she said. "Listen, since you're here, what do you think of my new slogan for the sign outside?"

She looked upward at an imaginary sign and raised her hands to bracket it. "Personal Leisure World," she said. "Where the Customer Always Comes First."

"Not bad, Wanda. Not bad at all."

"I stole it from the Girl Scouts, actually. Couple days ago I saw it on one of those license plate frames, you know? Kind of thing the dealer puts on your car for advertising, only this was for the Scouts. It said, 'The girl comes first in Girl Scouting.' "

"You're bullshitting me, right?"

"Bullshit I'm bullshitting you. I'm practically running off the road laughing. I'm thinking to myself, Enjoy it while you can, little Scout girls, because it ain't going to last."

"Let's get back on track here, Wanda. What about this exercise? How come you look about twenty-five years old all of a sudden? Who are you showing off for?"

"You got to know, smart-ass, I'm with this aerobics instructor now."

"I heard it ruins your knees."

"She does strictly low impact," Wanda said, and paused while she thought about that. "No impact at all, really. Like a feather. You know how some people feel heavy when you're getting it on with them, and some people it's like they don't weigh anything at all?"

"This sounds like love to me, Wanda. Is it love?"

"I'm afraid so."

"What's wrong, doesn't she love you?"

"I'm afraid so."

"Then what's to be afraid of?"

"Bethany, anybody's not afraid of love, they're a fucking idiot."

"You could get lucky. You could grow old with her, both of you live in a little cottage out on the Cape. Maybe raise dried herbs or something."

"Yeah, sure. That's me, all right."

"It happens. They used to call them Boston marriages."

"People like me and you don't wind up in cottages. People like me and you got to watch out for love. It'll fuck us every time."

I couldn't argue with that. For years Hope and I had been lucky, it was true. Even if our peculiar arrangement wouldn't suit most people, we filled the empty spots in each other somehow. But I never thought it would last anywhere near as long as it has, and I keep worrying one day I'll call up and she won't call back.

"Maybe this time it'll last for you," I said.

"Sure."

I wasn't going to convince her, anymore than I could convince myself. So the hell with it.

"Let me ask you a question on something else entirely," I said. "What do you think about abortion?"

"Kind of a question is that? You knocked up? I think it's a woman's own business."

"I was asking because you were raised by the nuns."

"Me and the nuns were a long way apart even then."

"You ever hear of the Reverend Howard Orrin?"

"Sure. I was in this motel in Wellfleet one time, it was Sunday morning and I woke up early and I couldn't get back to sleep. All there was on TV was assholes like him. One thing I got to say for my old home team, the Pope don't go on TV with a tin cup.''

"I met Orrin the other day. You're right, he's an asshole.''

"Of course I'm right. I know the guy.''

"You *know* him?''

"I don't mean actually know him. I mean I know guys like him. I used to run across them all the time.''

"Where?''

"When I ran away from the orphanage and peddled my tender teenage ass in the Combat Zone. That's where you meet guys like your buddy Orrin. The minute I saw him on the tube, I knew exactly what he'd look like with his clothes off, exactly what he'd say, how he'd act.''

"That right? Well, then, let me tell you what Orrin's up to these days, and maybe you can help me out with what I've got in mind for him.''

I told her about Hope's abortion, and about the little girl with the stuffed animal, and about the money machine the Pastor had built for himself, and about the way he was using the antiabortion issue to get to the Senate, and about my visit with him at his campaign headquarters.

"He didn't seem to be sorry at all for this kid that was dead?'' she said at the end.

"She should have kept her legs together.''

"This guy's a walking advertisement for abortion himself, huh? The day his mother flunked her rabbit test, she should have grabbed hold of a coat hanger. Been better off raising the rabbit.''

"You're a hard woman, Wanda.''

Which she was. In fact, she would be in the women's prison at Framingham for murder right now, if I hadn't gotten a policeman to agree with me that the killing had been a public service.

"So what about the phone calls to your girlfriend's house?'' Wanda asked.

"They stopped. I checked the next day."

"Asshole didn't have anything to do with them, but they happened to stop after you told him you'd burn down his garage?"

"I didn't say I'd burn down his garage. I just told him I knew where he lived."

"Whatever. The message got through, so it must have had the right address on it."

"Oh, I never doubted that for a minute. It was interesting how easy he scared, though."

"Made you want to scare him some more, didn't it?"

"It encouraged me, yeah."

"So what do you have in mind?"

So I told her. Among all the other things, I happened to mention about Susan Freedman's nipples standing out under her sweater.

When Wanda had heard me out, she went back to those nipples. "This reporter that said he was hitting on her, how old is she?"

"Midthirties or late thirties. Why?"

"Just wanted to make sure he isn't a little-girl freak."

"Would that be a problem? Couldn't you dig me up somebody that could pass for a teeny-bopper?"

"Yeah, but I couldn't pass for one."

"You?"

"Do I look that bad?"

"You look great. I told you that. But . . ."

"But I'm a dyke? Listen, I used to do men for a living. It's like riding a bicycle, you don't forget it. Especially if you're the bicycle."

"You got your job here to do."

"I got an assistant manager, too, which mostly it's a moron but I got a girl now that's actually fairly bright."

"There might not be any money in this thing."

"We'll see. Smells like money to me."

"Listen, all I wanted was for you to find me somebody smart enough to pull it off . . ."

"You don't think I'm—"

"Come on, Wanda. Jesus, you're twice as smart enough. It just never occurred to me it would be something you'd want to do."

"Let me tell you a story, Bethany. The first big love of my life was when I was eighteen. Me and Melissa worked for the same pimp. She got knocked up and he sent her to some old hag in Roxbury. When the poor kid started running a fever afterward, that pimp son of a bitch was afraid he might get in trouble if we took her to the hospital. It was raining out, cold. Late fall. She died about four in the morning. I was holding her hand. The pimp made me help him dump her in an alley in the Zone. Okay?"

"Jesus, Wanda."

"Jesus had nothing to do with it. It was that fucking pimp."

"The vice cops had to know she was one of his girls, didn't they?"

"They came around to see him the next day, but he was already dead of an overdose. So they tell me. I was on a bus to Cleveland, myself."

"Didn't that strike the cops as kind of a coincidence?"

"Why should they care? Nobody gives a shit about a dead pimp."

"People give a shit about television preachers that are running for the Senate, though."

"Hey, I'm a lot smoother now."

"I mean it. The idea is for nobody to get hurt." Actually I didn't care that much, but Hope would.

"I mean it, too," Wanda said.

"And you're sure you want to do it."

"If it can be done. These guys got to be kind of gunshy, after Swaggart and Bakker. I couldn't just walk in on him cold. Hey, big boy, let's fuck."

"No, I guess you couldn't. We'll have to think about that."

On the way back home, I stopped off to do my run around and around Fresh Pond. Hope says that sculling is complicated enough, with the balance of the boat changing all the time, that you can't let your thoughts wander far from the job. Running, on the other hand, requires about as much concentration as making your heart beat. You could compose sonnets while running. You could play imaginary chess games, or work out the theory of relativity. Or you could think about the Reverend Howard Orrin of the Holy Electronic Church and Wanda Vollmer of Personal Leisure World.

Wanda was genuinely tough, as I had every reason to know. And now it looked very much like the killing I already knew about had really been her second. But I wasn't an officer of the court, and to me it seemed as if the circumstances each time had been pretty damned extenuating. I also knew Wanda as a very decent and even kind woman, behind all the toughness. Life had dealt her a busted seven-high straight, and she had played it better than most of us could have.

I had got to know about Wanda's life, little by little, in the sauna. Normally I have access to the Harvard wrestling team's sauna, but it was shut down for repairs a couple of months last year. Meanwhile Wanda let me use the one in Personal Leisure World. Wanda is a sauna freak, too, and we'd spend an hour in there a couple times a week. Either she was starved for somebody to talk to, or there was something about being naked in 190-degree heat that lowered her guard. Anyway, I learned a lot about her.

She was the youngest of four children, only eighteen months old when her motorman father beat her mother to death with the cast-iron base of an electric fan. He got twenty years in Walpole, where he killed himself shortly after he arrived. Or so she learned years later when she called up Vollmers in the phone book one day till she came across an older brother she had never met.

Wanda herself was raised in a Catholic orphanage and educated in Catholic schools.

"I was always kind of a problem child," she said one day while she was slapping me with a bunch of birch twigs. That's what the Finns are supposed to do to each other in saunas, and we figured we'd give it a try. "So the sisters would use the steel ruler on me a lot."

"Ouch," I said. "What are you doing, playing nun?"

"Sorry. The nuns would smack me a lot harder than that, though. When you got a problem child, you got to really whack the shit out of her. Personally I always figured they was problem nuns, but nobody ever asked me."

"They should have whacked you harder, teach you to say *were* instead of *was*."

"They taught me, all right. I knew how, but I'd say it wrong just to bust their balls. Later I just kept on, the life I led."

The life was hooking when she was a teenager, then waitressing and bartending, then managing her shift at the bar, and for the last ten years running Personal Leisure World for the state legislator who owned it. She had met the guy bartending, and after a while he saw enough of her work so that he asked her to be the owner of record of the massage parlor and to manage it for him.

I saw a good deal of her work, too, on my visits to the place. She had a nice way with the girls, tough when they messed up, the rest of the time relaxed, but they always knew she was the boss. The place was clean, and it was honest as far as these things go. They didn't have Sunday dinners together or anything, but there was sort of a family feeling among the girls. Often enough, probably, it was as close to the real thing as these particular girls had ever come. So turnover was low for that kind of business, although it would have seemed high anywhere else.

"You got a retirement plan here?" I asked her one day.

"Yeah, sure. You make it to sixty-three, you get Social Security plus your own heating grate. So I'm taking bookkeeping and accounting three afternoons a week at Lesley College. Unless they're bullshitting me over there, you can always find work doing the books for businesses in small towns."

Wanda read the *Wall Street Journal* every day and had a few shares of this and that. Once she explained to me why she got into the market: "I tended bar for a year downtown and the place was full of riffraff like bankers. How hard can it be to understand this finance shit, I figured. I mean, these were stupid guys and they made millions."

"Well, can you understand it now?"

"Sure. It's nothing but bullshit and bribes."

So she understood money and men, and had had a good deal of religion whacked into her as well. What else would she need to take on the Reverend Howard Orrin? The only question was whether she could be counted on not to kill the son of a bitch, and I thought she could. The other two times had been personal, revenge taken in hot blood for the deaths of people she had loved. This time was just business, maybe mixed with a little pleasure. But nothing personal.

Besides, she had sort of promised to behave herself.

As I ran, I got to thinking about a way to get her together with the Pastor without him thinking it might end up with him on the front page of the *National Enquirer*. By the time I finished my second circuit of the reservoir I had the answer, or I did if everybody involved would cooperate.

Back home I settled down, still sweaty, to restore my precious bodily fluids with an India Pale Ale. About halfway through the bottle my system was back in balance enough so that I could turn my mind to other things. Roy Shipley answered the number he had given me on the first ring.

"Tom Bethany," I said to the kid.

"Hi, Mr. Bethany."

"Tom, remember? Everything okay?"

"Sort of, I guess."

"Were you able to talk to your mom about this business with Kimberly?"

"Sort of."

"Is she there with you now?"

"No, she's at work."

"The way you sounded, I thought maybe she was there listening."

"No."

"Can you tell me what 'sort of' means, then? Was she mad?"

"No, she just acted kind of funny."

"Funny how?"

"Well, she wasn't mad, for one thing. That was funny, because mostly whatever I do makes her mad. The other thing is she generally thinks I do worse stuff than I really do, but this time she believed me when I said that Kimberly and I never . . . well, you know."

"I know what you mean."

"At least that's one way I don't take after my dad, she said. She's always saying stuff about my dad. My dad is an electronics engineer in Oregon."

The way he said it, you could tell that the boy thought a man couldn't do much better than to be an electronics engineer in Oregon.

"Why do you think she wasn't mad?"

"I wondered about that at first, and then I figured she was glad because I was going out with a girl. Well, sort of. I wasn't, really."

"She's always after you to go out with girls?"

"She talks about it, yeah."

Time to back away from this particular subject. His mother had been pleased that he had a female friend, but unsurprised to learn that he hadn't been the one to get her pregnant. It sounded like she was afraid her boy was turning out gay. Logical enough. After all, he was intelligent and shy.

"That Pacer you were driving the other day," I said. "Is it yours?"

"Yeah, my dad gave it to me. For my birthday."

"A political campaign can always use volunteers with cars. What would you think about helping out with the Orrin campaign after school?"

"I guess I could. Why, though?"

"I was thinking about running kind of a sting operation on the Pastor. If you could get to be a familiar face around the campaign, then the guy won't be so suspicious when you introduce your sister to him."

"I don't have a sister."

"Sure you do. I just picked one out for you."

That stopped him for a minute, and then he said. "Oh, I get it."

"I think you're going to like her, Roy. She's not your average big sister."

I told him a certain amount of stuff about Wanda, but not enough to alarm him. "The plan's pretty vague at the moment," I went on to say. "Actually figuring out a good way for Orrin to meet her is as far as we've gotten. After that, we improvise."

"Can I ask you something?" Roy said. "Why are you doing this?"

"Because the Pastor pissed me off. Really pissed me off bad."

"Yeah, but still . . ."

"I know what you mean, only I'm not sure I entirely know what the answer is. I'll make a deal with you, though. I'll try to figure it out and we'll talk about it when I get down there."

"A couple of weeks, you said?"

"More or less."

"Spring break will be about to start."

"Good. The more time you can spend at campaign headquarters, the better. Listen, Roy, can I ask you to do one other thing? Go by the Arlington County welfare department and get me any kind of form or letterhead from them, anything official-looking like that.

"And listen, Roy," I said, "I don't want you to get in any trouble over this. If there's nothing laying around that you can pick up, just forget about it. It's something that would be handy, but nothing I can't do without."

"What's it for?"

"It's for some plans I have for Mr. Pearsall. Mr. Pearsall pisses me off, too."

After I hung up, I thought of calling Wanda with the news she had just become a big sister. But then I thought why call when I could draw down my precious bodily fluids again with a sauna. I phoned to tell her to turn the heating unit on while I drove out to tell her in person about her new status.

Business was slow at Personal Leisure World, and so Wanda joined me on the cedar benches of the sauna. It wasn't quite hot enough yet, but it was getting there. After fifteen minutes beads of sweat were starting to stand out on my shoulders. In another five minutes or so the beads would have run together, which was the signal that told me it was time to duck out for a cold shower before taking more heat. Wanda was slower to work up a sweat, although a sheen was forming on her breasts and stomach.

"It's amazing how good you're looking," I said.

"Yeah, isn't it?"

Before, she had been what they used to call matronly. Now her breasts had kept most of their size, but the padding on her stomach and hips had practically disappeared.

"You look like you lost a lot of weight, but I bet you didn't really lose so much," I said.

"How did you know that?"

"Wrestlers are all the time worried about making weight, so we think about it a lot. We know muscle is denser than fat. So you can lose more bulk in fat than you put on in muscle and still weigh the same. Only difference is you move better and you look better."

"That's what Diane says, too."

"Diane's your friend?"

"Diane Ackerly, yeah. The shit she has me doing in the gym, I wouldn't have thought it was possible."

"Possible you could do it, or possible anybody could make you do it?"

"Both."

"Anyway, it's a new you. Before you'd have had to be the kid's mother. Now you can be his big sister, easy."

"How old is he?"

"He's a high school kid."

"A good kid?"

"Yeah, I think he is. Smart. Real timid. Scared of girls."

"He won't be scared of his big sister. Watch how I do."

"I was thinking, what if Big Sis had an abortion she didn't want? Maybe her boyfriend or her ex-husband or something pushed her into it."

"Maybe she damned near died from it," Wanda said, picking up on it. "I could describe how that is, easy enough. I was right there watching, the time I told you about."

"So now, Wanda, you want to devote your life to seeing that no other poor girl goes through what you did. I like it a lot. I think the Pastor's going to like it a lot, too. If the boy can get himself hooked up to the campaign, we could go down to D.C. in a couple of weeks. That work okay for you?"

"Why not?"

"Good. Meanwhile, I'll try to find us a place to stay."

"Let me make a call. I've got a friend down there that's sort of in the real estate business in Washington."

9

SORT OF IN THE REAL ESTATE BUSINESS SORT OF described it. Wanda's friend turned out to be a pastry chef named Jeannie who worked nights at the Madison Hotel, a woman nearly as tall as my own five eleven and a whole lot wider. I'm not as good on women's weights as I am on men's, but I go 180, and she certainly weighed a whole lot more than that.

Jeannie had inherited a houseful of good furniture when her mother died. She had been about to put one or two pieces into her own small apartment and the rest in storage when she heard that the drop in real estate prices in the capital had created a weird little niche for her to fill. Apparently houses sell faster if they're nicely furnished than if they're empty, so a few of the upscale real estate firms hit on the idea of installing house sitters. You had to have references and you had to be able to fill the house with first-class stuff. And naturally you had to stay out of the way when the agent came to show clients around. But in return you lived rent free in a fancy house in an expensive neighborhood. If the house

117

sold, the real estate people sent the movers around for your furniture, and you started all over again in another fancy house.

Jeannie was working on her fourth, a half-timbered fake Tudor mansion sitting in a sea of ivy and pachysandra just off Foxhall Road. "It's the first one I haven't been able to fill up with Momma's things," she said when Wanda and I showed up in my 1987 Subaru wagon, which replaced my 1981 Datsun, which finally died in spite of the guys at MacKinnon Motors who kept it going well past the 200,000-mile mark.

"Looks full to me," said Wanda, inspecting the living room.

"That's only this floor and the second floor," Jeannie said. "The third floor is empty. I wouldn't even have had enough to fill the second floor, actually, except the nursery is already furnished."

"How come?" Wanda asked. "Why didn't they take it with them?"

"It's kind of sad," Jeannie said. "Apparently the wife of the couple who lived here was around forty and they went through all kinds of hell for years with some fertility doctor over in Alexandria."

"Not the guy in the papers?" Wanda said.

"That's the guy, all right. The fat one, although who am I to talk? Well, I don't know if the papers ran the stories up where you are, but using his own sperm wasn't the worst thing he did. Some of the patients said he strung them along by saying they were pregnant even when they weren't. Then he'd say they miscarried and start his fertility treatments all over again. The woman who lived here didn't know what he'd been doing to her till the trial came along.

"So anyway, these poor people had a nursery with no baby in it for three years. When they moved to North Carolina, they left all the nursery things behind. The agent said they couldn't face selling the stuff and they couldn't face taking it with them, either."

"Fucking doctor's lucky he's in jail," Wanda said. "I'd nail his balls to a stump and light the stump on fire." Which wasn't just a figure of speech, either. Not coming from Wanda.

Jeannie showed us around, starting with the pathetic nursery. Its windows looked out into the branches of a tulip poplar just starting to leaf out. The windows were childproofed with ornamental iron grills. The walls were painted pale yellow. The beddings and curtains and furniture were in bright colors, reds and yellows and blues mostly. Nothing was baby blue or pink. No stereotypes for the nonexistent baby. S/he would have grown up free to figure out his or her sexuality all by itself.

An expensive-looking black and white mobile hung above the expensive-looking crib. There was an antique cradle, too, and a ruffled bassinet. A hand-painted toy chest with puppies and kittens. The curtains had been designed by the same hand, as had the fabric on a big sofa that probably opened out into a bed.

"Really sad, isn't it?" Jeannie said. "See that thing on the table, looks a little like a clock radio? It makes a noise that's supposed to sound like the mother's heartbeat and help the baby sleep. They've even got a baby monitor."

"What's that?" I asked.

"There's a camera, and you can check on the baby from either downstairs or from the master bedroom."

I looked around till I spotted the lens, which was built inconspicuously into a lighting fixture on the ceiling.

"Is it a color system?" I asked. "You get extra yuppie points for color."

"What are yuppie points?" she asked.

"Jeannie, for Christ's sake," Wanda said. "It's ding-bat's idea of a joke, that's all."

"Oh," said Jeannie. "Well, I don't know if it's color,

119

but you could ask the agent. She demonstrates it to all the prospects. She says it's a big selling point."

We left the bright, sad nursery and took a look at the adult accommodations. Jeannie's parents hadn't left her any water beds, but there was something else I had always wanted to try. It was a feather mattress, on a big walnut coach bed that was dressing up a guest bedroom. Wanda settled for the adjoining bedroom, which just had a regular mattress. Each of our bedrooms had its own bathroom. It was that kind of house.

Each of them also had its own phone extension. I called Hope's office, and for once I caught her between meetings. I had already told her, before leaving Cambridge, what Wanda and I had in mind. Now I told her our address and read the phone number off to her.

"Are you sure this is a good idea, what you're doing?" Hope said.

"I can't see much of any down side to it. And it should be fun."

"What do you really hope to accomplish?"

"I hope to make the Pastor drop out of the Senate race and I hope to destroy Life Force and I hope to drive the son of a bitch off the tube. Realistically, though, I'd settle for just getting him out of politics."

"I guess what worries me is the entrapment aspect."

"It's no different from what the Justice Department did to Mayor Barry."

"Right. That's what worries me."

"Actually what the Justice Department did to Barry was worse. I'm not even setting the Pastor up to commit a crime. Look, do you want me to call it off?"

"I guess that's what worries me the most, that I don't want you to. I keep thinking of poor little Kimberly."

"Come on, Sandy baby, loosen up. If his heart is pure, nothing happens to him at all."

"Why do I remain unpersuaded?"

"On the other hand, if his heart *isn't* pure, it's a character issue and the press is required to splash the story all over the place because of the First Amendment."

Next I called Roy Shipley and told him where we were. The first part of our plan was already under way. Shipley had already sent me a small assortment of Arlington County welfare department forms. And he had signed on as a volunteer with the Orrin for Senate campaign a week earlier. I asked the boy if he could come by and meet his new sister or was he too busy at the campaign? The boy said he really didn't have to go to headquarters till later on, but he would tell his mother I was calling from the campaign for him to come in early. "Not that she cares what I do . . ." That way, he could drive straight on into the District, find our new mansion, and have the rest of the afternoon to get to know his new sister. His consciousness was about to be enormously expanded on the subject of big sisters.

"How do you like the place?" was the first thing Wanda said to Roy when he showed up at the door. He fielded that one with a mumble.

The second thing she said was, "Five bedrooms, each with its own full bathroom. You believe that shit? We're only using three of them, so feel free."

"Well, thanks, but . . ."

"Hey, you got your own bedroom at home. I understand that. But your mom could walk in any time, am I right? No mom here, is what I'm saying. You want to bring some cute girl around after school, you got total privacy here and no questions asked."

"Jesus, Wanda," I said, "you're embarrassing the poor guy."

"Is that right, Roy? Am I embarrassing you? See, asshole, he's shaking his head. He's not embarrassed. I just wanted him to know him and his girlfriend are always welcome. What's her name?"

The kid didn't say anything.

"You got no girl?"

The kid shook his head.

"Well, shit, we'll do something about that. Count on Big Sis. She'll find you some hot pants little Christer over at the campaign."

"Clinton wants to tax country clubs." I said. "Did you see that in the paper?"

"Hey, fuck Clinton, okay?" Wanda said. "And fuck the horse he rode in on. Don't you try to change the subject on me, Bethany. You said I could be Roy's big sister and I never had a shot at being a big sister, and I'm going to do it right. Before me and Roy here are finished, I'm gonna get him screwed, blued, and tattooed. Me and you, huh, kid?"

She threw an arm around his shoulders and squeezed, and the kid looked confused but happy. A definite smile. Maybe it was going to be all right.

"You're giving him a lot to absorb all at once, Wanda."

"He can absorb it, no problem. This is a hell of a guy, I can tell. You Catholic, Roy?"

Roy nodded.

"Me, too. You ever squeeze a tit?"

This knocked him so far off center that he couldn't even shake his head. Then Wanda knocked him even farther. She took his hand and put it on one of her large and bra-less breasts. "See," she said. "Now go ahead and squeeze it by yourself. That's a boy. I'm a little old for you, but hey, a tit's a tit. They all feel pretty much the same."

I wondered how long it would take for Roy to start wondering how come Wanda knew so much about the way all tits felt the same. For the moment, though, he was in a state of sensory overload.

"Don't mind me," Wanda said, punching his shoulder lightly to show they were just pals, even if this pal let you squeeze her tit. "I see a cute young guy and sometimes it's hard to remember he's my brother."

The boy smiled uncertainly.

"Now, see," Wanda went on, "at this point what you want to do is step into the conversation yourself, give the girl a compliment right back. Go ahead."

Roy was stuck for a while. At last he said, "I'm sorry. I guess I'm having trouble thinking of you as my sister."

"Hey, not bad at all." Wanda said. "See how easy it is?"

The kid looked surprised and relieved at the same time, like Calvin in the comic strip, the time he came up with the right answer in class without knowing why it was right.

"Come on into the living room and tell me about yourself, Roy," Wanda said. "Bethany can get us some coffee while we get acquainted."

It took me a while to locate what I needed in the huge kitchen. The only coffee turned out to be beans, kept in the freezer. In the pantry was a little whizzer to grind them up in. A coffee machine was out in the dining room. Fresh filters for it were tucked behind the silverware organizer in one of the kitchen drawers. Once I had assembled everything and turned on the coffee maker, I picked up a tray on the way through the pantry and set it on the kitchen counter. Might as well do this right, now that I was in a mansion. Might as well serve high tea, or high coffee, really.

Jeannie apparently brought her work home with her, since the refrigerator was loaded with enough different pastries to stock one of those carts they wheel around in French restaurants. It was also loaded with a wide selection of diet sodas. Jeannie seemed to be one of those people who eats a 600-calorie chunk of chocolate cake along with a zero-calorie Diet Pepsi, so the snack will average out to 300.

When the coffee was finally ready, I brought out my loaded tray. Wanda and Roy were evidently back on theology again.

"Roy turns out to be the same kind of Catholic I am,"

she said. "The former kind. Except I haven't been to church in an even longer time than him."

"Mom tries to get me to go sometimes," he said to Wanda. "But my dad never goes. He's an electronics engineer in Oregon."

"Yeah, you told me," Wanda said.

"A lot of the Life Force activists are supposed to be Catholics," I said.

"A lot of them are," Roy said. "I even see some priests around."

"So what do you think of this?" Wanda said. "Me and Roy were talking about the best way to get next to Orrin, and we figured being Catholic was the best way to do it."

"How would that work?" I asked.

"Well, Roy's an expert on microphones and stuff, so they've got him doing the sound at the rallies and all. Bottom line, he got to talk to Orrin a few times. So now the guy knows Roy was raised Catholic. You got to figure his big sister would be Catholic, too."

"Yeah, but so are lots of other people in the campaign," I said. "How would that get you next to the great man?" I had been in enough political campaigns to know that getting close to the candidate is the main aim in life of everyone from the campaign manager down to the guy who sweeps out the computer room. Competition is always fierce.

"How about because I'm a woman?" Wanda said. "We know he's a chaser."

"Not good enough. There's no shortage of women in a campaign who are dying to put out for their hero. All he's got to do is show an interest, and any candidate can get more ass than Howdy Doody in a puppet factory."

"Probably just about as good ass, too, but that's beside the point, Bethany. The point is I know about men, and I know about hard-shell Baptists, too."

"Actually the Pastor isn't a Baptist. He's some off-brand type of fundamentalist."

"To me, they're all Baptists."

"Besides, what do you know about Baptists anyway?"

"I was with this girl from a place called McCamey, Texas, for almost two years once and one time she dragged me down to meet her parents. She made me wear a wedding ring and pretend I was just an office buddy, 'Mrs. Vollmer.' You believe that shit? You want some more unbelievable shit? To make the parents happy, we went twice to services and once to fucking Sunday school."

"That's it? Now you're a Baptist expert?"

"Both sermons, the preacher spent the entire time hollering about the Vatican. The Pope this, the Pope that. The Pope wasn't just the servant of the devil, the Pope actually *was* the devil. This preacher used the two words like they were the same thing. I mean, not that I give a shit for the Catholic church myself, but this guy was totally deranged on the subject."

"Where are you going with this, Wanda?"

"Hear me out, okay? In Sunday school it was even worse. Apparently you can really get down and dirty in Sunday school, where you know there's no strangers sitting out front. It was a women's group, just us girls together. The leader we had was the preacher's wife. What we talked about was how all those nuns and priests are naked under their robes, so the priests can fuck the nuns easier."

"Oh, yeah? I always wondered about those robes myself."

"Yeah, well, did you ever wonder where nuns come from in the first place? From other nuns, that's where. The priests knock up the nuns so they can have a supply of young nuns coming along all the time when the old nuns wear out."

"What happens to the boy babies? They become priests?"

"Only the really evil ones. The decent kids, they sell them for adoption."

"That's too dumb even for Texans to believe."

"Trust me, they believe it. Those women were sitting there with their mouths open like baby birds. Anyway, it all gave me an idea how to get next to Orrin. Me and Roy were just talking about it. Tell him, Roy."

"You tell him, Wanda." Good. It was Wanda now.

"You might as well get the practice," she said. "You're the one that has to make the speech."

"Jeez, okay, I'll try. I'm supposed to go to the Pastor and say I've got this older sister and could he counsel her because this awful thing happened to her once that she still can't get over, you know? She was a nun and this priest made her do it with him, and then she was supposed to have the baby only she, what? I forgot why she didn't want the baby."

"On account of I lost my faith in the church and didn't want to have a baby around to remind me of the whole hideous experience," Wanda said. "I was half crazy by then, anyway."

"Right. She wasn't thinking straight or she would have wanted the baby. Only she was half crazy so she broke out of the convent and ran away and got an abortion, and she got an infection or something at the clinic so now she can't have any babies, and she wants to help other girls and women by talking about her experience."

"Don't forget about the counseling."

"Yeah, she needs to talk to somebody. Like counseling. Could she maybe sit down with you, Reverend, just to tell you about it?"

"A few minutes."

"Right. It'll only take a few minutes of your time, Reverend Orrin."

"Well, it probably needs a little work," Wanda said. "But what do you think so far?"

"I think it's fucking ridiculous," I said. "It can't miss."

And I couldn't think up any improvements. Nor could I think of any improvements on the way Roy Shipley was handling his assignment. Most people around political campaigns are technological illiterates, true enough. But it was still impressive that a slightly overweight, slightly clumsy, more than slightly insecure high school kid had been able to establish himself so quickly in the Pastor's operation.

"You couldn't have done better, Roy," I said. "I thought if you were lucky you'd wind up on the phones or a messenger or something."

"It was nothing, really. You should see some of the equipment they were using. I guess the press office needs to have tapes or something of every time he talks, and all they knew how to do was set this stupid little battery-powered Sony beside the mike when he gives a speech. You know the way you can run everything through a mixing board and record it as you amplify? They didn't even know about that."

"Neither would I."

"It's cinchy, really. I could show you in five minutes. I set it up that way in his office, too."

"How do you mean? Does he give speeches in his office?"

"I guess sometimes he likes to have a record of when he talks to people. Particularly press interviews."

"I interviewed him once for the *Reader's Digest*," I said. "At least that's who I told him I was. Suppose he's got that on tape?"

"That was you?"

"You heard me?"

"Nobody could hear you, that was the whole trouble. The Pastor had that stupid Sony in an open drawer of his desk. Only when they went to play it back you couldn't make it out, on account of the mike wasn't powerful enough to pick up somebody on the other side of the desk. What I did was I put a decent mike on his desk and then I ran the signal out to where the amp is. In this little kind of closet just off of his reception room where I store my stuff."

"Let me understand this, Roy. He's got a live mike on his desk and you're taping off it somewhere else?"

"Well, yeah, essentially. At least it's a live mike when he keys it."

"Key meaning when he turns it on?"

"Sure. If it's off there's no signal to record."

"Who collects the tapes?"

"I do. The press lady tells me when there's going to be an interview or something, and afterward I dub a tape of it for her."

"Politicians are always saying stuff into mikes they think are off. You suppose there might be a way of rigging that mike so it would pick up the Pastor when he thought it was off?"

"Let me think . . ." Roy said. "Okay, one way would be to reverse the switch so On was Off and Off was On. I'd have to look at the mike, but I think that would be pretty easy to do."

"How would that work?" I asked. "You couldn't tape the legitimate interviews because he'd really be turning the mike off whenever he wanted to record something."

"Yeah, let's see," Roy said. After a minute he had it. "Hey, this could be really neat if I can get it to work. Maybe I can sketch out a system with two recorders. When he thinks the mike is on, a regular recorder starts taking down the interview and I give a copy of that tape to the press lady like before. Only at the end, when he thinks he's switching the mike off, what he's really doing is diverting the signal to another recorder."

"And we get whatever else anybody says in the office? Is that what you're telling us?"

"That's right. The mike is always on, and all the switch does is direct the signal to the right recorder. It's kind of an elegant solution."

"It damned sure is," I said. "Basically you've got the guy bugging himself onto our private tapes."

"If I can only work it out," Roy Shipley said. "Let me think what all I'll need." He had a notebook in his shirt pocket, being the kind of kid that carried notebooks.

I wished I had had a kid like him back in the 1980 campaign. Insofar as the Carter people had a counter-intelligence operation then, I was it. You do your best to keep a credential like that off your résumé, though, since that was the campaign when Bill Casey had his career criminals stealing our debate books and trying to cut side deals with the Iranians so the hostages would stay locked up till Carter lost. All of which went on while I was supposed to be guarding the store. I could have used a Roy Shipley to wire Ronzo's campaign for sound.

"I have to buy a few things," Roy said, looking up from his calculations. "It might cost as much as two hundred, but they said they'd pay for whatever I need, within reason. You think two hundred is within reason?"

"Absolutely," Wanda said. "Two hundred for bugging yourself is cheap."

"Wouldn't they be able to tell from the receipts what the equipment was for?" I asked.

"If anybody with any brains saw it, sure," Roy said.

"Don't worry about it," said Wanda. "These guys are still having trouble figuring out evolution."

"That doesn't mean some guy over there might not know about audio equipment," I said. "Anything that's a legitimate part of what they think you're doing, Roy, let them pay for. Anything else, better put it on a separate bill and I'll pay for it."

"For now," Wanda said. "We'll get the dough back soon enough."

"Where from?" Roy asked.

"I'm no cheap date, Roy. Which the Pastor will be figuring it out soon enough."

Roy looked like he wanted to ask something, but didn't feel easy doing it. He knew roughly what we were up to, true enough. But I had talked in terms like "compromising situations," and so on, and perhaps he hadn't thought much about what was actually hiding behind the words.

"You know what the badger game is, Roy?" I asked.

"No."

"It's where a woman is in bed with a guy and her accomplice busts in on them and starts hollering he's her husband or boyfriend, or maybe a cop. Anyway, he shakes the guy down for his money."

"Like a sting?"

"More like blackmail. Wanda plays the woman and I play the cop."

"But she . . . Wanda . . ."

"Let me lay it out for you, Roy," Wanda said. "I manage a massage parlor up in the Boston area, and what I do in private with people nowadays is strictly because I want to do it. Been that way for years. But when I was about your age, I was on the street."

"You mean . . ."

"Exactly. I was a hooker. You know those hookers in the movies, with a heart of gold? Well, that wasn't me. I was just a hooker. Hey, hey, don't get that expression."

"I don't mean . . ."

"Sure you do. It's okay. Let me just explain you something, though, so you'll understand exactly where we are here. When I was your age, I got guys off for money, plain and simple. That was my job. Some job, huh? Some kind of weird? Not really, Roy.

"It's just one way of touching people. Think about all

the jobs you touch people in. What if I said I was a manicurist? Nothing wrong with that, huh? How about a doctor? How about a nurse, or somebody works in an old folks' home? How about a guy sells pants in a store, even? First time I saw one, I thought he was groping the customer. How about a wrestler, like Tom? Or listen, you want weird, how about an undertaker? See what I'm getting at here? Touching is touching. You do it, you don't think about it, it's over. You get used to it quick. Nothing so awful about it."

"I didn't say there was—"

"Hey, you don't have to say it. There's not a man in the world, he doesn't think to himself, What's a nice girl like you doing in a place like this? Well, she's there because he's there, you come right down to it. And what she's doing is the same thing wives do for their husbands, and plenty of times the wives aren't any more crazy about doing it than the hookers are. Plenty of times the husbands aren't either. If you can believe what they tell hookers. So what I'm saying here, Roy, is it's not such a simple world as it looks."

"All I was was surprised," Roy said. "I didn't mean I was shocked or anything."

"I understand what you're saying," Wanda said. She tousled his hair, which could have seemed condescending but somehow didn't. "You're a good guy, Roy. Some girl's going to be lucky to get you someday."

"Huh." He didn't believe that for a minute.

"It'll happen. What you got to remember is that most girls your age are stone assholes. Most guys, too. So the assholes ask each other to the proms and all that shit. Most of the guys are going to stay assholes, because that's what they're raised to be. But a lot of the girls are going to grow out of it, and then they're going to be looking for guys that aren't assholes. Wait and see."

This probably wasn't the general take on life that a kid Roy's age would have expected in a heart-to-heart with a grown-up. If he was like most kids, in fact, he had never had a heart-to-heart with a grown-up. Certainly not one who had let him squeeze her very nice tit practically immediately after being introduced. If I were Roy's age, I would have followed a woman like Wanda anywhere.

"Maybe it's the blackmail aspect of it that bothers him," I said. "Is that it, Roy?"

"I guess not so much," he said. "The Pastor does it, too."

"He does?"

"Well, he might be, anyway. I was trying to fix an old amplifier the other day and he was talking to this guy called something like Weeder. It's funny, they were talking just like I wasn't there. Some people do that around kids, you ever notice?"

"Sure. It's one of the ways you can spot an asshole."

"Anyway, this Weeder—"

"Wait a minute, you happen to get his first name?"

"Archie, I think."

"I'll be a son of a bitch. Archibald Weider."

"Who's he?" Wanda asked.

"Guy who used to give us trouble in the 1980 campaign. He's a right-wing political consultant and direct-mail fund-raiser. Started out back in the sixties with a mailing list he bought from a bunch of survivalist nuts after half of them went to jail for blowing up a courthouse in Idaho."

I wondered what a fund-raiser like Weider could do that would be any use to an operator like Orrin. The Pastor already knew more than Weider ever would about raising money from the theologically challenged.

"Blackmail sounds like Archie Weider, all right," I said. "Of course it sounds like us, too. Takes one to know one. Go ahead with your story, Roy."

"What happened was the Pastor unlocked one of the file cabinets in his office and pulled out a bunch of reports or something. He called them papers of purification. So anyway, he read one of them to Mr. Weider. I was off in the corner soldering stuff, but I was listening, too.

"It was all about some lady that was telling how she made her little boy eat a mouthful of pepper because he said a bad word, and he got to choking and coughing so bad he died. But she didn't tell the police anything about feeding him pepper and they just wrote down that it was an accident."

"Pepper, huh?" Wanda said. "That's one the nuns never thought of."

I asked Roy. "Were you able to figure out why Orrin had this purification stuff, and why he was telling Weider about it?"

"I don't know, really. But Mr. Weider looked over a few of the folders and wanted to know if the signatures on them were real, and the Pastor said absolutely. And Mr. Weider said those files were better than money in the bank. That's what made me think of blackmail."

"Does Orrin keep the key on him?"

"No, he got it from a little basket filled with paper clips and stuff on his bookcase. I guess I could get into the cabinet. Maybe."

"Well, somebody could walk in on you. Let's hold off, for now anyway."

"There was something else," Roy said. "The woman with the pepper? Her name was Mulholland. There's this campaign volunteer that has the name Mulholland on her desk. Mulholland isn't too common of a name, is it?"

"No, it isn't."

"If I was you," Wanda said, "I'd watch my language around Mrs. Mulholland."

10

*W*EATHER PERMITTING, HOPE LIKED TO BE OUT in her scull on the river by six o'clock. Normally she would drive straight downtown after her morning row, fully exercised, showered, dressed for power, and still the first one into the office. But my Tudor mansion— Jeannie's Tudor mansion, really—wasn't far from the Potomac Boat Club's boat house. The day before, Hope had cut her workout short and showered here instead. I had showered with her, helping her out with soaping and so on.

"Oh," she had said.

"Oh, what?"

"I'm still a little tender."

"Oh."

"No, go ahead. It's all right."

It wasn't, and I didn't. Couldn't, actually.

Now, the day after, I lay in the feather bed Jeannie's parents had left her and listened to the water run. I had taken my own shower before Hope arrived, so as to sidestep the whole issue. It wouldn't stay sidestepped in my head, though. I lay there thinking about how I had hurt her, not just in the shower the day before but back when I made her pregnant in the first place. Our love no longer looked like a no-money-down risk-free investment. Now what? I listened to the water run until it stopped, and then I listened to the silence until Hope stepped out of the bathroom, all rosy and naked except for the towel wrapped around her head.

She headed over to the feather bed. Not too many of us look good walking in the nude, and even fewer of us manage it once time starts to loosen up the wrapping on our packages. But Hope was one of the few. After all these years, all these uncounted scores or hundreds of times, I had never failed to respond to the sight and the feel of her.

Till now.

"Mind if I join you, mister?" she said, not waiting for an answer.

"No, I don't mind," I said. And I didn't, but at the same time I did. Could it be okay now, when it was hurting only yesterday? Worse, would it ever be okay? The soreness was bound to pass, but we had had one accident and we could have another. Dumb thinking, but a lot of thinking is dumb. "Maybe we should wait," I said.

"And just be good friends? Is this the brush, Bethany?"

"Well, if you hurt . . ."

"I don't hurt everywhere. You ever hear of lollipop? We could play that."

A long time passed, or it seemed long.

"I'm sorry," I said. I was about to say more, but couldn't quite manage. Hope said it for me.

"Nothing like this has ever happened to me before, he said wretchedly."

So I sort of shrugged. I could manage that much.

"You don't have to tell me, pal," Hope went on. "I

feel perfectly sure it never happened before. Remember election night?"

For us, election night would always mean the one that started out poorly at eight-fifteen, when NBC, with five percent of the vote counted, declared Reagan the winner over Jimmy Carter. From there on things got even worse, with Church, McGovern, Culver, and Gaylord Nelson going down. And even worse, although we didn't yet know just how bad, when Birch Bayh was beaten by a two-term congressman named J. Danforth Quayle III. By the time we finally got back to my room, it was spinning.

"I remember election night," I said. "Vaguely."

"Anyone who could function the way you did in the condition you were in," she said, "that person never had a problem before and he's got nothing to worry about now."

"Oh, yeah? Well, this is now and just look."

"I'm looking. You've still got nothing to worry about. Tom, listen to me. I wrestled with dysfunction for years. Dysfunction, hell. Nonfunction. Before Martin got up the courage to tell me he was gay, I thought it must be my fault. So I read, and I asked other women. I knew impotence personally and believe me, Senator, you're not impotent. All you've got is a little misplaced guilt."

"Like hell it's misplaced. Why shouldn't I feel guilty? It takes two to tango."

"True enough, but in this kind of tango the woman leads. Maybe she shouldn't or maybe they should both lead, but I'm not talking about the way things ought to be. I'm talking about the way things are."

"I could have done a little leading, too."

"Sure you could have. And I could have used two or three more methods at once, too. One of my classmates from law school is with the F.A.A. now. Once he told me they could easily put enough safety features into a plane so that it would never have an accident. Only it would weigh so much it couldn't get off the ground."

"Maybe that's best. Stay on the ground."

"Just say no, huh? Listen to yourself, Bethany. Jesus, you sound like the Pastor."

"I feel bad, that's all. I feel like I did something that wound up hurting you, which I did. And it can happen again."

"Oh, please. Of course it can happen again. So what?"

"So what? Don't tell me an abortion isn't a big deal."

"It is a big deal, and I still say so what. I'm the one it happened to, so that makes me the boss on this one. I don't want to stay on the ground the rest of my life, and I won't. If an accident happens, one-in-a-million or whatever, then it happens. Meanwhile, I want to fly. You want to, too, don't you? Well, don't you?"

"Sure I do. Of course I do. But—"

"Shut up a minute, then. Make yourself useful."

So I did, and at first she told me to do this and do that, until I got it right and she stopped talking.

"Shut up yourself," I said to her once she was quiet and her breathing had slowed down. "We're trying to run a respectable house here."

"Good. You're smiling." And she smiled back at me, down the familiar terrain of her. "You're okay, aren't you?"

"I'm okay."

"What are you going to do with the rest of the day? While I'm off earning a living?"

"I'm going to hang around outside the high school. Look at teeny-boppers and stuff."

C. W. Grizzard High School looked to have been built in what we think of so far as the Great Depression, although there's still time in the century for a greater one.

The school was an Art Deco pile of poured concrete and yellow brick identical in its ugliness to thousands of other power stations, post offices, hospitals, and courthouses built all over the country by the WPA.

Who was C. W. Grizzard? Perhaps a great poet who had set the mother tongue free to soar and circle? Or a philosopher who showed a troubled nation the path to reason and tranquility? A composer who set our dreams to music, or a novelist who held a wise and pitiless mirror up to our lives? Get real. What do you think this is, Europe or something? C. W. Grizzard was a politician.

"Chairman of the Arlington County Board of Supervisors, 1928–1934. Civic Leader, Jurist, Friend of Arlington's Schools" it said on one of the gate pillars. Underneath were the names of the six other politicians who had been supervisors when the school was dedicated, in 1937. Even the commonwealth's attorney, which is Virginia's way of saying district attorney, had somehow managed to get his name carved into the stone.

All over the names some kid had spray painted what might have been a couple of oranges and a banana, but looked more like a prick and balls. No disrespect intended, was my guess. The kid's work was probably a witty homage to that masterpiece of American commercial art, Joe Camel's face.

A few students started to come out, and then a few more, and quickly hundreds of them. The teachers seemed to be no more anxious to hang around the place after classes ended than the kids were, so there was an occasional adult in the crowd as well. It was tough to pick individual faces out of the stream, but I didn't think Roy Shipley and I could have missed connecting with each other. It would be hard for him to miss a grown stranger standing alone outside the gate. But the rush was soon over, and the boy hadn't shown up.

The plan was for him to follow William Pearsall out so that I could follow the English teacher home and begin learning his daily routine. Eventually I'd find or make an opportunity to get him alone. But not today, it looked like. By now only an occasional student was coming through the bank of doors at the top of the steps up to the school. One of them, at last, was Roy.

"I'm sorry," he said. "I tried to follow Mr. Pearsall out, but today he didn't leave. He scheduled a special rehearsal for some of the kids in *The Odd Couple*, and I never heard about it. I didn't exactly know what to do, so I hung around outside the auditorium for a while and then I thought I'd better tell you."

"No problem," I said. "I'll peek through the door to see what he looks like and then pick him up when he comes out. Just tell me how to get to the auditorium, and you can go on over to the campaign." Roy was volunteering every afternoon and some evenings at the Pastor's headquarters.

The few students in the halls paid no attention to me, probably because of my briefcase. In the real world carrying a briefcase does the same job that carrying a clipboard does in the army. It makes you look as if you're on legitimate business.

I found the auditorium with no trouble, and opened the door a crack to get a look at the drama coach. But he was sitting in the front row, slouching down, so all I could see was the back of his head. I thought it over and decided what the hell. If not here, where? If not now, when?

So I slipped through the swinging doors, eased them shut behind me, and sat down in the back row of seats. Only the stage lights were on, which left me not exactly invisible but at least inconspicuous. On stage, four boys were sitting around a card table covered with poker chips, soft drink cans, and cards. A fifth boy, a powerful-looking kid with sloping shoulders, was standing to one side. One of the poker players was saying, "Oh! Well, what do you feel like doing?"

The kid with the shoulders shrugged them and said, "I'll find something," and started to walk away.

"Hold it!" William Pearsall called out before the kid could get very far. "Felix, you're not walking like Felix."

"Huh?"

"You're walking like Bobby Flexner the linebacker, not Felix Ungar the compulsive neurotic."

"How can I walk like anybody but who I am?"

"That, Bobby, is the essence of theater. Did you ever see *Down and Out in Beverly Hills?*"

"Yeah."

"Remember how Nick Nolte walked?"

"Not exactly."

"Inexactly, then. Did he walk like a football player?"

"Well, he was playing a homeless guy."

"So he walked like a homeless guy?"

"I guess."

"He did indeed walk like a homeless guy. The same tired, hopeless, aimless walk that the homeless have."

"Well, he's an actor."

"He didn't start out as an actor, Bobby. Nick started out as a football player, just like you. For years he was a football bum, going from one college to another on athletic scholarships. He's hilarious talking about those days."

Pearsall paused for a second, and I had the feeling it was to give the kids a chance to ask him what old Nick was really like. But nobody did, and he went on.

"Before the shoot for *Down and Out*, Nick spent weeks on Venice Beach, watching the homeless hour after hour until he had their walk memorized in his bones."

"Who am I supposed to watch?" Bobby said. "What does Felix Ungar walk like?"

"He gives us a hint right in this same scene. Oscar says, 'Think of warm Jell-O.' Okay, go ahead, Felix. That's your cue."

"Isn't that terrible?" Bobby recited. "I can't do it. I can't relax. I sleep in one position all night. Frances says when I die on my tombstone it's going to say, 'Here Stands Felix Ungar.' "

"There you have it," the drama coach said. "Does anybody you know fit that description?"

"Mr. Roraback," one of the poker players said, and all the kids laughed.

"How so?"

"The way he stands in chem lab while we're doing experiments. All fidgety."

"There you have it, Bobby. Watch Mr. Roraback walk his fidgety walk, and then go thou and do likewise."

The rehearsal went on for another half hour. It didn't look like the show was going to be all that good. Maybe Nick Nolte had been a football player, but this football player would never be Nick Nolte. Still, Pearsall seemed to be doing the best he could with what he had.

At the end, William Pearsall climbed up on stage to help his players carry the props off into the wings—the same wings where Kimberly had told her secret to Roy. Now that I could see Pearsall, he was a tall man, right on the line between slender and skinny. Probably late thirties or early forties, trying hard to be ten years younger. He might have struck me as good-looking if I had come across him cold, not knowing anything about him. As it was, he struck me as looking weak and nasty and arrogant.

The boys leaped off the stage one after another, like kids jumping off the bank into a swimming hole. Pearsall sat on the edge of the stage and let himself down elegantly, feet together, as if he were being watched. Actually, the kids were charging out of the auditorium paying no attention to him, and he didn't spot his one-man audience till he was on the way up the aisle himself.

"May I help you?" he said when he was near enough. It sounded almost polite, but there was an edge of nastiness to it that suggested I was somewhere I had no business being.

"William Pearsall?" I said.

"That's right."

"T. W. Carpenter," I said. "Arlington County welfare department. Minor children's bureau."

Nothing alarming about that. He was a teacher of minor children, after all.

"What can I do for you, Mr. Carpenter?" he said.

"Sit down, Mr. Pearsall."

"I'm in a bit of a rush, actually."

"If I was you I'd slow down a little, Mr. Pearsall. You got a problem we got to talk about."

"What sort of a problem?"

"Sit down and I'll tell you." Now he sat down.

"You see what this is?" I said, holding up a book out of the briefcase that sat open beside me.

"A diary, by the looks of it."

"You got any idea whose diary it is, Mr. Pearsall?"

"Not the slightest. How could I?"

"You think of any minor child's diary you might be in?"

"Any number, I would imagine. I *am* a teacher, after all."

"You're some teacher, too. According to what's in this diary."

"I suppose you're eventually going to tell me just what imaginative child's diary this is?"

"It's Kimberly Butler's diary." Well, sort of. At least it was about her. And the handwriting might even look like hers from a distance, or so I hoped. It was neat, generic, good-girl handwriting, as taught by the nuns to Wanda Vollmer. My guess was that Pearsall had never seen Kimberly's handwriting, since Roy had told me she never took a class from him.

"Let me see that."

"Sorry, Mr. Pearsall. This is commonwealth's evidence."

"Evidence of what? Just what the hell is this all about."

"You know what it's all about. You got someplace where we can have a little privacy? Some place with a desk to write on?"

We wound up in the English department's office, which was a good-size room with a half-dozen desks, a wall full of filing cabinets, and another wall with ceiling-to-floor steel bookshelves painted dark blue. The shelves were a slovenly jumble of papers and old blue books and used file folders and textbook samples. When everybody shares, nobody cares.

"Which one is your desk?" I said, and he pointed. I sat down at it, opened my cheap briefcase, and took out a laser-printed forgery that was as official-looking as my Mac's self-publishing program back in Cambridge could make it.

"You come into my school and you sit down at my desk," Pearsall said. "Just exactly who do you think you are?"

"Let's face it, Mr. Pearsall. The girl was a fourteen-year-old minor. I don't know if you're familiar with the Virginia situation on statutory rape, but you got a very serious problem here. So don't waste either of our time with this bullshit, and just fill out this form, okay."

I shoved it over to him. He read standing up for a minute, and then he pulled a chair over from the next desk and sat across from me.

" 'Monetary or other considerations'?" he quoted from the form. "What the hell does all this mean?"

"Lots of times a girl wants money for clothes or something, or maybe some other type of consideration like maybe grades when the perpetrator is a teacher, that kind of thing. You know, monetary considerations. Like in the diary."

"Like what in the diary?"

I turned a few pages in the diary, and read, " 'I'm so disappointed about William and the money.' "

"What money?" Pearsall said.

"You tell me, Mr. Pearsall."

It took him a minute to figure out a lie to tell me. "I imagine what the poor child must have meant is money for an abortion."

"Now what abortion would that be, Mr. Pearsall?"

"I could see that Kimberly was troubled, and one day after rehearsal I asked her if I could help with whatever was bothering her. And it all came out."

"She was pregnant?"

"That's right."

"By you, right?"

"Certainly not. She didn't tell me the father and I didn't ask her."

"But you offered to pay for the abortion?"

"She asked me to pay. She had nowhere else to turn."

"Why would you pay for somebody else's abortion?"

"I might have. These kids ... Sometimes they just don't have any adult in their life, anyone they can go to for help."

"Including you."

"What is that supposed to mean?"

"What it says in the diary, here, she didn't get any help from you, either."

"If she had been able to wait only a few weeks, I could have helped her."

"Only momma was on a cruise and you couldn't get the money, huh?" Pearsall just looked at me. "It's right here in the book," I said.

"Let me see that book," he said, and I shook my head. "Where did you get it, anyway?"

"Think about it, Willie," I said. Time for first names. "A kid kills herself, who would find her diary?"

"The police?"

"It was the police, they'd be here, not me."

"Her parents?"

"If her old man got his hands on this, the police would be here, too. Or the old man would, probably with a shotgun. He struck me as a mean fucker."

"Then who *did* find this so-called diary?"

"Who's got it now? Any incident of suicide by a minor child, a welfare department investigator goes to the home to determine whether there was a possibility of abuse in the home that resulted in the incident. Waste of time, actually. Even if you find typical marks of abuse on the body of the deceased, the family always lies about it. Something like this diary, though, they'll naturally give it to you. If they find it. Only I found it."

"Where?"

"In her bedroom, hidden under the innersprings. I always ask if I can look through the bedroom."

"Do the police know about it?"

"Not yet."

"Are they going to?"

"Depends on you. Whether you fill out that form."

"I'm not signing anything without a lawyer."

"I'd think it over, Willie. You're not in court. Maybe you won't be."

"There can't be anything in that diary but the dream life of a very imaginative girl."

"You wish. The fact is, it's full of details, Willie. All I got to do, all the police got to do, if it comes to that, you know what it is? Just show pictures of you two lovebirds to certain desk clerks around Warrenton, you know? See if your handwriting is on the check-in cards. Talk to that other kid, the boy who was supposed to go with you and the minor female child on these little trips. Only somehow you never got around to telling him—"

"Now, listen, Mr. whatever it is . . ."

"Carpenter."

". . . anything that might have transpired between

Miss Butler and myself was strictly at her request and her desire, totally consensual."

"Sure it was, Willie. I talk to you guys all the time, I know how it is. She's just getting in touch with her emotions, right? Exploring her own sensuality. So you're a decent guy, you're just helping her find out what that little pussy is for."

"That's disgusting!"

"Hey, you said it, not me. Sit back down and cool off. This doesn't have to be so bad. Look, I don't give a fuck what you do, Willie. Somebody was going to break her in sooner or later anyway. Am I right or am I right?"

"Just exactly what do you want?"

"Nice watch, Willie. What is it, a Rolex?"

"As a matter of fact, it's something called a Patek Philippe."

I liked him all the more for taking it for granted that I wouldn't have any idea what a Patek Philippe was. Particularly since I didn't.

"Swiss," he added, in case I didn't know that, either. But I knew it had to be Swiss. No other watchmakers are so incredibly skilled that they can make watches thinner than a Necco wafer, and yet practically as accurate as my $12.95 Casio.

At last it occurred to Pearsall what was going on.

"You want my watch?" he said.

"I got a watch," I said. "See?"

"What do you want, then?"

"Your watch there, did momma give it to you?"

"What's the difference who gave it to me?"

"I was just thinking. Teacher's salary, kids, mortgage. That's a lot of watch there."

"As a matter of fact, it did happen to be a birthday gift from my mother."

"What do they call that stuff she paid for it with?"

"Well, that's not the sort of thing you ask someone

146

who gives you a gift, is it? Oh, I see what you're driving at."

"Right. I already know what time it is . . ."

"How much?"

"A thousand." That would let Roy pay back what he took from his college money and still leave him with a lot left over for his trouble.

"Five hundred is the most I can possibly do."

"Hey, Willie, I'm not bargaining with you here. I'm telling you what it costs you, take it or leave it."

"Exactly what do I get for my money? Plus the diary, of course."

"Plus the diary, you get to go into noncriminal rehab. I give you the name of a psychologist and you go once a week for counseling till she certifies you're cured of little girls."

"Which is how long?"

"It's never, actually. It's like a baldness gene with you assholes, no known cure. You'll be hustling jailbait till you can't get it up anymore, and then you'll be copping feels in the subway."

"I'll ignore that, except to say that you don't have the vaguest comprehension of what it's all about. Aside from that, you seem to be telling me that I'll be paying this psychologist forever."

"Did I say till you're cured? I said till she certifies you cured. Two different things."

"Give me an approximate time frame."

"Depends on you. You make that arrangement with her, Willie. I already told her about you. Said you'd be calling."

"My God, the whole process is corrupt, isn't it? I suppose you have an arrangement with this woman, too. Finder's fees, that sort of thing."

"We're wasting time here, Willie. Let me lay it out for you. It's my call if you go to the noncriminal rehab, which incidentally is all confidential, sealed records. Or if I turn you over to the cops.

"Suppose I do turn you over to the cops. What they do, they book you for statutory rape and under occupation they put down teacher. Once you're booked, it's an official record. So the reporters will print it and everybody knows. Then either you plead guilty, and the school fires you and your wife leaves you and your momma cuts off your allowance, shit like that. Or you plead innocent, and now the cops are pissed because they have to get off their ass and do some work.

"The cops know the same thing we do in child welfare, Willie. They know that when they catch guys like you, it's never the first time. They know you've been doing it all your life. So they start asking questions at school about any other little teeny-boppers you took kind of a special interest in over all these years. Some of them in college by now, am I right? Some probably married. Who knows who they're married to? Who knows who their fathers and their big brothers are? A lot of crazy bastards out there, Willie. Well, you see where I'm going, don't you?"

"I can't put my hands on that kind of money right away."

"I like to keep a clean desk, Willie. I can't wait long."

"Let's see. Monday? No, Wednesday's better. Wednesday?"

"Got to call momma for an advance on your allowance, huh? Okay, if that's the best you can do."

11

NEXT MORNING WAS THURSDAY, SO MY MEETING with William Pearsall was nearly a week away.

"How did it go with the teeny-boppers?" Hope asked. She was fresh from the shower and in my feather bed.

"Not too bad."

"You're thinking about them right now, aren't you? Don't lie. I've got the proof right here."

"Nothing to do with teeny-boppers. I'm queer for grown-ups."

"Oh, yeah? Prove it."

"Are you sure? I mean, I don't want to . . ."

"Oh, shut up. I'll close my eyes, and think of England."

A good while later Hope said, "I couldn't keep my mind on it after all."

"What?"

"England."

"Oh, right. England. I forgot, too."

"I could tell," Hope said. "Actually, I'm the one that's supposed to spring eternal."

"That's awful," I said, after the second or so it took me to get it.

"I know, but I can't help myself. Comes from reading Will and Safire."

We were lying on our sides front to back, fitted into each other like spoons, and before long the closeness had its old effect.

"I think you're cured, Bethany," Hope said. "It's just a feeling I'm getting."

"Maybe we should make sure."

"Oh, no you don't. I have to wash up so I can get to the office and start defending the Bill of Rights."

The shower wasn't running for much more than a quick rinse, and she was back in the bedroom dressing for the day. "We never got around to this Pearsall guy," she said, buttoning her blouse. "What happened with that?"

"I let him bribe me with a contribution to Roy's college fund. He's giving me a thousand bucks next week."

"A thousand dollars? The girl is dead and that's all that happens to him?"

"He just thinks it is."

"I know you'll do the right thing."

"I'll try. Tell you the truth, I didn't warm up to Pearsall very much."

I went downstairs in my bathrobe to see Hope off and was sitting in the kitchen waiting for my teakettle to boil when Jeannie came in with her tiny friend, Priscilla.

Priscilla worked nights, too—across the street from the Madison Hotel, in the press room of the *Washington Post.* She was barely five feet tall and must have weighed a good deal less than half what Jeannie did. They both ate like starving refugees, but Priscilla evidently had the metabolism of a humming bird. After a session of cholesterol loading, she and Jeannie would disappear promptly into the bedroom, and stay there all day except for occasional refrigerator raids.

Today Jeannie was carrying her usual load of pastries from the hotel, and went to stow them in the refrigerator.

"Are those really day-old?" I asked. "I mean, they always taste pretty fresh to me."

"What the hotel doesn't know won't hurt them," Jeannie said. "Just enjoy."

So I helped myself to a couple of éclairs. Priscilla did the same, only she found that this left a lot of space on her plate empty. So she filled it with ladyfingers and little glazed cakes. "I'll miss this kitchen," Priscilla said, and it was a pretty nice kitchen, sure enough. It had a TV, and sound piped in from the home entertainment center out in the living room, and a central food preparation island with a butcher block top, and a bunch of comfortable chairs you could sit in while you watched other people doing the work.

"Where are you going?" I asked her.

"We're all going. Tell him, Jeannie."

It turned out that the afternoon before, two bearded men had showed up with the broker. Without seeing any more than the downstairs, they decided the house was just what their royal highness needed to keep the rain off him when he visited Washington every year for the month of Ramadan. Their royal highness was a Kuwaiti prince now happily reunited by Bush with his offshore bank accounts and his Filipino house slaves. The parallels between Bush and Lafayette would be striking, except that Lafayette didn't sell his military services to George the Third.

Apparently the deal for rich Muslims was to be on a journey for the whole period of Ramadan, so they wouldn't have to observe the rules on daytime fasting. Normally this prince went to his places in Gstaad or London, but at the moment his eldest son was a student at American University, most likely having trouble with Problems of Democracy. Jeannie got all this except the Problems of Democracy part from the broker, who also told her that it would be another couple of weeks before the agency had another house ready for her and her furniture. Meanwhile, we could all stay where we were. Ramadan, it seemed, wouldn't start until next year.

Once Jeannie and Priscilla went on upstairs to begin their long day's night, I made a nice tray for myself. At home I don't even own a tray, but Jeannie's parents had had a whole collection. I was beginning to see the point of them, and even to consider maybe buying one for myself someday. I loaded a nice sterling silver number with my teapot, a cup and saucer and spoon, a honey pot, and a plate of lemon slices. The teapot, the spoon, and the filigree around the honey pot were also sterling silver. My previous life was starting to look a little low rent.

I put my silver service on the coffee table, which was another thing I lacked back in Cambridge, and went over to find the instruction booklet for Jeannie's home entertainment center. Once I had figured out what I had to do, I settled down with a notebook and a pencil to listen to the tapes of the Pastor that Roy was clearing from his hidden recorder every evening.

They were a mess, full of coughs, phones ringing, doors slamming and sirens outside—whatever random noise turned the recorder on. The noises were all run into one another, separated only by brief pauses when the machine switched itself on and off. Conversations had the same jammed-up quality, as the system shortened the normal pauses of speech into snippets of time all the same length. Telephone conversations sounded particularly odd, a run-together monologue of responses to a caller you couldn't hear. The only way to get both sides would have been to bug the phone itself, which Roy thought he could probably do without too much trouble. But we decided against it, in case the Pastor ever thought of getting somebody in to sweep the office. Roy's system with the microphone would probably breeze right through a sweep unsuspected, though. The mike was sitting right out in the open, supposed to be there.

The only way to sort through the stuff on the tapes was to listen to it all. After I was five minutes into the first cassette and had thought about how to attack the problem, I rewound the tape and set the tape counter to zero. Then I started over, noting down the number on the tape counter whenever I got to a worthwhile part.

Making my notes, I went through two hour-long tapes from two successive days. When each tape was filled up, that was it for the day, since Roy wasn't around to put in a new one. But this was less of a problem than I thought it might be. With the machine only running when people were actually speaking, an hour of tape covered a lot more than an hour of real time. And when it ran out, it ran out. We'd just have to wait till the next day to start eavesdropping again.

At the end of the first two tapes, I went through my little log, fast-forwarding till the good parts and recording just those onto a new tape. All this took longer than I thought. It was midafternoon by the time I had finished making my tape of highlights from a couple of days with one of America's top spiritual leaders. Roy himself was a feature player on my new tape.

"So that's what happened," Roy wound up saying, after telling Howard Orrin the awful tale of what the Papists did to his big sister, Mary Margaret. Actually, Mary Margaret was Wanda's real christened name, it turned out. Her first pimp was the one who picked Wanda for her, which says something about what a no-class guy he had to be. I mean, why not something fine like LaVonda or La Toya?

"I was telling her about you, Pastor," Roy's voice continued on the tape. "I was saying how she ought to come in and talk to you and all, and anyway, do you think you could? It wouldn't take but a few minutes. Really.

I told her how busy you were, and that's all we'd ask you for, just a few minutes."

"That's as terrible a tale as I've heard in a really long time," the Pastor said. "That baby goes in my prayers starting tonight, that tiny preborn victim that she was forced to sacrifice. And of course I'll offer your poor sister whatever comfort the Lord lets me give her. What does she do, your sister? What did you say her name was? Mary Margaret?"

"Yes, sir, Mary Margaret. She doesn't really do anything. She married this really rich guy, see? This really old rich guy, and he died and left her all this money, so now she just lives alone in this huge house out Foxhall Road . . ."

"Poor thing. She lost that pitiful unborn soul before it could know Jesus, and then before you know it she turns right around and loses her husband. How old is she?"

"Uh," Roy said. "Uh." He hadn't been expecting this one. "Uh, she's about twenty-eight. Yeah, twenty-eight."

Mary Margaret her very own self was listening to this section later that evening, sitting beside Roy on the sofa while I tended the tape deck. The boy had just come back from Orrin for Senate headquarters, where he had spent the afternoon repairing a couple of walkie-talkies used to coordinate Life Force demonstrations.

". . . Yeah, twenty-eight . . ." Roy's voice was saying to the Pastor.

"Well, if you ain't the sweetest thing," said Wanda to the real Roy. And then she tickled the boy, and grabbed him and wrestled around with him for a minute. Just kidding. Like a big sister might. Sort of. Roy looked flustered, and his hair was mussed when he broke away.

"Get a grip, Wanda," I said. "He just said twenty-eight because it was the oldest age he could think of."

She made a pass at coming over to tickle me, too, but didn't follow through the way she had with Roy. I had stopped the tape while they were horsing around, and turned it back on.

"A widow at only twenty-eight," Howard Orrin said. "Think of that. Old to you, son, but hardly more than a child to me. When can she come in?"

The Pastor was going to be out of town campaigning for the next couple of days, but they made arrangements to start saving Wanda's soul as soon as he got back.

Next on my highlights tape was the Pastor's half of a telephone conversation with his consultant and fund-raiser.

"What's coming up is Archibald Weider," I explained to Wanda and Roy. "The same guy that Roy heard when he was talking to the Pastor about those papers of puri-fication, isn't that what he called them? The things you figured were for blackmail, Roy. I know Weider going back to the '79 campaign. We had our moments."

That time, Weider had won. Reagan's people had crossed their hearts and hoped to die that those slimy last-minute scare ads from Weider's "independent" po-litical action committee were total news to the Reagan campaign and deeply offensive to the candidate himself. People like Archibald Weider had no place in an Ameri-can political campaign, and you could quote Governor Reagan on that. Sure. In an earlier kind of campaign, Weider would have been the trader who sold blankets infected with smallpox to the Apaches. I figured I owed him.

"I understand it's just a mailing list for fund-raising, Archie," the Pastor was saying on my tape. "But it's a mailing list from the Ku Klux *Klan*, and naturally I'm a little nervous about it. Can't you fiddle with your com-puter programs somehow so the Klan names are just stuck into some other list and nobody here can tell where they actually came from? . . . All right, fine. Slide them onto the NRA tapes and I'm a happy man, Archie . . . No, on that *Reader's Digest* matter we don't know a thing that's new ... I couldn't agree with you more. Some fella shows up at one of our demonstrations and next thing he's in here looking the office over? No way he's from some neighborhood crime watch ... Well, what do you expect from me, Archie, I'm just a poor country preacher. None of my people's got any investigative background. I'd think that would be more in your line ... Well, yeah, he's been trying. Joel's his name, Joel Hamilton ... Yeah, you're right about that, but being big enough for a cop doesn't mean you know what you're doing. You got to remember the dinosaurs were big, too. Joel's dumb as a stump ... Well, that's true. He's the only one that knows what the fella looks like, all right. Aside from me, and I'm kind of tied up right now running for the Senate ... Oh, yeah, that boy'd walk straight off of a cliff for me, Archie. I got his purification paper all signed, sealed, and delivered in my special files ... Sure you can borrow him. I'll send him over this afternoon. Just remember to spell everything out for him real slow, then go over it with him again just to make sure he's with you. Once he understands what he's supposed to do, he'll go ahead and do it till you tell him it's time to stop and go do something else ..."

I stopped the tape to go put some more hot water on, and to drain off some of the tea that was already in me. When I got back, Wanda said, "This Joel is the kid you broke his thumb when you chased him off of Hope's place?"

"Actually I broke it outside the clinic."

"So what does this Weider guy want him for?"

"Listen for yourself," I said. "The Pastor called the kid in right after he got off the phone with Archie." I turned the machine back on and we heard Howard Orrin's voice again and then Joel Hamilton's.

"Son, I want you to go to work for Mr. Weider for a while. You know who Mr. Weider is, don't you?"

"Yes, sir. I know the gentleman by sight."

"Well, that gentleman does the Lord's work as a world-famous political consultant and fund-raiser. He worked for President Reagan and he worked for President Bush. You might not have heard that said, because Mr. Weider is a very discreet gentleman and anybody who works for him has to be very discreet, too. You follow me, son?"

"Yes, sir, Pastor."

"Mr. Weider's arrangements with his clients are private. His arrangements with me are private. You'll be sure they remain private, won't you?"

"Yes, sir. Can I ask what I'm supposed to do for Mr. Weider?"

"You're supposed to find that so-called *Reader's Digest* man, the fellow that ran you off of the devil-woman's place."

"Yes, sir. Only, how?"

"Well, driving around the devil-woman's neighborhood hasn't done it, has it?"

"No, sir. Most people won't even talk to me, but one of those guys you see them in uniform but they're not regular cops? They're like cops that you see outside of embassies? He told me he never heard about any neighborhood crime watch or anything like that."

"I'll bet he didn't. Mr. Weider and me, we never believed that story for a minute anyway. Sending you to look around was just a way to make sure it was horse manure."

"What should I do next, then?"

"He has to be linked to the devil-woman somehow. Nothing else makes any sense. Let her lead you to him."

"How do I do that?"

"Not my area, son. I'm just a country preacher. Mr. Weider will tell you what to do."

"What am I supposed to do if I find him? I mean, he knows what I look like, too. What if he sees me?"

"What if he does?"

"I don't know what I could do if he was to come after me. He's not that big, but he's awful strong."

"Would you say he was as strong as Our Lord?"

"Nobody's that strong, no, sir."

"Well, the strength of the hills is yours also, son. When you're serving Our Lord Jesus Christ you're as strong as those hills."

"Yes, sir."

"Look at yourself. Look at that great, big, powerful body Our Lord Jesus Christ gave you."

"Yes, sir."

"I didn't tell you to say yes, sir. I told you look at yourself. Do it! That's right. Look at those thighs. I'll bet your legs are as big around as that fellow's waist. Well?"

"Maybe not quite, sir."

"Close enough. You're half a head taller than that fellow, probably got him by fifty or sixty pounds, too. Do you think Our Lord created you with all that strength so the devil could whip you with a little squeeze to your thumb?"

"No, sir."

"Did you think the devil was going to hurt your thumb worse than Our Lord suffered for us on the cross?"

"No, sir."

"Are you proud that you wouldn't suffer a little pain for Our Lord?"

"No, sir. I'm ashamed. I think about it all the time. I pray for purification."

"You ever think maybe that's why the Lord let your thumb be broken in the first place?"

"Huh? I mean, no, sir. Should I think that?"

"That's the hand, isn't it?"

"What hand?"

"The hand you used to pollute that other boy's body at church camp. The hand that committed the sin of Onan on the body of an innocent youth of only thirteen years of age. The very hand that was polluted with the seed he spilled on it. THAT'S THE HAND I'M REFERRING TO, BOY!"

"Please, please, sir. Please, Pastor. I wasn't but eleven then."

" 'I wasn't but eleven then.' Are you telling me you didn't know AT THE TIME that what you were doing to that lad was a foul and filthy sin?"

"I knew, I knew. Help me to be purified, Pastor!"

"Why do you seek purification, boy? Do you hope for life everlasting, is that it? Do you think prayer will get it for you?"

"I pray all the time, Pastor."

"That's not enough, not by a long shot. You can't just sing the Lord's song. You have to do his work, too."

"Yes, sir."

"Well? Do you know what the Lord's work is?"

"No, sir, not all the way I don't."

"Do you at least know who his shepherd on this earth is?"

"My Pastor is Our Lord's shepherd on this earth."

"That's right, Brother Joel. Now tell me if you know what the devil looks like."

"No, sir."

"Why, son, he looks just like that fellow took you by the thumb and led you around like a pitiful lost lamb. The next time you let a little pain stop you from fighting the devil, ask yourself if the agony of Our Lord Jesus Christ turned him into a coward."

"Yes, sir. I'm sorry, sir."

"Our Savior doesn't want to know how sorry you are. Our Savior just wants to see the devil whipped."

"If I see him, Pastor, he'll get whipped. You got my sworn word."

Orrin must have pointed the kid to the door, because the next sound we heard was a slam. Then came Orrin again: "Damn moron. Why is it everybody around here is such a damn moron?"

"You'd think he'd be able to figure that out," Wanda said. "Guy goes hunting for ducks, he's liable to catch ducks."

"Who's the devil-woman?" Roy asked, and it struck me that he had no way of knowing about the brief demonstration outside Hope's house. I killed the tape.

"Hope Edwards," I said. "The woman in the car with me when we brought Kimberly to the arcade. Her picture was on TV, so next night the Life Force picketed her house. This big kid, this Joel Hamilton, I talked with him and got him to lay off."

"Bethany here is an excellent talker," Wanda said. "Maybe you should talk to this big kid again, Bethany."

"Probably not worth it," I said. "At least this way we know where he is. I already called Hope this morning to keep an eye open for a guy with a cast on his thumb, and she called me back five minutes later. She spotted the guy right out of her office window, down at the end of the block. Pretending to be one of those hot-rod bicycle messengers, you believe that shit? While she was watching he got on his bike and drove to the other end of the block and tried to blend in over there for a while. Looked like one of those bears in a circus, tooling along on a kiddie bike."

"Yeah, but he could still screw up everything," Wanda said. "What if he followed her here some morning?"

"On a bike?"

"He must have a car, too."

"Shouldn't be a problem, now that Hope knows to

check the rearview mirror for him. That time of day, the streets are empty. She could either lose him or drive straight on to the office instead of coming here."

"Lose him probably be easy enough," Wanda said. "Kid sounds like he's got the brains of a zucchini. How'd he ever get into college?"

"College is full of zucchinis," I said. "Even Harvard."

"I feel sorry for him," Roy said. "He doesn't sound too swift."

"You're a good kid," said Wanda. "I wish I was as good."

"I wish I was, too," I told Roy. "But the truth is, most of the harm in the world is done by dumb people."

Roy thought about that for a while and didn't like the sound of it. "Would that mean that most of the good in the world is done by smart people?" he asked.

"Good for you, Roy. You're right. Most of the good in the world is done by dumb people, too. Most of everything is done by dumb people, or at least ignorant people. Good and bad don't have anything to do with dumb and smart."

"Guys like the Pastor are what you got to watch out for," Wanda said. "Bad and smart. This Joel, though, he's probably just a good soldier."

"In fact, he'd probably be just as good a soldier in any other army," I said. "Like most people. The big thing to remember isn't just that the average IQ is a hundred. It's that half of the world is below it."

"Still it's sad," Roy said. "About Joel and this other kid."

And it was. I thought of Joel Hamilton as a fat eleven-year-old boy at camp, afraid of an older kid or wanting to make friends with him or just curious. And terrified ever since that now he was a fruitcake and somebody, someday, would find out. One day somebody did, and it was like handing a fiddle to Jascha Heifetz.

I wondered how the machinery worked. Maybe the

people who took the pledges for the Pastor down in Newport News were supposed to pass the names of any troubled callers up the line. More likely, though, there was some kind of confessional process involved in joining the Church of Our Redeemer Risen, with Orrin's assistants passing the best prospects along to the boss.

The beauty of it was that the sin didn't have to be much of a sin. Like Joel's silly little hand job. The important thing wasn't how big the sin was, but how guilty the sinner could be made to feel about it. Enough guilt, and you had yourself at the very least a part-time volunteer for the Senate campaign or for Life Force. And no doubt you often had much, much more. A Joel Hamilton or a Mrs. Mulholland, the pepper lady, could be counted on for heavier duty than just handing out leaflets or stuffing envelopes.

"Maybe I should turn Mr. Pearsall over to the Pastor for purification," I said to Roy and Wanda. "He could spend the rest of his life staging demonstrations outside abortion clinics. Probably be good at it. What the hell, it's all show biz."

Wanda's counseling session with the Pastor was the next morning. "How'd it go?" I asked when she came home afterward, looking good in a rich young widow outfit she had picked up in a Georgetown consignment shop.

"Fantastic," she said. "I'm going to be washed in the blood of the lamb. He told me so."

"Tell me about it."

"Oh, no," she said. "I want you to hear it live on the tape. I was great. Fantastic. Roy's got to make me a copy of it. This shit is Academy Award stuff. I want to thank all the little people, okay?"

"Come on, Wanda," I said. "Did he ask you to the prom or not?"

"Wait till Roy brings the tape over this evening. We

can listen to the blow-by-blow after supper. First we eat
Boston cream pie and strawberry tart from Jeannie, and
whatever else she's got. Then we sit around with the
brandy and the cigars and listen to the great Wanda."

And that's what we more or less did, except for the
cigars and the brandy. Instead I had gone out for a six-
pack of John Courage for Wanda and me, and a big bottle
of Coke for Roy, whose taste buds were still unformed.
I fast-forwarded as quickly as I could through the earlier
parts of the Pastor's day, but it wasn't quick enough for
Wanda. "Come on, pedal to the metal," she kept saying.
"Let's get to the good stuff."

When we got to it, she took over the controls of the
tape deck on the grounds that she knew the best spots to
stop the tape for voice-overs from the outraged maiden
herself.

"Check this out," she said at last. "Here's where it
starts getting good."

"No, he wasn't wearing anything under the robe.
What I was thinking, Father—"

"Not Father. Call me Pastor."

"Oh, right. It's just like a habit, you know. Funny,
habit is what they call it, what they wear . . . Anyway,
I remember I thought at first there was something
wrong with him, you know? Because of this like knob
on the end of it? I never saw a man down there before
except only in the museum on school trips and like
that. So on the statues they don't have that sort of big
knob on them, you know? More like a string or something hanging off? Because in the museum they're not
what do you call it, circumscribed—"

"Give me a break, Wanda," I said, and she held the
tape. "Circumscribed!"

"Hey, I'm no dummy. I took geometry."

"—the statues aren't, I mean. So Father Feeley says go ahead, touch it, and I thought it was okay, being that he was a priest, right? And he says don't be afraid of it, that's it, and I moved my hand like he said but I didn't dare look until I felt this wet all over my hand."

"What were your feelings at that point, sister?"

"That's when I knew I had him," Wanda said. "Son of a bitch was so excited he was squirming around in his seat."

Roy didn't look particularly calm, either. He was flushed, but I doubted if it was embarrassment. Or at least not mostly.

"Father Feeley?" I said. "Jesus, Wanda, have you no shame?"

"Actually, no. But I wasn't really making it up, exactly. I was sort of telling yo-yo what it looked like the first time I ever saw one. Jimmy Feeley in the eighth grade. I was only in the fifth, just a little eleven-year-old punk."

"Getting an early start, huh?"

"Well, my hands were already fully developed."

Roy was warmed up all right, although not to the point he couldn't laugh. Wanda smiled back at him, but not the way any of my sisters ever smiled at me. She hit the button on the machine.

"I was kind of afraid, Pastor. But kind of curious, too. I mean, at first I thought he was doing you know, number one, but it was all white, kind of like blobs of wax or something. 'We call that the Word,' Father said, 'because that's what life comes from.' "

"Compose yourself, sister. We're in no rush here. Take all the time you need."

"It's all right, Pastor. I'm okay now."

"What did he make you do then?"

"Nothing, really. That was it for that time. He pulled his robe down and then he gave me ten Hail Marys."

"He gave you a penance for what he made you do to him?"

"No, for having bad thoughts. That's what I went in to confess, remember? That I had bad thoughts about Kathy Donnelly's brother Kevin, that was off to college."

"Then later there was another time?"

"Oh, yeah. Lots."

"Tell me about them."

"Well, the first couple times it was like I just told you, that I would touch him with my hand and he would go off practically right away, okay? Then he would say this was the staff of life, and I should kiss it, and all, and so he taught me to do him like that. He said I had to learn to do that first, so afterward we could do the other thing. Because we could only do the other thing if I made him go off first, because that meant the seeds would all be gone the first time and then we could do the other thing and there wouldn't be any babies. So then we went along like that each time I went to confession and I'd do him with my mouth first, he liked that better than the hand, and then we would, well anyway he'd take me into this little room they had like a closet where they kept all the robes and everything and we'd lay down on them like a bed, right, and then we'd . . ."

"Why didn't you just tell him the guy jumped your bones right on the altar, Wanda?" I said. "I mean, shit!"

"Hey, this is my story, do you mind? In my story, people might walk into the church and see you, if you do it on the altar. You got to keep things believable."

"I wouldn't believe any of this shit was believable if I wasn't listening to this dork apparently believing it."

"I told you, Bethany. Fucking Baptists, they'll believe anything. Wait till you hear the number I lay on him about the orphanage where they send all the nuns' babies to raise them to be priests."

We heard that one, and then we heard about how Father Feeley didn't even want her to give birth to a baby priest, murdering Papist that he was, but instead he insisted on a botched back-alley abortion when he got her pregnant. This calamity had sterilized poor Mary Margaret and denied her the joy of fulfilling her holy destiny as a woman, which otherwise would have been to spend the years between puberty and menopause either pregnant or lactating.

Fortunately, though, the Reverend Howard Orrin had been able to come up with another way for poor, mutilated Wanda to serve the Lord.

"Sister Mary Margaret, will you permit me to speak to you honestly?"

"I hope you will, Pastor."

"Any son of a bitch says he wants to talk to you honestly, that's when you want to get a good grip on your purse," Wanda said. "Remember that, Roy."

"I feel like you have been denied the joys of motherhood so as to perform an even greater service to our Lord Jesus Christ. I feel like you have been chosen to bring motherhood to hundreds of other young women and to give the greatest gift of all, the gift of life, to their innocent unborn babies. I feel like that is why our Lord Jesus Christ led you to me his servant today, and I call on you to throw yourself with ecstasy into his purpose and his power. Will you do that for your Lord, Sister Mary Margaret?"

"I will, I WILL!"

Roy and I broke out laughing as Wanda stopped the tape. She looked as satisfied with herself as a baby that's just filled its diapers.

"Hey, could Meryl Streep do any better than that?" she said. "We're cooking now. Right here he grabs hold of my hand and looks me straight in the eye and tells me that all I got to do is sit down and sign my ass over to him for the rest of my natural life. Check this out."

"Sister Mary Margaret, you know from your Holy Bible that Jesus wants you to let him into your heart and accept him as your personal savior. But first he wants that heart to be pure. When he commands us to give up all we have, part of that is our past sins, sister. That's the only way we can have a pure heart for Our Lord to enter into. Jesus wants you to sign a pact of purification with him. Will you tell Jesus this story you've just told me, Sister Mary Margaret? Will you put it on paper for Jesus in your own hand and give it to the Lord Jesus Christ that he may enter into your purified heart? Will you do that, sister? Will you?"

"You mean just write it down all about Father Feeley and killing my baby and all that?"

"And all you feel about that preborn baby's murder, and how you mean to dedicate your life to saving babies to give the gift of life to more babies than any one mother could bear in a lifetime. Yes, that's what Our Lord Jesus Christ wants. He knows. Jesus knows you want to live your life for your Savior, that you want to live your life that souls yet uncreated will be created, and given the spark of his holy life, and enter up into God's kingdom in that final rapture, and each one of them a soul that you gave the gift of life everlasting to. You, Sister Mary Margaret. Yes, that's what Jesus wants."

"I'm not too much of a writer, Pastor."

"I'll guide your pen and the Lord will guide me as I guide. Will you do it, sister? Will you enter into a pact of purification with our Lord Jesus Christ?"

"I'll do the best as I can, Father."

"Pastor."

"Yeah, right. Pastor."

"Do you feel like you're ready to let the Lord Jesus enter you?"

"I feel like I'm just about ready, yes. Do we do the writing now?"

"I need to pray. We both need to pray to make ready our hearts. We will pray for Our Lord to receive your purified soul, and I will see you tomorrow evening at six at the place of purification."

"Where is that?"

"For the moment the place of purification is in my temporary quarters on Williamsburg Boulevard, here in Arlington."

Stop tape.

"I argued with the son of a bitch a little," Wanda said. "But he said it was a very personal, private thing, and this and that, and finally I figured fuck it, I'll go on out to his place. I mean, what's the difference after all. We won't be able to get it on tape, whatever the hell he says there, but I'll remember it."

"Remembering won't cut it," I said. "We've got to have more than just your word against his."

"Look, Bethany, it's just not a problem. After tomorrow night, this son of a bitch will meet me anyplace I say."

"How are you going to manage that?" Roy asked. He sounded like he didn't want her to do it, whatever it was.

"I'm going to blow in his ear."

"I don't get it."

"Blow in a man's ear," Wanda said, "and he'll follow you anywhere. Watch."

HEAD LOCK

Wanda took Roy's head in both her hands, bent toward him, and blew in his ear.

"So come on," she said.

Roy looked confused, so she took one of his hands and pulled him to his feet.

"Follow me," she said. "Upstairs."

12

AFTER HOPE HAD GONE OFF TO WORK THE NEXT morning, I was getting myself breakfast by nuking a big chunk of something Jeannie had identified as *coulibiac*. It turned out to be an uptown version of salmon loaf, baked in pastry.

"Hot water on the stove," I said when Wanda came downstairs. "There's cereal and eggs, like that. Or Jeannie brought home some kind of big fish ball that's pretty good."

"I'll just go with the cornflakes."

"Sleep well?"

"What's that supposed to mean?"

"Hey, it's just a thing people say."

"I shouldn't be robbing the cradle? Is that it?"

"I didn't say that, Wanda. I didn't even think that. Well, I did, but it was just envy. My own first time I was a couple years younger than Roy and it was a big disaster. I don't know why I kept on with the whole business, tell you the truth."

"Well, this wasn't a big disaster."

"Hey, hey. Me. I'm the one had the big disaster, not Roy."

"You had the wrong woman, that's all."

"I damned sure did."

"I didn't want the kid to have the wrong woman. He's not like you. He might not keep on."

"Look, I'm not his mother. I'm glad you showed him what goes where. You don't have to explain anything to me."

"I'm explaining, so shut up. I did it a little bit because I'm sorry for the kid. And a lot because he's a really good kid. But mostly, really, because I learned early that good deeds normally don't get you squat. So when I see somebody that does something decent, I'll try to do something nice for them. I don't believe in that pie in the sky bullshit the church hands out. Pie while you're still around to eat it is my motto."

"This good deed we're doing with the Pastor, it could turn out to be a lot more than pie in the sky for the kid."

"I'm talking about the good deed Roy did for that poor little girl, what was her name?"

"Kimberly Butler."

"Yeah. Cashing in his college money to pay for an abortion when he didn't even screw her, that's what I'm talking about."

"Are we okay now, Wanda? Can I ask you again how it went with the kid, or is that going to get me a whole other ration of shit?"

"Yeah, I guess we're okay, except don't call him the kid. It went real good, actually. The trick on somebody's first time is to keep the temperature down. Laugh. Explain things a lot. Go slow. You know?"

"Only in my dreams. Mine was a wham-bam-thank-you-ma'am in a crib in Hudson, New York."

"Well, you know. In that kind of a situation, the girl has to turn over the tricks fast."

"You sent him home, I hope? So his momma wouldn't worry."

"Oh, yeah. He was back before midnight."

"School day tomorrow."

"No, you prick. His spring break just started. Now he can hang around the campaign even more, change tapes during the day so we can get everything down."

"How long does the break last?"

"Just through next week."

"About when we've got to move out of the house, too. We could have a time problem."

"Jeannie will get another house," Wanda said.

"Yeah, but I like this one. I particularly like that nursery. The penny just dropped last night when I was going off to sleep and I happened to think about that monitoring system."

"What's the matter with the original plan? Roy could wire up a room in some hot bed motel just as easy, couldn't he?"

"Not for pictures."

"Pictures over the monitoring system in the nursery, huh? Hey, good thinking. Only are you sure you can make videotapes off those things?"

"I don't know, but Roy will. If he can rig it up, would you do that Wanda? Go on TV?"

"Sure, why not? Might be fun to play it back when I'm in the nursing home."

Roy Shipley came to the house early that evening, full of nerves. He was embarrassed that I knew about him and Wanda, I imagined. And he had to be worried about her being out in Howard Orrin's house, alone with him for some weird pact of purification. Presumably jealous, too. Right at this minute, the first woman he ever went to bed with was out in Arlington, very possibly getting it on with a famous TV preacher practically three times his age.

"You think she's all right?" the boy said once I had settled him down in the living room with a glass of Coke.

I couldn't help him with jealousy, maybe, but I could help him with whether she was all right. "You want to worry about someone, worry about old Orrin," I said. "She could swallow him whole." Once I said it, I realized that this might not have been precisely the best way to phrase it. But Roy didn't seem to notice.

"What if he didn't really believe her story?" he asked.

"Then he didn't believe it."

"Maybe he'd hurt her, you think?"

"I saw a guy try to hurt her once, Roy. She blinded him with Mace."

"What if the Pastor has a gun, though?"

"This guy had a gun."

"Still."

I didn't think he was really worried about the Pastor as a physical threat. Howard Orrin came across as a soft, grown-up sneak. A let's-you-and-him-fight type like Kissinger. He'd leave anything risky to the Joel Hamiltons or Archie Weiders. And Roy Shipley probably knew that as well as I did. What the boy was really worried about was something I no doubt couldn't help him with, but what the hell.

"Roy," I said, hearing in myself that same tone of voice I always hated to hear from my father. The one that meant some kind of shit was headed my way.

"Yes." It meant the same thing to Roy; he sounded wary.

"Wanda's pretty nice, isn't she?"

"Yes." Still wary.

"Well, sometimes a thing can mean a lot to one person, and it still means a lot to the other person involved, but maybe not as much as it would to the first person if the first person had ... Aw, shit, Roy, all I mean is Wanda's been around a lot more than you, and she's done more things, and they mean different things to her than they might to somebody else, but that doesn't mean she . . ."

"She explained to me about all that. She told me she actually went, you know, with women mostly."

"She *did!* She did, huh? Well, then you see what I'm saying. But you'd still have it in your head what she might be doing with Howard Orrin right now. I mean, it would be natural to think about that."

"I am thinking about that."

"What are you thinking about it?"

"I was wondering how she would make him, you know . . . go in his pants."

"Huh?"

"She said that's what she would make him do if he tried to go too far. So I was wondering exactly how she would do it."

"Oh. Well, maybe rub up against him or something, huh?" Every topic I blundered unhelpfully into, it seemed as if Wanda had already been there before and taken care of everything.

"Maybe," Roy said. "Anyway, she says it's easy for a woman to get rid of a man once he ejaculates. She says the only trick is for the woman to make him think she didn't notice what he just did. That way he saves face."

"Jesus, one or two little episodes from high school are beginning to make sense now."

"I never even had any episodes like that."

"You jumped directly into the big time, kid. You're lucky."

"I know I am. I still can't believe it. Wanda's so wonderful."

"Long as you know it's just a stop on the road for you both."

"Oh, I totally know that. We talked about all that before."

So I was wasting my breath.

I shifted gears and asked him whether it would be technically feasible to videotape the nursery. We spent a half an hour looking over the system together, and he decided it wouldn't be much trouble. Then the phone rang.

"Hello," I said.

"Hi, Roy," said Wanda. "Look, a friend is just about to drive me home, so I'll be there in probably twenty minutes. You can call Mom and have her come pick you up."

"Do I sound like Roy?"

"No, stupid," Wanda said, and waited for me to think things through.

"You mean asshole is driving you back?"

"Right."

"Probably I should stay out of sight?"

"That would be nice, yes."

"But it's okay if Roy is still around, right? Your brother, and all?"

"Oh, sure. See you in a few minutes, Roy."

So after a while I headed upstairs and stood by a darkened window that overlooked the front door. I had the timing figured about right and only had to wait a few minutes till headlights lit up the white gravel drive that curved through the pachysandra to the front door and back out again. I've been confused about brands of cars since they stopped calling them Chevvies and Fords and started calling them things like Furies and Cougars, but the dark four-door that turned in the drive was probably a fairly new Chrysler. American, anyway. Like any good politician, Orrin would have garaged the Mercedes for the duration of the campaign.

The car stopped. Light suddenly came from the direction of the big front door. Maybe Roy wasn't insane with jealousy, but he wouldn't have liked the idea of them sitting in the car too long. Wanda got out and waved at the doorway where the boy was standing. The window on the driver's side went down. By then Wanda had crossed in front of the car. She waved again, this time saying good-bye to the Pastor. Howard Orrin waited like a gentleman till the front door of the house closed safely behind her, and then his big car crunched over the gravel toward Foxhall Road. I headed downstairs so Wanda could tell me all about her night out.

By the time I got there, she was getting out a bottle of wine for herself and a bottle of John Courage for me. Roy still had the Coke he was working on. "Yo-yo was all business at first," she said. "We got down on our knees and he prayed for me. He's a hell of a pray-er. By the time he was through, God didn't have no choice but to let me into heaven. It was a done deal, once I just signed this little piece of paper. Then we went over to this big desk he had in his study, and he had me sit right beside him while we went to work on the confession. It was kind of funny, two people sitting on the same side of the desk.

"He'd get me going with questions, kind of organizing what I told him the first time, and I'd write it down on a yellow pad, all that stuff the priest had me do, and me just a pitiful little girl like that. I had given him a pretty lot of blow-by-blow stuff the time before, remember. But this time he had me put down even more. Practically every second.

"Then he had me start in on my rich husband, which we never got into before at all. He liked it when I told him it was just basically greed that made me go after the old guy and marry him, and how sorry I was over what a bad girl I had been, and how Jesus didn't like greedy little girls and all that shit. What he really liked, though, was when I talked about making it with that poor old man. We got right down to the nitty-gritty you might say, how I'd have to work on the senile old fart for an hour or so before he could get it up to where I could climb aboard. And then sometimes he'd fall asleep right in the middle of it."

Wanda had to stop to laugh.

"I even told him the poor old guy died while I was riding him," she went on. "Rode him completely to death and at first I didn't even notice. Thought he just fell asleep again. When I said that I was afraid for a minute I was going too far, but by that time the son of a bitch was so horny his little head was the one doing all the thinking. He just took hold of my hand and kept saying, You poor thing, and had me write all this wild bullshit down like it was gospel."

The kid seemed to be taking all this pretty well, which surprised me at first. But by now I saw what Wanda had been up to, being so blunt and open and humorous and matter-of-fact about sex. She was inoculating him against taking their relationship too seriously. Or taking her too seriously. Or taking sex itself too seriously.

And it was working. Roy wasn't quite as amused as I was over Wanda's adventures, but he didn't seem to be in pain, either. When it came to learning about the birds and the bees, it looked to me like a boy couldn't do much better than Wanda.

"Did you get him to, you know . . . What you said you were going to do?" he asked her.

"Actually, that was the greatest part of all. While we were at the desk I kept looking over at this couch, which I figured was where we were going to end up once I was done writing. And I don't want him to score, of course, because why bother? It wouldn't be on tape."

"What if he forced you, though?" Roy asked, worried.

"No big deal. I mean, what are we supposed to be doing here, right?"

"Well, yeah, I guess," he said, because what else was there to say? How do you ride to the rescue of a damsel when she's trying to get the dragon to bang her on videotape?

"But the point is," Wanda went on, "on account of I'm such a genius it never got to wrestling around on the couch. Ask me how come."

"How come?" I said.

"I talked him off!"

"You what?"

"I gave such an unbelievably great confession that the son of a bitch creamed his jeans without me even touching him. He was getting more and more excited and finally I heard him kind of take a sharp breath and he squeezed my hand harder for a second. I didn't let on, but after a while I sneaked a peek and saw the pecker tracks on his pants. When we were finished at the desk he stood up kind of facing away from me, and he couldn't get me out of there fast enough.

"So I called up dim bulb here and after a while he caught on and said he'd get out of the way so Howie wouldn't wonder why I kept some other guy stashed away in the house. And here I am. I spent the whole trip back not looking at his lap, on account of it's impolite to stare."

"Did he ask you for another date?" I said. "The sock hop or something?"

"He's coming by at nine-thirty, day after tomorrow. I told him I was nervous at his place, somebody might come in. But I'd arrange it for us to talk all alone here, and it was just better all around, and yatatayatata.

"I think he was starting to feel horny again, particularly after he saw the size of this little place I got. I told him I was thinking of getting something smaller, a woman alone like me. A real estate guy told me I should ask a million-two for this one, what did he think? Asshole thought that was just fine. Even said he knew a good broker, a guy that happens to be his campaign finance chairman. Wonderful guy. Good Christian.

"Only Roy was standing in the door like he was my father, and I was half an hour late, and so the Pastor had to say good night in the car. 'I know we're going to be very, very close,' he goes. 'Remember, when you help the shepherd you're helping the sheep.' "

"We'll help the shepherd, all right," I said. "Can we be ready to videotape by then, Roy?"

"I guess we could."

"You got some work to do, too, Bethany," Wanda said.

"Take Pearsall's money off him?" I asked. My meeting with the father of the preborn was tomorrow night, at the high school.

"Plus you got to round up some stuff for my TV debut."

"Stuff like what?"

"Bethany, this guy is into stocks and bonds."

"Sure, he's a multimillionaire."

"Stocks and bonds, Bethany. Stocks like the pilgrims put you in. Bonds like chains and handcuffs."

"He told you that?"

"He didn't have to. I put a lot of different shit into my purification paper, so I could see what raced his motor. I told him Father Feeley had me do it to another priest one time, and then the priests did each other. I talked about different positions and so forth. He liked all of it, but then when he came in his pants, I figured he was telling me which part he liked best of all."

"Which part was it?"

"When I was telling him about how I used to tie my poor old husband's hands to the bedposts with neckties, and he asked why in the world I did that, and I said sometimes the old goat was a bad boy and needed to be punished. Right then was when the Pastor popped."

"You sure that means he's a bondage freak?"

"Trust me, Bethany. I don't know everything, but what I know, I know good. This I know."

When I go to do any kind of little handyman job and screw it up, I wind up flinging the tools around and banging stuff and swearing at whatever's broken. My old man did the same thing, except that he took it out on people instead of things. Whenever he got out his tools, the whole family found something to do someplace else.

Roy was different. Once he got started on the nursery monitoring system the next morning, he found out there were things he had forgotten to pick up when he stopped at the store on his way to the mansion. But instead of blowing up, all the boy said was, "Hm, I should have thought of that." Then he put the missing things down on a list, and spread the stuff out that he already had, and figured there were another couple of things that might come in handy, too. And so he added them to the list. "Want to come along?" he said to me. "Few things I forgot to get."

"No, thanks," I said. Probably he wouldn't swear at the other drivers on the way downtown, either, and I felt inferior enough already. "I want to listen to yesterday's tapes for a while."

We figured Roy should keep bringing in the tapes from Howard Orrin's office as long as he could. Although they were really a sideshow now that our main program was under way, you never knew what might come up that we could use.

The principal thing that was coming out of the office tapes was that the Pastor's political show was essentially a one-man operation. He had the regular lineup of campaign officials: a manager, a deputy manager, finance chairman, issues chief, and so on. But he kept them at a distance and dealt formally with all of them.

The only one he let inside his guard at all was Archie Weider. The dirty tricks expert filled what was almost a stock part in a political entourage. He was Skippy, the evil twin. The infantile, premoral, greedy ego. Grabbing, eating, drinking, biting, hitting, screaming. A guy a candidate could let down his hair with, because no matter how rotten the candidate was, Archie would think he wasn't nearly rotten enough. A restful kind of guy to have around.

"Tell me something, Howard," Weider said on one of the tapes, "do you actually believe this shit about abortion?"

"That it's murder? Of course I do."

"What if it is murder? So what?"

"I don't follow you, Archie."

"Well, for instance, I was reading in the *Post* that they had six drive-by killings in Chocolate City already this month. What does that tell you?"

"That there's a crisis of values in America."

"Tells me we need more abortions. We ought to put clinics all over the city. Thin the bastards out before they get big enough to be dangerous."

"Archie, Archie." Fondly, as if to a bright but impractical child. "It's still murder."

"Archie, Archie, bullshit," said Archie. "War is the health of the state. Which is to say murder is the health of the state, too. That's why we've got the Pentagon and the CIA. That's why we've got the electric chair. The state's into death. Why do you think it lets bums freeze to death on the sidewalk? Why do you think it lets every homicidal asshole in America buy an assault rifle? It's all murder, Howard, and it's all good for us. It's the evolution of the species. *It's just thinning 'em out.*"

"It's a good thing I know you're kidding."

"I'm not kidding."

"You don't believe in a strong defense? You don't believe in the people's right to bear arms? You don't think the death penalty is God's law?"

"Come on. All that stuff is bullshit to get the suckers inside the tent."

"I wonder why you're a conservative, Archie."

"Same reason Willie Sutton robbed banks. Because that's where the money is."

"Archie, Archie. You're some kidder."

"I never kid. I especially never kid myself."

I almost liked Archie, compared to his client, anyway. I knew Archie would understand later on, when I circulated this tape anonymously to the newspapers. He might even be able to explain it to the partial satisfaction of his more fanatical clients, but something fine and wonderful would no doubt be gone from his business relationships.

Or maybe not. Howard Orrin knew that Archie wasn't a true believer, after all, but the nonbelieving consultant still seemed to be his only confidant on the campaign. It might have been because Archie was the only one on the tapes who didn't let himself be pushed around.

The truth was that Orrin seemed to be a nasty guy to work for. He had a petty, tyrannical manner with his people, and went easily into pissy little rages. He belittled staffers in front of other staffers. His system was the one he had used with Joel Hamilton: to make the offender feel that he hadn't let the boss down, he had let God down. The Pastor would say things like, "We're fighting the Lord's battles here, not our own little personal battles. The life of every unborn baby is important to our Lord Jesus Christ. Isn't it important to you? Can't you hear the cries of those unbaptized babes in hell? Jesus can, why can't you?"

In that particular case, the poor staffer didn't get a mailing out in time to catch the four-thirty pickup, and now millions of preborn babies were going to burn for all eternity.

"Everybody's scared of him," Roy had said after we listened to one of the Pastor's tantrums. "He's real strict. A lot of times he makes people cry, and not just the women, either."

HEAD LOCK

When Roy got back from his high-tech shopping trip, he set to work rigging things up while Wanda and I went upstairs to redecorate the set. We figured that a nursery might strike the Pastor as being a weird place to screw, so we began hauling all the baby stuff out and replacing it with furniture from the other bedrooms.

Afterward the nursery looked more or less like a love nest. I had sacrificed my feather mattress to dress up the set, and Jeannie had plenty of frilly and puffy pillowcases and other feminine bedding. The curtains we brought in from Wanda's bedroom didn't quite fit the nursery windows, but a man like Howard wouldn't notice things like that. But he would certainly notice the little couch upholstered in a fabric covered with puppies and kittens. So we dragged it into the empty room next door, along with the mobile, the toy chest, the bassinet, and so on.

"Something's wrong," Wanda said when we were done. "Looks like a hotel room." So we raided her room and Jeannie's for books, magazines, clothing, toiletries, and various other odds and ends to scatter around.

By the time we had the room looking more or less like a boudoir, Roy was ready for a test run of his equipment. The two monitors were in the master bedroom and on the ground floor, in the living room. Roy watched the bedroom monitor and I stood in the hallway outside to relay directions up to Wanda while she moved around in the old nursery, saying things like, "Testing, one two three, six, seven, eight, nine, Why Howard Orrin, you stud, you. I can't believe it's so huge."

We had to move the bed a little to get it centered in the camera. The sound pickup was nothing special, but okay. Actually I couldn't see why the former owners had planned to wire their baby for sound anyway. I had left my own baby girl behind me in Alaska when my ex-wife and I divorced many years ago. But my recollection was that the slightest sound made by a baby carries hundreds of yards and passes through walls like gamma rays. The noise could even penetrate the worst hangover, as I discovered morning after morning in those days.

The system for taping from the monitor camera didn't work at first, but Roy quickly found out what the trouble was and fixed it. Without swearing even once, show-off that he was. I called Wanda to come on downstairs so she could watch herself horsing around on the tape Roy had just made.

"Not bad," she said. "Be better in color, though."

"You can't shoot color on these surveillance systems," Roy said. "You'd need floodlights."

"I could live with that," Wanda said. "But I guess the Pastor might wonder what they were for."

From the looks Roy kept sneaking at Wanda, I figured I wasn't really needed around the house. I made a thing out of picking a movie out of the *Washington Post* and wasn't surprised when none of the matinees out at Seven Corners was anything either Roy or Wanda felt like seeing.

So I left them alone and off I went.

13

IT WAS JUST AFTER DARK WHEN I GOT TO C. W. Grizzard High School, where I was supposed to exchange the fake diary for the real money. I followed my directions to the field house out back. A chain link fence surrounded it and the football field. The service gate was unlocked, as Pearsall had said it would be. There wasn't much light, but enough for me to see my way. I headed toward the field house, crunching along the cinder track that ran around the playing field. As I got near, I made out a form standing in front of a small outbuilding that was probably an equipment shed.

"Pearsall?" I called out.

"Over here," he said.

"Be right there." He seemed to be alone, but I took a minute to walk around the small building just in case. Nobody. Pearsall was standing a couple of paces from the door to the shed. I tried the door, but it was locked.

"Looking for someone?" Pearsall said.

I turned toward the English teacher. "Just you, Willie."

"Did you bring it?"

"Right here in my briefcase."

"Let me see it."

"Let me see the money."

"Well, it seems there's a problem with that . . ."

I heard movement, but I didn't sort out the direction of it until too late. A hard shock knocked me off my feet, and then came a much harder one when I smashed into the ground on top of my cheap briefcase. For a time that seemed much longer than it was, I couldn't breathe.

"Jesus," Pearsall said. "You've killed him. Is he dying?"

"He'll be okay."

"He can't get any air. Shouldn't you do something?"

"Bill, will you just shut the fuck up?"

I was making noises that would have frightened me, too, if I hadn't had the wind knocked out of me plenty of times before. Only before there were always coaches and trainers running onto the field, and everybody hollering, "Give him air," as if the crowd was airtight. And those other times, whoever had flattened me always got up right away, not like this guy. I felt like I was under a 250-pound beanbag.

But after the usual agonizing wait, my electrical system kicked in again. I stopped making dying noises and started making living noises, a drowning man who just made it up to the surface. I started to feel the pain from my face, where it was mashed into the cinder track. The beanbag said, "Let's have that briefcase, shithead."

By now I had sorted out what went wrong, which was that it hadn't occurred to me that a locked door can usually be opened from the inside. And so now I was in a position that I had been in a hundred times in all the years of wrestling, except no coach was hollering at me, "Get back to your base." This meant to heave yourself up till you were back on your hands and knees. Maybe I wouldn't even have to heave much.

"I'm on top of the damned briefcase," I sort of groaned, and he started to lift his weight off.

I went right up with him, only faster, got hold of an arm, and gave him a hip roll. I worked it so that he came down hard on his back and helpless in a head lock. A head lock is something you don't generally try with a real wrestler, but I knew from the way he had handled himself on top of me that he wasn't a real wrestler. So now I had him with his right arm captured and his left arm free but useless behind me, and me right in his face with my own cinder-gouged face, dripping blood down on him. He started to thrash around a little, so I put pressure on his neck.

The head lock is what wrestling coaches call a submission hold. Once you get it on a man, even a much bigger man, you can keep him where he is as long as you want, and eventually cut off his circulation till he passes out, if you want to do that, too. Until he dies, I guess.

This was a much bigger man, and his efforts to get loose showed that he knew how to move his body well. But after a while he grasped the point that there was nothing he could do about things except let me bleed on him.

"Christ's sake, Bill, get off your ass!" he said, once he remembered he had a partner. "Pull the son of a bitch off me."

"Go ahead, Bill," I said. "Touch me and I'll break your fucking arm."

Pearsall stood there.

"For Christ's sake," my prisoner said again.

Pearsall stood there.

"What's your name," I asked the big guy.

"Paul Starzynski."

"He's the head football coach," Pearsall said. Maybe he thought I'd let the guy go once I knew how tough and important he was, but the fact is I played for two head football coaches back in Port Henry and they were both stone assholes. It felt good after all these years, having Coach in a head lock.

"Listen, Coach," I said, "what did you think was in the briefcase?"

"Blackmail pictures, shithead."

"That's what he told you? Slick Willie here?"

"Don't try to get out of it, mister. The county welfare department doesn't have any investigator named Tom Carpenter."

"That's because I don't work for them."

"Who do you work for, then?" Pearsall asked.

"Use your head, Willie. Who could have given me the girl's diary?"

"What diary?" Starzynski asked.

"The one you're lying on." The coach had wound up on top of the briefcase, which was probably kindling by now. "Kimberly Butler's diary."

"It's natural he'd have her diary," Pearsall said. "Probably they were working together. Probably he was her boyfriend."

"Still, he told you it was pictures, didn't he, Coach? Why you suppose he said that? Pictures aren't diaries, are they?"

"Well, why?" Starzynski asked the English teacher.

Pearsall wasn't coming up with an answer, so I helped out. "Because he's bullshitting you, Coach. He knocked up this little Butler girl who killed herself, and the family learned about it from her diary. The family hired me to have a talk with asshole here, make him wish he never got started fucking little girls."

"What about the thousand dollars?" Starzynski asked.

"Hey, this way I was going to get paid twice, the parents and prick, here. Prick here should've given her the money for her abortion anyway."

His face all speckled with drops of my blood, Starzynski looked over at his colleague. "There's a lot you didn't tell me, Pearsall," he said. Not Bill anymore. Pearsall. It was time to let the coach up.

Starzynski wasn't more than a couple of inches taller than my own five eleven, but he was a whole lot wider and thicker. Probably 250 now, and 230 back in college. In the dimness he looked a lot like Jerry Lewis, only not as handsome. He wobbled his head around to loosen up his neck, and then remembered the briefcase that was lying on the cinder track. It was crushed and one of the latches had popped open.

"Tell me about this diary," he said to Pearsall, but I answered.

"You can have it," I said. "Read it for yourself."

"What do I want it for?"

"Tell you what I'd want it for, if I were you. To give to the principal or the superintendent, whichever. That way you won't be dragged down with this guy when he goes."

"Goes where?"

"Think about your position, Coach. Your pal here has been fucking little girls for years—"

"That's not true! He's lying, Paul."

"Shut up," I said, making a quick movement toward Pearsall. He moved back in alarm and shut up. "Figure it out for yourself, Coach. The family is going to go to the police with the information from the diary, which is easy to check no matter who has the actual diary. Then the vice squad starts asking questions not just on the Butler girl, but going back years. When all the shit starts coming out, the question is going to be how come the coach is helping this cradle robber conceal evidence. How about Coach? What's he doing hanging around the showers so much—"

"Now wait a fucking minute here, mister!"

"Hey, I'm not saying it's true, I'm just telling you the way they're going to start thinking. Unless as soon as you realized there was any funny stuff even possibly going on, you grabbed hold of this diary and turned it in to the authorities."

"We had a deal," Pearsall said to me.

"Till you said there was a problem with the money."

"There's no problem."

"You've got it?"

"Of course I've got it."

"There was a problem when you figured Coach here was going to kick the shit out of me and grab the diary, but now there's no problem?"

"No, no problem."

"Let's have it, then."

Pearsall took an envelope out of the inside pocket of his jacket and held it out to me at arm's length, as if he were offering a chunk of meat to an alligator. The envelope felt like it held a thick-enough sheaf of bills, so I stuck it in my own pocket.

"How about the diary?" Pearsall said.

"Right there on the ground over by the coach," I said. "See if he'll give it to you."

"Hurt?" Hope asked, touching the abrasions on my face almost too lightly to feel, let alone hurt. And they had scabbed over anyway, during the night.

"Not really. Just tender."

"I can't let you out alone, can I?"

"Come on, anybody can fall off his bike."

"That going to be your story?"

"Happens all the time. Cyclists call it road rash."

"The rash part is right. What were you doing meeting this guy alone at night?"

"I only thought he was alone."

"Even if he *was* alone. You have no idea what he might be capable of and you were threatening to ruin his life."

"I just didn't think he was dangerous, and I was right.

He wasn't. His idea of a tough guy was the football coach."

"What about this coach?" Hope asked. Now she was running her fingers feather-light down my chest, but she wasn't serious. She was showered, dressed, and ready to go to work. We had already made love. "What's he going to do, this Starzynski?"

"I think he'll be okay. He picked up immediately that Pearsall was spinning him. He'll read the diary, and once he sees what he's being used for, he'll turn the thing over to the school."

"The diary's a forgery, though."

"Doesn't matter. The information in it is true, and it's easy to check."

"After which they let Mr. Pearsall resign quietly to avoid scandal, and he pops up later teaching in some other state. That's the reality of it."

"Except that I'm going to tell Susan Freedman to call Roy Shipley and the family and the cops and the school, and by then there won't be any way to keep it quiet."

"Who's Susan Freedman?"

"A reporter at the *Globe* bureau here."

"Yeah? How come I never heard of any Susan Freedman before? What does she look like?"

"A lot like you used to, actually. Except her tits are much . . . Hey, that hurts!"

After breakfast I sat down with the previous day's audiotapes from the Pastor's office. For a long time I heard nothing but office routine: Orrin discussing his schedule with aides, dictating letters to his secretary, talking to what seemed to be his broker, talking to his assistants at the Church of Our Redeemer Risen and at Lordland. In the compressed-time world of the voice-activated tape, the phone rang again, practically immediately after the Pastor had dealt with Lordland's problems of the day. "Good," Orrin said. "Send him on in. And listen, Cindy, hold all calls. No interruptions, and I mean none."

This usually meant something interesting was about to happen. I snapped my attention back into focus, the way you do when the teacher starts talking about something likely to be in the test.

"Brother Weider," the Pastor said. "Come in and sit down and tell me what's so important."

I had seen Weider once or twice in the past, and judging from newspaper pictures he looked pretty much the same now. He was in his fifties, bald and short and fit-looking. You could imagine him as a park ranger, or a high school principal. He wore rimless glasses. His skull was round, and his face was solid and bulging, with muscular dimples in his cheeks and chin. It was the kind of face that looks like a small, rosy apple, lumpy from worms. He was a high-energy, high-aggression bantam rooster. Nasty things seemed to happen whenever Archie was in the vicinity, but the tracks always petered out before they led to him.

"What's important to you, Howard?" Weider asked the Pastor back. "For instance, this Senate race. Are you willing to give up every waking hour to it?"

"I have the church, Archie. I have Life Force. I have Lordland."

"That's what I mean."

"Are you suggesting I give up my ministry?"

"Hell, no. Keep on preaching. Stay on TV. That's what's going to get you into the U.S. Senate. But you've got to give up the day-to-day stuff. Delegate for the duration. Can you do that?"

"I'd lose my ministry. There are un-Christian people even in the church, people who would take advantage if I turned my back."

"Well, it's one or the other. If you won't give full attention to this race, neither will I. Your choice."

"I don't see—"

"Before you make that choice, let me tell you why I'm aboard right now. Two little words, Howard, two little words. *White House*. I got it for George Bush and I can get it for you."

"You're serious, aren't you?"

"Damned right. Aren't you?"

"I won't say I haven't thought of it."

"It means your whole life from now until probably literally the millennium. Unless Clinton steps on his dick, and we go in '96. Every vote you cast in the Senate, every word you say, every hand you shake. Every waking moment, and when you have those fucking rapid eye movements at night, that's what you'll be seeing in your dreams, too."

"Tell me why it's even possible."

"Because you're good on TV, better than anybody in politics today. They say it's a cool medium, but that's bullshit. That's just because nobody's figured out how to use it hot. Nobody except you guys, you preachers. Listen, the last politician in America that could really get a crowd on its feet was George Wallace. Beside him, everybody else since has been dogshit. Cuomo, Reagan, all of them. Dogshit. And you know what? Beside a guy like you, Howard, *Wallace* is dogshit."

"You're exaggerating a little, aren't you?"

"I told you once already, Howard, I never kid. Never. I'll tell you something else I'm not kidding about. There's another preacher that makes even you look like dogshit. Jesse Jackson would be president today if he was white. And I'll tell you another thing. If I could figure out a way to bleach the son of a bitch, I'd walk straight on out of here and go to work for him tomorrow."

"My God, man, Jesse's a hard-core liberal!"

"Politics isn't about liberal and conservative. It's about power."

"Archie, you've worked for conservative causes all your life."

"That's because I don't do pity as well as I do fear."

"What's fear and pity got to do with it?"

"Everything, that's all. You get all that direct mail from Ralph Nader and Amnesty International and the ACLU, what's it all about? Pity. They want you to feel sorry for some poor bastard that's starving to death or he's in jail or big business is fucking him over.

"The poster child for liberal causes is always somebody else that you're supposed to feel sorry for. The poster child for conservative causes is me, myself, and I. So pity isn't really necessary in my mailings. The guy that tears open my envelopes, he already feels sorry for himself. My job is to make him feel even more sorry, which means to frighten the shit out of the guy.

"Only what has he really got to be afraid of? The fact is that he doesn't have any real worries. His taxes are lighter than practically any other country anybody would want to live in. He's got most of the dough around. He sits on every board, he holds every office, he runs the courts and the schools and the churches and the police and the military. He owns the banks and he sells the insurance and he rigs the markets. He's got no natural enemies at all, so what am I going to make this guy afraid of?"

"You tell me, Archie," Howard Orrin said.

"No problem. Deep down he knows he didn't do anything to have all this good stuff except get born white, male, and American. Since he got it so easy, why couldn't somebody else take it away just as easy? So I make him afraid of the poor kids from the other side of the tracks, which is everybody who isn't white, male and American. I tell him those kids are all smarter and meaner and hungrier than he is, and they're on their way over right now to grab off all his toys.

"That's why when you get a letter from the NRA or

Jesse Helms or me, it's all about fear. The blacks or the foreigners or the libbers are going to take away your job or ruin your neighborhood or trash your schools or spend all your tax money on food stamps instead of atom bombs to keep the Commies away. Fortunately I can save you by keeping the women barefoot and pregnant, closing off the border, and throwing the black bastards in jail. See what I mean?

"So take it from an old direct mail specialist, Howard. Pity and fear, that's the only two places where the votes are. And fear is a lot easier to work with than pity. As you should know."

"Why should I know?"

"You think anybody would ever send you a nickel if they weren't scared shitless of dying?"

"Fear of death is a natural and universal emotion."

"Especially if somebody tells you the next stop is hell. Face it, Howard. If you got up there next Sunday and told the folks that death is just like going to sleep for good, how much do you think you'd find in the collection plate? Religion is built on fear, just like politics. That's why you're going to be president, Howard. President Howard Orrin. Because you understand fear."

"I also understand faith, hope, and charity. They're part of the Christian message, too."

"Not your message. You're just not listening to yourself out there, Howard. You're not talking about faith and hope and charity when you're out there hollering about secular humanism, family values, law and order. Come on. Welfare queens, AIDS is God's judgment on gays, tuition grants, the right to bear arms?

"That's not faith, hope and charity, Howard. No, it's plain old fear. You're just stirring up the natives."

"Sometimes the natives need stirring up," the Pastor said. " 'Strait is the gate, and narrow is the way, which leadeth unto life, and few there be that find it.' "

"Spare me the Scripture."

"Archie, I can give you Scripture for every one of those issues you've mentioned. The Lord God makes us feel fear because he loves us, the same as an earthly father chastises his son because he loves him, and wants to keep him from sin."

"Good," said Weider. "Stay as sweet as you are, Howard. It's better that way, adds credibility. That was Reagan's strength, too, never understanding his own message."

"Archie, sometimes you can be a real—"

"Prick is the word. When a fella needs a prick, he calls Archie Weider. And Howard, if you really want to get to that big white house across the river, you need a prick."

"What would a prick tell me to do?"

"First of all, start putting some distance between yourself and this abortion stuff."

"This abortion 'stuff,' as you call it—"

"Don't worry what I call it, Howard. Just step back from it. Read the numbers on abortion, for Christ's sake. There's a big down side to it. The votes you're chasing are votes you're going to get anyway. The votes you're losing are votes you could pick up. Look at this shit on the TV with the schoolteacher."

It had been on last night's news and this morning's, too. Very satisfying stuff. Pearsall was suspended from his job, pending the outcome of statutory rape charges against him. The TV cameras had staked out the school and eventually nailed him. Pearsall had been dumb enough to pull his jacket up around his face, so that he looked guilty as hell. My only regret was that Kimberly Butler's father, interviewed sympathetically on all channels, had come across as a victim instead of a perp.

Apart from that, it had been a good evening's work for me. The investigation had been triggered by a diary turned over to school officials by another teacher, unidentified. Using leads from the diary, police had been able to verify its contents from various witnesses, identities undisclosed. Surprisingly, nobody mentioned that the diary was forged. Either nobody had thought to verify the handwriting, or Wanda's was enough like the dead girl's to pass. Nor was there any mention on the news of who had given the diary to the unidentified teacher. Probably the cops didn't see any reason to look a gift horse in the mouth.

"This so-called shit with the schoolteacher has nothing to do with me at all," Howard protested, a little loudly I thought. "Life Force hasn't got the slightest connection with that man, or with the girl either. And neither do I."

"You do now, Howard. You got the tightest connection there is in America. You were on TV together."

"Come on, Archie."

"You come on, Howard. Pictures are the only things that register on the monster's brain. Your picture was on last night's news, in the same segment with a dead girl and a child molester and a bunch of screaming loonies being dragged off by the police. That's all that matters, Howard, not whether you ever saw that teacher before in your life. Politics is pictures."

"I can see that—"

"And that's one particular picture I want you out of. So start delegating, like I said, and begin with abortion. Pick medium-smart guys to run Life Force and Lordland and the Newport News church for you day-to-day. Guys just smart enough to run them and not quite smart enough to steal them. Pay those guys plenty, and find an accountant to see they don't steal you blind on top of that. Put somebody right next to each one of them to report back to you. Not somebody smart, just somebody totally loyal. That's where those purification files come in, Howard. You wouldn't happen to have an accountant in there, would you?"

"As a matter of fact, I do. He's half of a two-man firm in Newport News. Royal Carberry."

"What did Mr. Carberry do?"

"He ran a stolen car into a baby carriage when he was in high school. Hit and run. The baby was killed."

"Perfect. Hire him for twice what he's making and let him crunch the numbers."

"You understand that you're asking me to give up my ministry, don't you?"

"Hell, no. That's the last thing I want you to do. I want you to keep overall control, just let go of the day-to-day. Particularly keep on preaching, so you can keep that cash flow up. *Even after you get to the Senate.*"

"Is that legal?"

"Sure it is. Just don't use public funds for church expenses. And you won't have to. We'll have money sloshing around between the theme park and the church and the new PAC we'll form, until there won't be a way in the world to figure out where the stuff came from in the first place. In two or three years you'll be in a position to do what Perot did. Independent candidate. Tell the print media to shove it, and buy all the TV time you need."

"Can you believe that voice Ross had?" said the Pastor, who himself had an easy, powerful baritone. "And those boring charts of his?"

"And the guy didn't have the slightest idea how to use the camera," Weider continued, "and he sounded like Mickey Mouse, and the asshole shot himself in the foot by dropping out halfway through the race—"

"And he still pulled nineteen percent," the Pastor finished.

"*Now* you're catching on."

I ran off a couple of copies of the tape, tagged them with the date, speakers, and subjects discussed, and put them away with the others Roy had brought home. Then

I had a light lunch of assorted Viennese pastries, lemon sponge cookies, date macaroons, and almond meringue kisses. I was just cleaning up when Wanda came in.

"There's a couple million calories left in the refrigerator," I said.

"Good, because I just got through working off a couple million calories. This is a pretty rough class. The instructor looks like some cute little button-nose cheerleader, but she's a real Nazi."

"Are you sure this is okay, going to some rival class with a cute cheerleader? Have you cleared this with the home office?"

"With Diane?" Diane Ackerly was the new lover, the aerobics instructor back in Boston. "Diane was the one who recommended the class."

"That's good, Wanda. Indicates a solid relationship. Indicates Diane is confident. Secure. Trusting."

"Indicates Diane is buddies with the Nazi's girlfriend. If I touched either one of them, I'd be dead within minutes."

Wanda let her workout bag fall on the floor, and herself fall onto a chair. "I might have a little taste of Ben and Jerry's," she said. "Any of that rain forest crunch left?"

"I'll bring you a bowl. Then there's something I want you to listen to."

Once we had finished listening together to Archie Weider's pep talk, Wanda asked, "Could he really make it?"

"Who knows?" I said. "Who would have believed how far Perot got?"

"Perot's probably into bondage, too," she said. "There was something weird about the guy."

"Well, if you're right about Howard Orrin and bondage, whether he could make it to the White House is strictly hypothetical. He won't even make it to the Senate once we're through with him. They're going to give him the Pee Wee Herman treatment if we send that tape around to the networks and the papers."

"I was thinking something, though," Wanda said. "Who's ever going to see this tape? Even Fox doesn't run hard-core yet."

"Reporters will see it, and they'll describe it."

"You think they're going to describe shit like that in the paper? What if the guy likes golden showers or hot wax on his dick? They're going to run it in the paper?"

"They'll talk around it, but close enough so people will get the idea."

"It's not the same thing as seeing it, though."

"Nobody has to see it. Having these tapes is going to be sort of like having an atom bomb. It's no more use once you explode it."

"What use is it if you don't?"

"Well, hear me out and see what you think."

And I told her what I had been thinking about after listening to Archie Weider's plans for Howard Orrin. Archie was no fool. Maybe the Pastor had real potential. Maybe we ought to set our own sights a little higher. At the end, Wanda agreed with me. The Pastor deserved better than what our original plan had called for, which was merely driving him from politics and the pulpit.

"I like it," she said when we had it all worked through. "I like it a lot. It's a big career move for both of us."

14

ROY SHIPLEY DIDN'T WANT TO WATCH THE SHOW he had helped set up, which I understood. But on his way back from the campaign he had dropped by to make sure everything was working right, and that I remembered what to do. Not that my part was very complex. All I had to do was sit in the master bedroom watching the monitor in the refurnished nursery, and then turn the taping machine on at the right time.

No doubt I should have felt pity, like one of Archie Weider's liberals. Instead, I was looking forward to it eagerly. After all, this was the Reverend Howard Orrin who sucked millions of dollars out of poor and ignorant people who couldn't afford it, who kept a blackmail file on people who came to him for help, who had harassed at least one pregnant and terrified girl into suicide, and who was using the subjugation of women to get himself elected to the Senate.

If he made it, he would become one more dependable vote for war, racism, censorship, greed, injustice, oppression, cruelty, and murder. And every vote would be cast in the name of our Lord Jesus Christ. Two thousand years ago Howard Orrin, as a good law-and-order man, would have voted to crucify that same Jesus Christ.

I heard the doorbell ring, and Wanda's voice when she opened it, and both voices as the pair came up the stairs a few minutes later. On my television monitor the would-be senator came through the nursery door. I switched the taping machine on. Howard Orrin stopped just inside the door to look around him. "What a lovely, lovely room!" he said. "You have a very lovely home, Mary Margaret, which just goes with a very lovely little girl."

"Shut up," Mary Margaret said, not kidding a bit.

I thought the Pastor would at least look surprised, but she knew her man better than I did. He just stood there, and even looked down at the floor.

"Who said you could speak?"

"Nobody, sister."

"Do I look like your sister?"

"What should I call you, then?"

"Call me mistress."

"Yes, mistress."

"Now take those filthy clothes off!"

She turned away to the closet, where I had put a bundle of bamboo plant stakes I had found for her in the gardening shed. They were somewhere between a pencil and your little finger in thickness, thin enough to have some whip in them. Wanda had said to bring the whole bundle, because they broke.

Orrin was hustling to take his clothes off, hopping and almost falling as he got out of his pants, and then actually falling when his feet got tangled in his underpants.

"Get up, you clumsy brat," she said, her tone icy.

"I'm sorry, mistress."

He got to his feet, naked except for his socks. He had

the body of a ten-year-old, still pudgy with baby fat, who had been enlarged to man size without ever firming up. I never believed that part in the Bible about God creating man in his own image. No God would have taste that bad. More likely God looked like an ocelot, or a Baltimore oriole.

"I'll give you something to be sorry about," Wanda said. She touched his underpants with the tip of the bamboo cane, where they lay on the floor. "Now pick your clothes up and fold them over the chair."

When he had followed orders, she eeled out of her own dress with the speed that comes with long practice. Under it she was wearing the special underwear she had made me go shopping for. "Do you good to learn something about ladies' lingerie," she had told me. "Just tell the man you want something nice in a size ten harness."

Even though Wanda was a good-looking woman, the black straps that framed and exposed her breasts and her crotch almost made her ugly. The gear looked like fake leather even in the grainy TV picture I was watching, but it made the fashion statement we were after.

Certainly the sight of a nearly naked Wanda in spike heels was having its effect on the Reverend. Back in high school we used to call it a lazy hard on, what Howard had.

Without a word of warning, Wanda slashed at his legs with her cane. He leaped and screamed.

"That really hurt!" he said, bent over and rubbing the spot.

"That's what happens to bad boys."

I had asked Wanda earlier whether S & M freaks let themselves get really hurt, and Wanda said some did and some didn't. You had to play it by ear. But she hadn't done any experimenting to figure out which kind the Pastor was. The whistle the cane made in the air was loud enough for the mike to pick up. It must have felt like a hot iron. And while he was still bent over, Wanda gave him another cut, nearly as hard, across the rump. He howled again.

"Get over to that bed," she snapped, pointing with her switch.

He got.

"Sit," she said. He sat, a pudgy, naked, full-grown kid.

"You want some more?"

"No," he said, and she hit him across the thighs.

"No what?"

"No, mistress."

"You're a pig, you know that?"

"Yes, mistress."

"A fat, pink little pig."

"Yes, mistress."

And the horrible thing was that he was responding to it. Her contempt was making him fully erect. I had thought the scene would play funny, but it wasn't funny, and yet it wasn't sad, either, and it certainly wasn't arousing. Just nasty. Worst of all, the nastiness on the monitor spoke to a nastiness in me, and I kept watching instead of turning away and just letting the tape roll. There's a kids' joke: "I saved your life yesterday. I killed a shit-eating dog." Shit-eating dogs are everywhere, and sometimes they're us.

"You remember what I told you about the neckties, piggy?"

"Yes, mistress."

"You liked the neckties, didn't you?"

"Yes, mistress."

"Reach under the pillow."

The Pastor pulled out a fistful of two-for-a-dollar Salvation Army neckties I had picked up on my shopping trip for Wanda.

"Tie your feet to the bedposts," she said, and he did it.

"Now give me your left hand." She tied it to a bed-post, too, all the time making an obvious effort not to touch him any more than she had to. Now he was lying flat on his back with his right hand free. An erection rode the soft swell of his belly. Wanda poked at it with her bamboo switch.

"Start pulling your little weiner, piggy," she said.

She moved up by the head of the bed to give the camera a clear shot at the action. The Pastor was following orders enthusiastically. Now we're getting some-where, he seemed to feel.

A minute passed. Actually probably less than a min-ute, since a minute is longer than we think. Suddenly, for no reason that I could see, the bamboo whistled and Orrin screamed. The cane had hit his right forearm. He strained to grab the hurt place with his other hand, but of course it was tied. The cane was broken, hanging at half-mast. So was Orrin.

"What did you do that for?" he said. He was on the point of crying.

"You were about to make a mess in your bed, weren't you?"

Orrin nodded. He looked ashamed and proud at the same time.

"You'll have to be punished."

Wanda went to the closet for a new switch and came back to the bed. She cut the Pastor free from the neckties with a pair of scissors I had wondered about when she brought them up from the kitchen and stashed them in the bed stand.

"These assholes like sharp things," was the explana-tion she'd given me.

Now Howard Orrin was free, but he just lay there obe-diently, like a beached sea mammal with cellulite for blubber. Wanda whacked her cane hard onto the bed beside him, making him jump.

"Onto the floor!" she ordered. "Down on your hands

and knees, piggy. You're going to give me a piggyback ride, aren't you, piggy?' She swished the bamboo.

"Yes, mistress."

Wanda straddled his back, facing backward, and the Pastor started to crawl. "Faster," she said, and cut him across the naked buttocks in front of her. Orrin crawled faster. Although her feet touched the floor for balance, most of her weight was on his back. She hit him again, and round and round he crawled.

"My name is Piggy," she said.

"My name is Piggy," he repeated.

She gave him a sharp cut with the bamboo. "Don't forget who you're talking to."

"Piggy, mistress."

"Go oink, oink, piggy."

"Oink, oink."

She made him keep saying it as he crawled along. Either the Pastor was in terrible shape or crawling was hard work, or most likely both. Anyway, Orrin was breathing hard and moving slower and slower. He'd try to pick the pace up each time Wanda laid another stripe across the pale moon of his buttocks, but he didn't have the strength in him anymore. After a while he just collapsed.

Wanda got up and stood there with her high heels spread wide as she looked down at the naked televangelist. "One of these days these boots are gonna walk all over you," she said, doing Nancy Sinatra.

"Yes, mistress."

"Get up and put your clothes on and get out of this house right now, piggy."

"When can I see you again, mistress?"

"Want more, do you, piggy?"

"I deserve it, mistress."

"Yes, you do, piggy. And next time you're going to get it."

Once he was dressed, she prodded him out of the

bedroom with the slender bamboo cane. I heard them going downstairs, and heard the front door she slammed shut behind him. I heard his car driving away, and then Wanda came back upstairs.

"Want to watch the show?" I asked.

"Shit, no. I was there."

"Want a drink?"

"Shit, yes. I was there."

"That bad?" I said as we headed downstairs to the liquor.

"I didn't really mind doing it. After all, I'm no cherry, right? What was bad was that I caught myself enjoying it."

"Either that or you're a hell of an actress."

"It came across, huh?"

"To him, too. He was legitimately scared."

"Yeah, and he loved it. I was doing the son of a bitch a favor. Hey, so what, though? Was I right about the guy or not?"

I nodded.

"Practice, that's all," she said. "After a while, you get to where you can spot 'em coming."

"Speaking of which, Wanda. When you whacked him so he wouldn't come, how could you tell he was about to?"

"His balls drew up tight."

"Huh?"

"You know. The way they always do when a guy's getting ready to come."

"They do?"

"You mean you never noticed, Bethany?"

No, I hadn't.

"Jeez," Wanda said. "Men."

"I shook my tail," Hope said when she joined me at my table for lunch the next day. I didn't understand what she was talking about.

"Isn't that what you say? Shake your tail? The big kid with the messenger bike? Hey, Bethany, snap out of it."

I had forgotten about the Pastor's young rugby player who was on temporary detail to Archie Weider. "Oh, yeah," I said, when Earth finally got through to Bethany. "Right. Joel Hamilton. He's still around, huh?"

I shouldn't have forgotten him. I didn't want her connected in any way with what was about to happen to the Pastor. It would have been a major problem if Hamilton had seen me meeting Hope. And we were at the Iron Gate Inn, which was only a mile or so from the ACLU office. It would have been an easy tail for a cyclist in midday traffic.

"He was outside with his bike as usual, so I went out the back way," Hope said. "The cab I got circled the block and we went right by him. I was going to wave but I thought it would be mean."

"Did he see you?"

"He could have. But we were moving and he was stopped, and we turned the corner and the next few lights were green. If you think about it, it must be pretty hard to tail somebody."

"It's practically impossible for somebody alone. Just about completely impossible if the person knows you're there. Weider's got the kid for free, though, and I think he's just parking him outside your office in case I show up some day."

"And then what?"

"I don't know. Get my license number. Try to follow me. Hope to get lucky somehow."

Hope hadn't come by the mansion that morning. She was having her period, which was the good news, and hadn't felt like rowing at dawn, which was the bad. But I had asked her to lunch because I wanted to tell her what was on the Pastor's tape. And what Wanda and I had decided last night to do with it.

"It must have been awful," Hope said when I was finished telling her about the taping. By then we were finished with lunch, too.

"It was a lot of things. Fascinating. Repulsive. Yeah, awful, I guess. This wasn't playacting for Wanda. Afterward she told me that all she could think of the whole time was her first love, Melissa."

"She was the one who got killed in the back-alley abortion?"

"That's her. Melissa and Wanda were both kids when it happened, not much older than Kimberly. So Wanda connects Melissa with Kimberly, and figures a guy like the Pastor is basically responsible for killing both girls."

"Not a concept the law recognizes, Bethany. Retroactive responsibility."

"It wouldn't recognize his responsibility for pushing Kimberly off the Calvert Street bridge either, would it?"

"Nope."

"I guess this is something we ought to talk about here, Hope."

"What?"

"The law."

"Why?"

"Because what Wanda and I have in mind for Orrin, it probably breaks dozens of laws."

"It probably does."

"And now I've told you about it, and you're an officer of the court."

"You think I'm obligated to turn you in?"

"Aren't you?"

"I might be once you did something. It's not an entirely clear point, ethically. Why? Do you think I will?"

"No, but I wonder about putting you in the position."

"Well, don't. I don't believe in the law very much, or at least not always. It's a pretty blunt instrument. I believe in other things just as much or more. You, for instance."

"I'm not following you."

"Well, I've argued before the Supreme Court three times, as you know. The first time I won, the next time I lost, and the third time the decision was maybe sixty-forty in my favor."

"It'd be a hell of a batting average."

"The point is that the time I won I should have won, because my side of the argument was right from the point of view of morality and public policy and common decency and so on and so forth. But legally I was on pretty shaky ground. The time I lost I was right, too. Only this time I was on rock-solid ground, legally, but I lost anyway. Same way with the time I sort of won. Do you see any pattern here?"

"No."

"That's my point. The law is only marginally about justice and right and wrong. Centrally, it's about itself. The only consistency in those three decisions is that all of them are now the law. They were made by the highest court in the land and all of them are final in those particular cases."

"Why be a lawyer, then?"

"Because of the case I won, and the other one I sort of won. It feels good to beat the law, so to speak. Sometimes you can do that by being a part of it. Sometimes you have to get entirely outside of it to make the right thing happen."

I thought I was hearing my name in all this, but I didn't say anything. And she went on. "For instance, I'm with you on who killed Kimberly. In a properly run world her father and Orrin would be guilty of her murder. I'm even with Wanda on retroactive guilt. In a properly run world, Orrin would be guilty of killing Wanda's girlfriend, too, even if it happened while he was still in Bible college. But being an officer of the court means I can't do anything official about either murder. Within the system, they aren't even murders. You and Wanda have a different system, though, and in this case yours is better. Personally, I believe in the ad hoc approach."

"So you come out on Howard Orrin the same place Wanda does?"

"Right. I don't really care what happens to him."

"Thank you, counselor."

15

*N*EXT DAY WAS WHEN WE WERE ALL SUPPOSED to move out so the Kuwaiti prince's agents could take possession of the mansion. Ramadan was still a good ways off, but maybe the prince's son wanted to throw beer parties for his buddies at American University.

Moving day turned out to be no trouble at all. Jeannie slept over with her friend, Priscilla. Wanda and I let the movers in and then drove to Annapolis to see the sights. When we got back to our new address, out by Tenley Circle, the movers were just leaving. A woman from the real estate firm had spent the day overseeing the operation, and so everything was in some more or less appropriate spot. The real estate woman left the keys with us, and left us with our new house. It wasn't as big as the old one, but it was plenty big enough. Wanda called the Orrin-for-Senate headquarters and told Roy where we were, so that he could bring by the day's tapes from the office.

These would be the last tapes we'd get from him, not that it mattered. The office tapes were interesting, but basically surplus. Our new videotape was the ultimate submission hold. We had the preacher in what amounted to the head lock from hell.

Today was also Roy's last day as a volunteer. He had told them spring break was over. It still had a few days to run, actually, but we wanted him safely out of there before we opened negotiations with the Pastor.

When the doorbell rang Wanda went to bring our agent in from the cold.

"What do you think of the new place, Roy?" Wanda asked.

"It's really nice," the kid said. "I guess I liked the other better, though."

"You'll like this one all right," Wanda said. "Come on up and take a look at my bedroom. Bethany here was just leaving. You got an errand, am I right?"

I did, actually. And so I borrowed Roy's clunker and went off to deliver a copy of our videotape to the Reverend Howard Orrin. I knocked for a while at the front door of the house on Williamsburg Boulevard where he was staying. When no one answered, I just found a rock, smashed out one of the two little windows near the top of the front door, and shoved my package through the opening.

The note with the package was in Wanda's handwriting, which of course he knew from the purification pact she had dictated. It told the Pastor to come by Mary Margaret's Foxhall Road mansion to discuss in a civilized manner the disposition of the enclosed tape, copies of which would of course go instantly to all major media outlets if he brought the police into the affair. Mary Margaret and a gentleman friend would be expecting him alone at nine-thirty the following evening.

At nine o'clock the following evening, though, Mary Margaret-Wanda was in fact watching television at our new home near Tenley Circle. Or she had been when I left her shortly before. I had run to the empty mansion on Foxhall Road from the new house. It was not a long way and mostly downhill, and I had given myself a lot more than enough time. I had underestimated William Pearsall, but I wouldn't underestimate the Pastor. I wanted to look the situation over carefully before I showed myself.

So I was sitting in a cast-iron lawn chair inside the open door of the gardening shed where I had found the bamboo canes for Wanda. It was tucked in among hemlocks, inconspicuous by day and almost invisible at night unless you knew it was there. The mansion was a black mass against the sky. My navy blue sweats and running shoes were swallowed up in the darkness. The only thing I could see inside the shed was the paleness of my hands.

The idea had been to draw Orrin away from his house or his headquarters so I could deal with him on my turf rather than his. I didn't really think the Pastor was foolish enough or tough enough to try violence, but I didn't really know, either. And Orrin had a lot of loyal followers, some of them probably pretty crazy. I kept quiet and still in my dark shed, in case any of them showed up.

Nothing happened, though. Cars went by now and then on Foxhall Road, right behind the shed. A couple of joggers went past. Nine-thirty came and went.

At about nine-forty, a car slowed for a moment and then went on. I heard it pull into the next drive, fifty yards or so down. It backed out and came back and slowed again. I heard a voice saying something that might have been, "Gotta be it." The car came into the drive and crunched to a stop on the gravel outside the front door.

A big man got out of the driver's side. The dome light went on just long enough for me to see that there was someone in the passenger seat, but not long enough for me to see who it was. I couldn't really see the big man standing beside the car, either, but he had the size and build of Joel Hamilton. It made sense that the Pastor wouldn't have come alone. I hadn't expected him to.

The big man reached through the driver's side window and the headlights went out. "Looks like nobody home," he said. It was Hamilton's voice. "You want to pass me the flashlight in the glove compartment, Mr. Weider, I'll take a look."

Weider and Hamilton. Very sensible of the Pastor. This kind of nastiness was Weider's specialty.

Sooner or later I'd want to find out what message the Pastor had given them for me, but for the moment I kept quiet to see what they would do. Hamilton rang the doorbell, and then knocked. The shape in the dark that was Archie Weider got out of the car to join him at the door, and Hamilton tried ringing and knocking again for a few minutes.

"No cars, no lights, nobody home," Hamilton said. "You suppose we got the wrong place, Mr. Weider?"

"It's the right number, kid. It looks like the house Orrin described. How many three-story houses with six chimneys could there be at the same street number the note said?"

"Maybe we got the day wrong."

"Something's wrong, but it's not the day. Go take a look around, kid."

Joel Hamilton came back down the steps that led up to the big front door. The beam of his flashlight disappeared around the corner of the house. Weider was still visible, but just barely. All I could see of him from my distance was the lighter spot that his bald head made against the dark door.

Hamilton was probably behind the big house by now, since I couldn't hear his progress anymore. But I heard a new noise, from behind me on Foxhall Road. A sort of shuffling and snuffling, with pauses. Had Weider brought along backup? Were they finding cover for them-

selves now? If so, they were likely to try the shed, just
as I had. I got up, trying not to rustle, and held myself
ready for anyone who might show in the doorway. The
noise continued as I held my breath.

At last I sorted out what was going on: a dog was
taking his human for a walk. The human would shuffle
along unenthusiastically for a few yards and then the
dog would make the human stop while it sniffed at a
new set of piss markers. And so they moved on down
Foxhall Road, man and master. They had made it almost
to the driveway entrance when Hamilton and his flashlight reappeared from behind the house.

"It's empty," he called to Weider. To demonstrate,
Hamilton stood on tiptoes and shined the light through
one of the living room windows. "Not a stick of furniture or anything," he said.

From behind my shed, as soon as Hamilton had first
called out, I heard a woman say, "Come here, boy." Her
voice was hardly more than a whisper, and sounded
scared. While the light was flashing around, she made
no more noise. Then I heard her whisper again, "Come
on, boy, *please*. Home, home. Back home." I could hear
the dog scuffling in the leaves as she evidently tugged
on his leash. Whatever was going on at the big house,
the woman wanted no part of it. Luckily for her, the
dog wasn't a barker. In a minute even the dog's faint
scratchings were gone.

I had barely heard the woman and her dog; plainly
Weider and Hamilton hadn't heard her at all. They were
discussing their problem.

"Maybe we should leave a note," the big kid said.

"Son, you don't know what this situation is that we're
dealing with here, but believe me, this is a situation that
doesn't call for leaving a piece of paper behind."

"I was only asking."

"This is a situation that calls for talking face-to-face.

Maybe they're just late. All we can do is wait for a while and see if somebody shows up to talk with."

"I can't believe this woman would bear false witness against the Pastor. Who would believe her? She must be crazy."

"She's not crazy."

"Satan must have sent her."

"Save it for Sunday school, kid. There's no Satan in politics. There's just the other guy. You've got the seat and he wants it, or he's got it and you want it. That's all there is to it."

"You mean this is political? The woman is working for one of the other candidates?"

"What else? Come on, let's sit in the car."

"I'll be there in a minute. I forgot to check the garage to see if there's any cars there."

"What if there is? We can't talk to cars."

"I just thought . . ."

"Shit, go ahead and check, if it makes you happy."

The big man and his light went along the side of the mansion, and then disappeared behind it.

A moment later, a Metropolitan Police Department cruiser rolled quietly to a stop across the driveway entrance and cut its lights. The car must have been right in the neighborhood when the woman with the dog reported a burglary in progress.

Both doors opened and policemen got out. Like most cops, they had rigged the interior lights not to go on when the doors opened, so as not to make targets of themselves. And they left the doors open, so as not to alarm anybody with the slams. I might not have seen them myself, if I hadn't happened to notice the headlights before they were doused.

But Weider was sitting inside his car facing away from the cruiser. He must have been watching Joel Hamilton. A moment before, Hamilton had rounded the corner of the house, dragging a patio chair. He was up on it when the police arrived and was playing the beam of his flashlight through the dining room window. The light would have destroyed his night vision, and he would have figured that what little noise the police made was coming from Archie Weider. Or so I pieced it together later.

"FREEZE, MOTHERFUCKER," one of the cops shouted. He was crouching in firing stance just behind Weider's car. He was so busy concentrating on the big man with the flashlight that it hadn't occurred to him that anybody might be in the car.

You'd think that a sensible motherfucker caught outside a house by police in the dark would freeze when told to. But Joel Hamilton had been conditioned by a thousand movie and television chases. All that vicarious experience had taught him that when somebody shouts freeze, you don't freeze like somebody sensible. You run, like an idiot. He dropped his flashlight, jumped down from his chair, and ran.

Probably he wouldn't have run if the cop had calmly said, "Would you mind stepping over here, sir," but the cop had watched the same thousands of television shows. Everybody had his role to play.

So did Archie Weider. He was one tough son of a bitch, and no two-bit bureaucrat in a blue suit pushed him around. So like another idiot, he got out of the car on the same side the cop was standing—a cop who was already pumped full of adrenaline and maybe about to try a warning shot at the fleeing perp who had challenged his authority by not freezing. Suddenly another perp popped up out of nowhere, right in front of him, reaching in his pocket and saying something the cop probably never even registered. But I did. Weider's last words before the cop shot him, were, "Who the hell do you think—"

Weider took a step backward and fell down on the gravel. By now the second cop had come up. He looked older, although it was hard to tell in the dark. He acted older, certainly. He stood well back from his partner, and spoke very slowly and carefully. "All right, Harry," he said. "You can put your gun away now."

"I shot him," Harry said, astonished at himself.

"I know you did, Harry. It's okay. It's all over now, Harry. Holster your gun." Harry holstered his gun absently, looking all the time at the form lying dark against the gravel that was white by day but light gray now.

"It just went off," he said, still wondering.

"No shit, Sherlock." The older cop didn't need to be soothing anymore, now that the gun was safely holstered.

"I didn't mean for it to go off."

"Well, it did."

"It went off by itself."

"Will you shut the fuck up, kid, and let me figure out what we got here?"

The older cop shone his heavy Maglite on Weider's body. There was bright red all around the back of his bald head, on the white gravel.

"I thought he was going for his gun," the young cop said.

"Now you're thinking. Maybe he was." The cop with the Maglite crouched down and reached inside Weider's jacket. He came out with a wallet.

"No gun," he said. "Shit. Well, let's see who he was, anyway." They learned that he was Archibald Weider of such and such an address in Chevy Chase, but neither of them recognized the name.

"Hadn't we better call in?" the young cop asked.

"Take it easy, kid. Let's get together on what happened before we have to start answering questions."

While the cops were working on their story, I slipped out of the gardening shed and got it between me and them. Moving slowly in the dark, with my hands before me, I felt my way through the hemlocks and onto Foxhall Road. A streetlight around a bend in the road gave enough light to see by once I was clear of the trees. I started to run, just another jogger in my navy blue sweats and New Balance shoes.

Maybe the cops didn't know the dead man's name, but the reporters who covered police headquarters did. The local television guys were there on the eleven o'clock news, standing in front of the camera as the emergency squad technicians rolled Archie Weider to the ambulance. Channel 9 had called in their top crime reporter, Mike Buchanan, but he hadn't been able to get much more from the cops than Weider's name and that the circumstances of the shooting were still under investigation. But Buchanan had no trouble filling air time with background stuff on the dead consultant.

Roy had gone home, and Jeannie was at work as usual. Wanda and I were alone in the living room of the new house, watching the news.

"This Weider was a real heavy hitter, huh?" Wanda said after Buchanan went off. "I thought he was just another asshole."

"You can be both," I said. "In fact, they go together quite a lot."

"What are we going to do now?" Wanda asked.

"About the Pastor? Just go to sleep, I guess. We'll have to see tomorrow morning whether he decides to go to the police, or Joel Hamilton turns himself in, or whatever."

At the moment all the reporters had was a mystery—a dead prowler at an empty house who turned out to be a nationally known political consultant, and a second prowler who had disappeared. The flashlight he'd dropped would have fingerprints on it, but Hamilton's fingerprints wouldn't be on file anywhere.

If the media people or the police were able to make any connection between the visit to the mansion and the Orrin campaign, Wanda and I would want to disappear back to Cambridge, mission unaccomplished. If the mystery stayed a mystery, though, we might still be able to move ahead with our plans.

We were both up early the next morning, to see what the reporters had come up with overnight. Hope had come by, too. She still didn't feel like rowing, but she had heard the early news on her clock radio. I told her what had happened the night before, and we started channel-surfing.

On Channel 7, Greta Kuz said, "Among his many clients were political figures as diverse as televangelist Howard Orrin and former President Ronald Reagan." Fortunately this was the only mention on any of the broadcasts of a link between Weider and the Pastor. Most of the talk was about his skills at direct mail fundraising and his fame as a dirty trickster for the right.

"Archie Weider was the man you brought in through the back door when your campaign was in trouble," Linda Lopez said on Channel 4, "but you didn't want to advertise that he was on your payroll. It's widely believed that he was behind the false rumor that Michael Dukakis had been under a psychiatrist's care, for instance. And yet nobody will admit for the record that the slain consultant had any official connection at all with the unusually vicious 1988 campaign."

On the Fox channel, Lark McCarthy said, "The big mystery is what Weider was doing at the old Fairweather mansion, which was recently purchased by a member of the Kuwaiti royal family. Agents for the property said the new purchaser has not yet moved in, however, and the house was empty at the time of last night's shooting. A second mystery is the identity of Weider's companion, who is still at large after fleeing when police ordered him to halt. A third mystery is why the political consultant was carrying the pistol he allegedly drew when police ordered him to halt. The dead man had no permit for the unfired .32 caliber revolver found in his hand, and police have so far been unable to trace its ownership . . ."

"Weider was charged with assault for allegedly slugging a Democratic campaign worker during Reagan's first gubernatorial campaign, but the charges were reduced to disorderly conduct and ultimately dropped," Mack Lee said on Channel 9. "He was said to have occasionally carried a gun during his years in California politics, but associates denied he had done so since moving to Washington in 1979. The arresting officers, however, said he disobeyed an order to halt and moved toward them while reaching inside his jacket. When his hand emerged with the gun, Officer Harry Parker fired. Parker, who has only been on the force eleven months, was placed on administrative leave pending the outcome of an inquiry into the circumstances of the shooting . . ."

After a half hour, we had learned all we were going to learn from TV. There would be more from the later editions of the *Washington Post*, but the outlines were clear.

"The other cop, what's his name, Preston, must have got a throw-down gun out of the cruiser after I took off," I said.

"Will they get away with it?" Hope asked.

"They probably will. Who's going to say different? If Joel Hamilton hasn't turned himself in yet, it's got to mean he went straight to Orrin. I'm assuming Orrin would have told him to sit tight. The last thing the Pastor would want is to get dragged into this."

"I suppose you're right," Hope said. "No reason for the police to think that Orrin's anything but just another client of Weider's. Probably nobody but Orrin and Hamilton could make the connection to that particular empty house."

"Don't forget us," Wanda said. "We could. If you think about it, this gives us even more to use against the son of a bitch."

"It does, doesn't it?" I said. "We know whose finger-prints are on that flashlight, and we could tell the cops. That would make it look like Orrin sent a couple of guys to burglarize a house."

"Except they weren't burglarizing a house," Hope said. "Why would they be?"

"That's what the police want it to look like, though. It's bad for morale if you don't let the troops lie their way out of a little thing like killing a trespasser."

"To be fair, though," Hope said, "the officer was prob-ably scared to death when somebody popped right up in front of him in the dark."

"Another question is why Weider popped up," I said. "My view is it was a sort of semi-suicide. Every now and then you see that."

"How do you mean?"

"Like this TV guy I ran across once in Laos, always hollering about his twenty million viewers and their right to know, and all of us at the embassy were insig-nificant scum that better get out of his way. Later he was stopped at a road block in Cambodia, and nobody ever saw him again. I always figured the Khmer Rouge listened to about thirty seconds of his freedom of the press bullshit and then decided to blow him away."

"Those Khmer Rouges were kids, too, weren't they?" Wanda asked. "Just like this cop. Nothing scarier than a kid with a gun. You're right, this Weider asshole should have stayed in the car and never moved a muscle."

"I wonder why he did get out?" Hope asked.

"To let this insignificant scum know what a big shot he was," I said. "Didn't I tell you what Weider was saying when the kid shot him?"

"I don't think so."

"His last words were, 'Who the hell do you think . . .' "

"Maybe you're right," Hope said. "Maybe it was semi-suicide. In any event, I imagine we'll all learn to get along without Mr. Weider pretty easily."

16

*W*ANDA AND I HAD SUPPER WITH JEANNIE, WHO knew practically nothing about our dealings with the Reverend Howard Orrin. All I had told her was that I was doing background research on the televangelist. If everything started to fall apart, the less she knew the better off she'd be.

"These guys will do anything, won't they?" she had said after the news had run an in-depth, for TV, update on the mystery of the dead hardball expert for the far right.

"What guys?" I asked.

"Politicians."

"You think it was political?"

"The guy they shot was political, wasn't he? Or maybe it was those Arabs that shot him. Maybe a slavery thing."

"Slavery?"

"Why not? The guy who bought the place was a Kuwaiti, wasn't he? I heard they have slaves over there."

"I don't know, Jeannie. I like your politics theory better."

"So do I, really. Maybe they were trying to break in and find pictures, like Watergate."

"She was getting pretty close there," I said to Wanda after Jeannie had taken off for work.

"Yeah, well, Jeannie's strong suit is really pastries," Wanda said. She was silent for a minute, something on her mind. "I wonder where Roy is?" she said after a while. "He was supposed to come by a half an hour ago."

"Half an hour isn't long," I said, and instantly knew I was wrong about that. If I were Roy's age and Wanda was expecting me, a half an hour would be impossibly long.

"Could you call him, Tom?" Wanda said. "A man's voice is better, in case his mother answers."

"This is a new side to you, Wanda. This sensitive side."

"Fuck you, too, Bethany. Just call."

Roy's mother did answer, and said he left to play video games a couple of hours ago. Then he was going to the campaign. Presumably he hadn't told his mother he had given notice at the campaign. Presumably he was using the campaign to explain his visit to Wanda.

"Actually I'm calling from the campaign," I said. "We were expecting him but he never came."

"Maybe he's with that other fellow."

"What other fellow is that, Mrs. Shipley?"

"The other fellow from the campaign. The one that called just after Roy left this afternoon and said he was looking for some keys he had."

"Some keys Roy had?"

"Right. I told him he might could catch Roy at the arcade."

"Which arcade is that, Mrs. Shipley?"

She told me, and it was the same one where I first met him.

"I wonder where that boy has gotten himself to," Mrs.

Shipley said. The notion that there might be a problem had finally percolated through. I remembered Roy saying that his mother didn't generally give a damn where he went or what he did. "You don't suppose there's anything wrong, do you?" she said.

"I wouldn't think so. When you said about those keys, it made me think he must be in our other building. One of the guys was looking for the keys earlier."

This didn't make much sense, but it satisfied her. I thanked her and hung up. Of course, I thought now that it was probably too late. Of course Orrin would go after the one person who had links to his blackmailer. Of course the campaign would have addresses and phone numbers for all volunteers. And of course I was a damned idiot.

"I fucked up big time," I said to Wanda. "Roy has disappeared. It should have occurred to me that the campaign would know how to get hold of him."

"The hell with what should have occurred to who. What do we do now?"

"You wait here and I go looking. First the arcade, then campaign headquarters."

"Bullshit. We both go."

"You got to stay, Wanda. Probably we're wrong and he'll show up any minute. If you're not here to answer the phone, I could be running around all night while he's here okay."

"Okay, go. But hurry up."

I didn't know how late arcades stayed open, but evidently late. At eight-thirty, this one was nearly full of kids playing the games I've never tried, even on my own computer. I'm afraid if I once get started I might never get stopped. And my brain would die. It's a danger, like daytime TV, when you don't have to work for a living.

The man who ran the arcade didn't know Roy Shipley by name, and my description didn't help much either. "He would have been here just before supper time," I said. "His uncle might have come by to pick him up. Was there any kid that somebody came after?"

"Yeah, there was, come to think of it."

"What did the guy look like that came for him?"

"Great big son of a bitch, about all I remember."

"Young guy, probably early twenties?"

"That sounds about right. He seemed pissed off at the kid, had him by the elbow. I didn't pay much attention. I figured his mom sent his big brother to drag him home, something like that."

I hadn't seen Roy's old Pacer in the parking lot of the shopping center when I came in. Now it occurred to me that the lot might have been full earlier in the day, and I set out to check the neighborhood. There turned out to be a row of spaces behind the shops as well, and that's where I found his car.

I went back to the front and used the phone booth on the corner. "Joel Hamilton took him someplace," I told Wanda. "At least it was somebody his size, and I don't know who else would be that big."

"Should I call the police?"

"They wouldn't look for him. The two of them might be out getting pizza, for all we know."

"So we lie to the cops. Tell them we saw somebody shove him in a car."

"It's no good, Wanda. Even if they believed us, what could they do?"

"Well, what can *we* do?"

"First I'm going to check every other place I can think of, then I'll go to Hamilton's house."

"How are you going to find out where he lives?"

"I went through his ID when I chased him and the rest of those assholes away from Hope's house."

Next I called the Hamilton house. I told the woman who answered that I was calling from the campaign, and was Joel in? She said no, and no, he hadn't said when he'd be back.

So I went to the campaign headquarters, instead. The only one around was a uniformed security guard, who said the last staffers had left a good two hours before. The Pastor himself practically never came in the evenings and had already gone when the guard's shift began.

Next I went out to the Pastor's big house on Williamsburg Boulevard. No lights showed. His car could have been in the two-car garage, but it had an automatic door and was windowless. I went up to the front door and rang and hammered for a while. I could hear the chimes inside, but no one came.

I went to find a phone and called Wanda again, to be sure the boy hadn't shown up there. He hadn't. "All I can do is head out to Joel Hamilton's house and just camp there till he gets back," I said. "Maybe I can find someplace nearby that I can call from, but maybe not. So if you don't hear from me, don't worry. What am I saying? Go ahead and worry. What else can you do? I'll call when I can."

I found the Hamilton house in Springfield after a while, eight or ten miles away but a good deal more than that by the time I was through with getting lost. Once I located the address I backtracked to a convenience store, and called Hamilton's mother to make sure that he wasn't already inside. He wasn't. Next I called Wanda to tell her I was on station.

The Hamiltons lived in a ranch house development old enough so that you didn't notice for a minute that every house in sight had started out identical. By now there were carports with green plastic roofs, aboveground pools, brick barbecue pits, plastic flamingoes, bedroom additions, aluminum siding, planters made from truck tires painted white, and various other modifications to make each house a little different from its neighbors but not different enough to be, well, different. It was the American way.

The house had a reflecting sign out front that said The Hamilton's House. In the middle of the lawn was a small cement column with a mirrored ball on top of it. It was too dark to see what color the sphere was. The one we used to have back in Port Henry was green, and it looked pretty elegant till my father came home drunk one night and smashed the pickup into it.

I parked up the block, in front of a house that showed no lights. The lights were still on at the Hamiltons'. Probably my two calls had got Mrs. Hamilton worried about where her son was. Or maybe the lights were just on. It was only a little after ten, and the lights were on in most of the other houses, too.

I considered my problem, which would be to get to Hamilton before he could get to his house, and then to get him into my car before anybody saw what I was doing. A thought struck me, and I walked down one side of the block and up the other to see if I was right. Sure enough, there was no bluish light from televisions coming from any of the front windows. This was likely to signify that in the development's master floor plan all the living rooms faced out back. Which meant that the Hamiltons probably wouldn't see their son drive up. And he couldn't park in his house's short driveway, because another car was already parked there. The logical place for him to park was directly across the street from his house, where enough space was free, at the moment, for three cars.

I moved my own car to one of the free spots, which still left plenty of space for Joel. I got various things I might need from the trunk. And then I got into the backseat on the passenger side, leaving my door unlatched so that I could get out without making any noise. Like the cops, I fixed the dome light so it wouldn't go on with the door open. And I waited.

I was lucky. Before long a car with Hamilton at the wheel turned into the street, slowed down, and pulled into the curb in front of me. I was out of the door and crouched out of sight by my right fender almost before the car stopped moving. As soon as I heard the door open, I moved fast to take advantage of those few seconds when his back would be to me. He had his hand on the door to slam it shut when I reached him.

I took the big man in a choke hold, breaking his balance backward so he couldn't exert any real strength forward. He did his best to resist for a few seconds, but then his conscious brain, starved for oxygen, stopped telling his body what to do. The unconscious brain made his feet jerk, in that weird little dance that the Los Angeles police call "doing the chicken." This was the tricky part, holding on long enough to knock him out, but not long enough to cause brain damage or kill him. When his legs stopped jerking, I shoved him into my car.

He started to stir almost as soon as I turned the corner out of his block. Down the street was a church, and I pulled into the parking lot behind it. By now Joel Hamilton was conscious and just coming back into focus. "Hi," I said. "It's me again."

"You?" he said, slow and baffled. "Why? Who are you?"

Before he could get the world sorted out enough to resist, I forced his arms behind his back and wrapped a bungee cord in a figure eight above his elbows. To keep tension on the hooks so they wouldn't come loose, I ran another bungee cord around his neck and attached it to the narrow part of the figure eight. It wasn't much of a way to tie somebody up, but that wasn't the point. The bungee cords were only the first step of another plan.

"What does that sticker mean on your bumper, it takes leather balls to play rugby?" I asked.

"It's just a joke."

"Means you have to be tough, is that it?"

"Kind of."

"You think you're kind of tough?"

The big man didn't answer.

"Well, we'll find out. Tough makes me think of something from the war. One day the ARVN guys caught this VC and they buried the poor bastard alive with only his head sticking out of the ground. So he would talk, you know? All day in the sun and flies and bugs and shit he never said a word, so finally everybody racked out. Next morning, man, there was nothing there, and when they come to look, his head was gone. What happened, they got these sway-backed pigs, they must have come by and eaten off his whole fucking head and the guy was so tough he never even hollered loud enough to wake anybody up. Wouldn't give the bastards the satisfaction, you fucking imagine?"

Joel was starting to look like he woke up in the twilight zone, which was where I wanted him.

"True story, Joel," I said. "I was sleeping in a hooch not twenty yards away."

He spoke at last. "You must be crazy," he said. "What do you want?"

"Where did you take the Shipley kid?"

"He was a spy."

"I didn't ask was he a spy."

"I didn't take him anywhere."

"Oh, shit," I said. "Okay, then." I got some of the rest of the gear I had put in the backseat, a pair of side-cutting pliers and a piece of heavy wire. I cut one end of the wire at an angle, so that it had a sharp point. Then I did the same to the other end. Now I had about two feet of stiff wire, sharpened at both ends.

"What are you doing?" Hamilton asked, sounding the way anybody else would under the circumstances. He knew I could hurt him; I had done it before.

"I'm going to tie you up better, the way the Nungs used to," I said. "You know who the Nungs were? They were these mean Chinese pricks that Johnson hired to fight in Vietnam. When they transported a prisoner, they'd stick a wire through his cheeks and then run the ends through the palms of his hands and then twist everything together, you know? You do a guy like that, he doesn't even think about trying to get away."

Hamilton was thinking about it, though. He was heaving at his bungee cords.

"Hold still, will you?" I said. "I got to think whether to start with the hands or with the cheeks. I never saw them actually wire the VCs up, you know. Only saw them after. I guess through the cheeks first, huh? Hold *still*, for Christ's sake."

Now he held still. The sharpened end of the wire was jabbing into his cheek, not quite breaking the skin but making a deep dimple.

"Or you can tell me where you took the kid, and you can walk right across the street and go home. If it turns out you lied to me, I know where to find you and your family. Come on, Joel. Either you tell me here or we take a ride and I let Roy's sister go to work on you."

I kept the pressure on the wire but he didn't say anything. His teeth were clenched against the far worse pain to come.

"Fuck it, then," I said, when I saw it wasn't working. You can't bluff a martyr. "But let's take a ride, anyway."

I used the wire and the pliers to tie his elbows together properly and tossed aside the bungee cords. Then I put duct tape across his eyes, and drove back toward Washington.

"Well, what have we got here?" Wanda said when I pushed Hamilton ahead of me into the living room.

"I thought Joel here might like our home movies," I said. "You want to turn on the VCR, Sister Mary Margaret?"

"You'll burn in hell, and your lying brother with you," the kid said to her.

"Oh, shut up, Joel," I said and peeled the tape off his eyes along with some of his eyebrows. "Just watch."

"The voice of the Lord is speaking through me."

"Let's see how he speaks through duct tape," I said, pulling out the roll again.

It turned out to be only in mumbles, and even those stopped once Joel Hamilton began to watch the show. Nor did Joel or the Lord or whoever have anything to say once I pulled the tape off his mouth afterward.

I wanted us all to be pals now, so I untwisted the wire that held Hamilton's elbows behind him. He sat silently, massaging the spots where it had bitten in. The cast was off the thumb I had broken, but he still held it stiffly.

"You understand what you've seen here?" I asked.

The huge kid nodded his head to show he did. Tears were shining in his eyes.

"What did you think of when you saw the Pastor jerking off?"

"The sin of Onan."

"Son, we know about the files."

"What files?"

"The pact of purification files. You at the church camp."

"Oh, God, God."

"God doesn't really care, Joel. First of all, you've got to learn not to take the Pastor's word for what the Bible says. Go read it for yourself. The sin of Onan wasn't jerking off. It's a pretty confusing story, but basically Onan's sin was that he wouldn't knock up his brother's widow when his father told him to."

"The Pastor may have sinned, but he knows Scripture better than you."

"Wake up, Joel. People like Howard Orrin have been twisting the Bible around to suit themselves for two thousand years. He's been playing you for a total sucker. How about it? Now that you've seen the video, don't you feel a little like a sucker?"

"Maybe." It was just a whisper, but it was a start.

"All right. The first thing for you to understand is that what you did when you were eleven is what maybe fifty million other kids did when they were growing up. Don't mean a thing.

"Second thing is that the Pastor has got a whole file full of confessions like yours, most of them a whole lot worse. He uses them the same way he did with you, to keep people in line. We're going to get them back from him, and then we're going to destroy them. You can watch them burn. That's a big part of the reason why Mary Margaret got Orrin in front of the camera, to make him give us all those files."

No use telling Hamilton that her name was Wanda. The less he knew about either of us, the better.

"Son," I went on, "what's your understanding of the videotape you just saw?"

"It's disgusting."

"As disgusting as what he did to people like you?"

"He didn't do anything disgusting to me."

"He took a person who wasn't evil and tricked him into doing evil things."

"What evil things?"

"We'll get to that. For now, what did the video make you think about Howard Orrin?"

"I guess that the Pastor is kind of a hypocrite . . . and a liar. A sinner, I guess."

"You see any connection between the video and this antiabortion stuff?"

"I guess I don't. Doesn't seem to me they're anything like."

"You don't see that Life Force and all the rest of it, it's not about murder at all?"

"What's it about then?"

"It's like that video. It's about domination."

"Women dominating men?"

"Other way around. But it's different sides of the same coin . . . Oh, hell, forget it."

It would take more time than anybody had to make Joel Hamilton, rugby player for Christ, understand that sadism and masochism were the same disorder, that both tied love to pain, that it wasn't illogical for Orrin to be the abuser in most of his relations but the abused in others. Better keep it simple.

"Now that you've seen the tape, Joel, do you think Orrin is a good Christian?"

"I don't see how he could be."

"If he's not doing the Lord's work, then, whose work do you suppose he is doing?"

"Looks to me like maybe Satan's. But the Pastor's brought a lot of folks to Jesus. I don't know what to think anymore."

"If he's doing Satan's work, would he really be bringing those folks to Jesus? Or maybe to a false Jesus?"

"A false Jesus?"

"A man working for Satan wouldn't go around admitting it, would he?"

"I reckon not."

"Well, think of that man you saw on the tape. The one crawling around on the floor like a pig. Masturbating in front of a woman who came to him for help. Do you think for a minute that man works for Jesus? Don't you know who that man works for? That man works for the devil himself!"

I found myself falling into the cadence of the Pastor's own broadcasts.

"Think of that young boy you delivered bound unto his enemy," I went on. "What do you think Satan wants that boy for? What do you think Satan is doing to that boy while we're sitting here, son? WHERE IS THAT IN-NOCENT BOY?"

"I only took him to the house, just like the Pastor said to."

"Which house?"

"The Pastor's house."

"On Williamsburg Boulevard?"

"Yes."

"When?"

"Just a little while before you jumped out at me. I came straight home after I dropped the boy off with the Pastor."

"You took Roy from the arcade hours before that. Where was he the rest of the time?"

"The Pastor was never home when I'd go by to let him off."

That was true. He hadn't been there when I was searching for Roy, either.

"So what did you do?" I asked.

"I drove by every forty-five minutes or so to see if he got back yet, and the rest of the time I parked and read my Bible down by the nature center where nobody wouldn't hear him."

"What do you mean, hear him? What was he doing?"

"I had him tied up in the trunk with a rag in his mouth, but he could make these like sounds, you know. Not really talking."

More like strangling, probably, although so far it sounded as if the boy was alive.

"Then finally you drove by one time and the boss was home?" I said.

"Yeah, at last I saw a light. The Pastor answered the doorbell and told me to take the boy around back to the cellar door, so wouldn't nobody see him go in."

Now that the big kid had begun to talk, I got him to back up and start from the beginning. The Pastor had sent Joel off to do some campaign work for Mr. Archie Weider. Everything with Mr. Weider was on a need-to-know basis, and he didn't seem to think Joel needed to know much. Consequently Joel didn't really know what he was supposed to be doing at the empty mansion on

Foxhall Road, except that Mr. Weider had told him to come along while he talked to Mary Margaret. Then the police showed up and Joel ran, and they shot at him. Apparently they hit Mr. Weider, according to what was on the news later.

But at the time, Joel didn't know that. He escaped in the dark and was lucky enough to catch a bus on MacArthur Boulevard. He called Howard Orrin at his home for instructions. The Pastor was disturbed to hear about the police and the shooting, but he volunteered no more than Mr. Weider had about why they were supposed to go to the mansion in the first place. He told Joel to go straight home and stay there till further notice, saying nothing to anybody about what happened on Foxhall Road.

Earlier today, the Pastor summoned him to his house on Williamsburg Boulevard. He gave Roy Shipley's address and phone number to Joel, with instructions to bring Roy to the Williamsburg house and leave him off. The Pastor and Roy would pray together for as long as it took, and sooner or later the Lord would make the boy reveal where his sister could be found. Then Joel would be able to go and find Mary Margaret so she, in her turn, could be cleansed.

"Be what?" I said.

"Cleansed. He said we would cleanse her of all her sins, and probably her brother, too."

"What did you understand by that, Joel?"

"I didn't want to think too hard about it. I guess it was like Abraham and Isaac."

"Did he say it was like them?"

"Not exactly, but he said I was the one who was supposed to do the Lord's work and put the rams in the thicket."

"Did you know what he meant by that?"

"Not for sure, no. Catch Roy and his sister, I guess."

"Well, do you know what the ram was in the thicket for?"

"For Abraham to sacrifice when the Lord told him he didn't have to kill his own son after all."

"And so you were supposed to do the sacrificing?"

"Well, he didn't come right out and say that. I couldn't believe it would come to that."

"What if it did? Would you have done it?"

"I don't know what else I could have done, if he'd have told me to."

"Because it would have been like God saying to do it?"

"Well, sort of. Yeah."

"You thought God would ask you to kill?"

"He's always slaying his enemies in the Old Testament, isn't he? I don't know. I just don't know. It's got to where I feel like my head is all twisted up. That video has got me all confused."

"I don't think so, son. I think it's starting to get your head untwisted. You think you could come along with me and turn Roy loose from Satan?"

"Satan?"

"Satan's got the Pastor, and the Pastor's got Roy. We've got to get them both back."

"I could go there with you, but I don't want to talk to the Pastor. He'd get me all turned around again."

"He won't talk to you. All I need you for is to get him to open up the door."

"All right, then. Only . . . sir?"

"Yes."

He lowered his voice, embarrassed to say it in front of Wanda. "Before we leave, can I go to the rest room?"

"That door over in the corner."

When he had gone, Wanda said, "That stuff about noise in the trunk, I had trouble keeping my hands off him."

"It'd be like kicking the dog. It's the dog's owner we want."

"That's scary shit about sacrifices, Bethany."

"Yeah, but what I think it meant is that Roy is okay for now. It sounded like the Pastor would put somebody else up to it fast enough, but he wouldn't kill anybody himself."

"What about that part where the Pastor was going to pray with Roy till he told where I was? Just what kind of prayer is that supposed to be?"

"That's the part that worries me, too. Considering what the Pastor gets off on."

"Hey, you in there," Wanda hollered at the bathroom door. "Stop shaking hands with the son of a bitch and let's get going!"

17

THE BIG HOUSE ON WILLIAMSBURG BOULEVARD sat back from the road, behind low hedges. I parked down the street and we walked in so Howard Orrin wouldn't be alarmed by seeing a strange car in his driveway. I stood so that I would be hidden by the door when it opened, and Joel Hamilton rang. The chimes sounded inside, just like on my first visit, but no one came.

"You stay here in case he tries to escape this way," I said to Wanda. "You can handle him, can't you?"

"Are you shitting me?"

"Now you and me, son," I said to Joel Hamilton, "we're going around to that back door where you delivered Roy."

The big man was too confused or too upset to do anything but keep quiet and do whatever I said. He took me around back to the rear entrance. There was a light over the door, but it wasn't on. No light showed under the door either.

"Open it," I said.

"It's locked," Hamilton reported after trying it.

"I see it is. You got fifty or sixty pounds on me. Go ahead and kick it in."

"I don't know how."

"Use your heel and get all your weight behind it. The only trick is to aim right above the doorknob."

I did that one time back in my Alaska bush pilot days, when a man who had just fired me for drinking on the job tried to escape by locking himself in the bathroom. The door had exploded open in such a satisfactory way that my drunken honor was satisfied, and I got off with just paying for the door instead of an assault charge.

It worked just as well for Joel Hamilton. The splinters flew and the door blew inward to show steps leading downward. Dim light showed from the basement. We waited at the top, to see if anybody would come to see about the noise. Nobody did, so I led the way down the stairs.

The light was coming out of a hallway at the far end of the basement. As we went to it a frightening sound stopped us. It seemed to be a cry or a groan coming from a distance, although from the direction of it, the source had to be just down the hallway. We heard it again, a little louder, when we had started down the hallway ourselves. It came from behind an odd door made out of tongue-and-groove cedar. It could have been a sauna door, except for not having a window.

"Roy's alive anyway," I whispered to Hamilton. "This is where we save a soul from Satan, kid. Stand to one side of the door so that when he opens it he sees you. Then knock."

"What will I say?"

"Say you're sorry to interrupt but something important came up and you've got to talk to him. I don't know, Joel, just wing it."

He knocked, and a silence followed that seemed to last forever. Fifteen or twenty seconds, maybe. Then Orrin's voice, muffled but understandable: "Who is it?"

"Joel Hamilton," the big young man shouted.

"How'd you get in?"

Hamilton looked at me, and I shrugged. So he said the handiest thing, which was the truth. "Nobody answered the bell, so I had to break the back door down."

"Nobody answered because I didn't want visitors, you idiot. Now go away."

"I got to see you. It's real important, Pastor. It's something awful has happened, is what it is. Real awful. You got to come out and tell me what to do."

"Oh, for . . . I'm warning you, son, you better have a good reason for this or you're in real serious trouble. Now you go on around the corner into the main basement, and I'll come on out and talk to you in a minute."

Hamilton looked at me for instructions. I gestured down the corridor with my thumb.

"Yes, sir," he hollered, and went on down the hallway. From around the corner he shouted at the top of his voice, "I'm where you told me, Pastor."

As soon the cedar door opened the merest crack, I smashed into it.

The Pastor was knocked backward but didn't quite lose his feet. I was in an enormous cedar closet, with rows of woolens and furs hanging against the wall on racks made from steel pipes. Roy was hanging from one of the racks, too.

"You hurt?" I said.

"Not really," he said. He sounded as if he had been crying, and his face was swollen and very red. His hands were cuffed to the pipes so that his arms were spread in a crucified position, but his feet were on the floor so that his weight wasn't hanging from his arms.

"I heard noises," I said. "What was he doing to you?"

"Just slapping me some."

"That right?" I turned to the Pastor. Now he was making noises himself, a kind of whimpering. His hands started to come up, but before they got high enough I smacked my right palm against his left ear with all the force I had. He screamed and fell down.

"Like slaps, do you, Howard?" I asked.

But he didn't. Howard Orrin was sitting on the floor where he fell, crying. His cheeks were wet and his upper lip was slick from his nose running. He might have liked boutique pain, but he didn't like what he had now, the kind of pain that gets deep inside and lives there. Maybe his eardrum was broken. I didn't care.

"Fuck with me even one little bit, Howard, and I'll kick your ribs in. Every time you take a breath for the next two weeks, it'll be like somebody's sticking knives in you. Now get up on your feet and unlock that boy, you goddamned pus bag."

Joel Hamilton was standing in the doorway now. We both watched as the Pastor, fumbling in his hurry, took out the key and unlocked the handcuffs that held the boy to the pipe rack.

The boy stood there chafing his wrists, still snuffling a little.

"He do anything else to you?"

"No, but he said he was going to stick safety pins in my penis if I didn't tell him where she was. You know. Mary Margaret."

"You can say Wanda. It doesn't matter anymore."

"The worst part of it was I was going to tell him."

"You shitting me? So would I."

"No, you wouldn't."

"Safety pins in my cock? Hell, yes."

"Really?"

"Really. And incidentally, Wanda's outside, by the front door. She was hoping the Reverend would run out, so she could Mace him. Joel, go get her. She'd probably like to come down here and Mace him anyway."

"Does she have to come now?" Roy said. "I mean, I'd like to wash my face and kind of clean up."

"Take Roy upstairs and find a bathroom for him," I

told Joel. "Then bring Wanda down here and show her what we've found."

"Joel . . . ," the Pastor began, and then he fell silent.

The large young man looked at the Pastor, and then at me, and then left to do what I said.

"He's found another daddy on the Wabash Line," I said to Howard Orrin once we were alone. The Pastor wiped his nose with his sleeve, like a kid.

"Go over by that rack, Reverend," I said, and he went right over. Anything I wanted him to do, he wanted to do. He knew he had another ear for me to work on. So I told him to click his own wrist into one of the handcuffs that had held Roy, and he did that, too. "My ear hurts," he said. "Real bad."

"Yeah, I'll bet it does.'"

"I should see a doctor."

I took his free wrist, and clicked that into the other handcuff. Except for where the Pastor was, woolens and furs filled the racks around the walls.

"This is some cedar chest, Howard. The woman that owns the house is really rich, huh. You fucking her? I asked you a question. Howard. You fucking her?"

"Of course not."

" 'Of course' is kind of smart-ass, Howard. Don't get smart-ass with me. It was a natural question. Why wouldn't you be fucking her?"

"She's in her seventies."

"You could still fuck her. People in their seventies fuck. Why aren't you fucking her?"

"She's too old, for God's sake. What do you want me to say?"

"I just told you she wasn't too old. Or do you mean she's too old for you? Is that it?"

"Yes, that's it. Sure. Yes. What is it you want?"

"What is it about her age that bothers you? Specifically. I mean, she's still got everything, doesn't she?"

"What is it? What do you *want*? WHAT DO YOU WANT FROM ME, ANYWAY?"

"I've come to help you, Howie. I just want to bring you to Jesus."

"Don't hurt me," he said. "Please, please don't hurt me."

I just stood and watched him, not understanding at first why he was starting to cry again.

"What did he do?" Wanda said from behind me. "Hurt you? You ain't seen nothing yet, if you so much as laid a hand on Roy."

"Come on in," I said to her. To Joel, behind her in the hall, I said, "Close the door and leave us alone, will you, kid?"

"I didn't hurt him," I said. "Not real recently, anyway. I think he just misunderstood. I told him I was going to bring him to Jesus, and he must have taken it the wrong way. We don't want to kill you, Howie. Last thing we want to do."

Wanda nodded.

"You look funny with your nose running, Howard," she said. "I wish I had my video camera."

"In fact, the whole point is keeping you alive and well," I said to Orrin.

"Whole point of what?" he managed to get out.

"Of bringing you to Jesus."

"How much do you want for the tape?"

"And the affidavits?"

"What affidavits?"

"We're getting sworn affidavits tomorrow, too. From Joel and Roy Shipley about the kidnapping."

"The affidavits, too, then. How much?"

"Why would you want to give us money for the affidavits, Howie? We could just get new affidavits next week, and then you'd have to pay for those too. Same thing with the tape, of course. We'd just keep selling you copies."

"What do you want, then? Just tell me what."

He wasn't crying anymore. He was on familiar ground, a millionaire negotiating with people who didn't have as much money as him.

"Well, Howie, all we want really is a relationship."

"A partnership? A percentage? I don't follow you."

"Let me put it another way. We've already got the relationship. All we need now is for you to understand it completely."

"What relationship?"

"We own you."

"You want a hundred percent?"

"We've got a hundred percent. Not money, Howard. You. Think of it like a corporation, and Wanda and me vote all the shares. Or else."

"Or else what?"

"Or else there's no corporation at all. Copies of the videotape go to the supermarket tabloids and the networks and everybody else you can think of. You've seen the tape, so you know. Once it's out, everything collapses, like the PTL Club."

"And you don't want money?"

"No, not to speak of."

"What, then?"

"We'll start tomorrow. Me, you won't see anymore unless you fuck up. Wanda here—that's her real name, not Mary Margaret—she'll meet you at campaign headquarters at ten. Then you collect Mrs. Mulholland and Joel Hamilton and any other appropriate volunteers who might be around and you ask them to start shredding the purification files. Following which you work out a way to tell each person who was in those files that the files no longer exist. Tell them any shit you like. Tell them the Lord told you to shred them, and it's allee-allee-in-free."

"All right. Those are acceptable conditions."

"You still don't get it, do you, Howard? You're Jonah,

and you're inside the whale. The whale doesn't give a fuck whether something's acceptable to you or whether it isn't."

"But it so happens that this is acceptable, so everyone's happy."

"Good, Howard. Now you see the way to happiness. Okay, the next big thing is on Saturday morning, ten o'clock press conference. Plenty of time to make the Sunday papers and panel shows. You drop out of the Senate race."

"Now wait just a minute—"

"I told you to cut that kind of shit out, Howie. That kind of shit is not acceptable to the whale."

The Pastor wasn't stupid. He was handcuffed to a clothes rack, and that was only the beginning of how we had him tied up. His only intelligent course at present was to smile and be agreeable to his captors, and try to figure out what the hell was happening.

"What direction is the whale going?" he asked. "Just in general terms."

"You'll begin to see as we go along," I said. "After a while, you'll probably get to like it."

"Sure you will, Rev," Wanda said. "We're going to mindmeld with you and you won't be able to help liking it."

"Here's the general direction for you," I said. "You ever hear of liberation theology, Howie?"

"It's leftist Catholics isn't it?" he said. "Communist priests in Latin America?"

"Close enough, at your present stage of theological development. Now try works. You're familiar with the concept of works?"

"As in good works, I guess you mean? As in, 'Let your light so shine before men that they may see your good works.' Matthew five, sixteen."

"No, as a concept, Howie. Did the Bethel Bible Institute teach you anything about the historic battles between works and faith?"

"Jesus commands both faith and works. There's no real conflict, it's just a question of emphasis."

"Would you say the emphasis in your ministry was on works or faith?"

"Faith has to come first. For a man to accept Jesus Christ as his personal savior is an act of faith."

"Okay. Now what we want you to start doing here, Howie, is to kind of turn that around in your head. You see, we want you to think about ways of getting Jesus Christ to accept *you*. Do you catch the subtle distinction here?"

"Accept Jesus Christ, and Jesus Christ will accept you."

"This isn't a debate, Howie. These are instructions. From now on, your emphasis is on works. 'Faith without works is dead.' You know that one?"

"James two, twenty-six."

"Whatever. Anyway, from now on, you let Brother Falwell and the rest of the boys worry about faith. Works is where your whale is headed."

"But—"

"But is not a word in your language anymore, Howie. Now let's unlock you so you can get a good night's sleep, be all ready for the big day tomorrow. After the shredding party maybe you can start pulling your resignation statement together, and then you've got a whole lot of other things to get going on. Don't worry, though. Mistress Wanda will be right beside you to help out."

"Every step of the way," Mistress Wanda said.

18

SUNDAY MORNINGS WHEN THE WEATHER IS FINE I like to walk down to Harvard Square for my *Boston Globe*. The Sunday *Globe* weighs about as much as a small suitcase packed for a weekend trip, so the Out-of-Town newsstand is a good place to buy it. Right outside the newsstand are trash cans you can strip the paper into, until it gets down to readable size.

The fliers and inserts from Lechmere's and Fretter's and Bradlee's and Grossman's, and Staples, the Office Superstore, the coupons from Star Market and CVS, all in the can. The real estate section, since I rent. Home & Garden, ditto. The want ads, since I've trained myself to cut down on wants. The employment ads, since I manage to stay unemployed. The sports section. For years sports were the center of my life, but being a sports fan is another matter. Having a favorite team makes no more sense than having a favorite oil company.

Into the can with the sports section, then, and with travel, and weddings and automotive. And with the *Boston Globe Sunday Magazine*, except wait a minute. Look at this week's cover boy, with those once-plump cheeks and that little cupid's bow mouth. And that little gold cross in the powder blue lapel by Armani. "From Anti-abortion to Pro-Orphan," a special report by Susan Freedman.

Saved from the trash, and off I went across Mass. Ave. to digest my load of reading at the lunch counter of The Tasty. Cambridge is a town that gets up late, and it was only just after seven. Except for a cop and a cabbie, both regulars, I was the only customer in The Tasty. Joey Neary, the counterman, greeted me warmly.

"What the fuck do you want " he said. "You fucking retrograde."

"Retrograde? You don't even know what the word means, Joey. Come on, what does it mean?"

"What is this, a quiz? I don't have to know what it means. I just like the sound of it."

After a while we settled on eggs over light, hash browns, and bacon.

"You got it," Joey said. "One cholesterol special."

First thing, even before *Doonesbury*, I turned to Susan Freedman's magazine profile of the Reverend Howard Orrin.

A year ago, televangelist Howard Orrin was the probable winner of a U.S. Senate seat from Vir-ginia—an antiabortion activist who appalled mil-lions and was applauded by millions more when he brandished a pickled fetus during demonstrations.

Today Orrin holds live babies in the $6,000,000 orphanage just completed at Lordland, his religious theme park near Virginia Beach. The former darling of the religious right has undergone a conversion unequaled in religion since Saul, and in politics since Strom Thurmond learned to love his black brothers.

Or so it seems to many baffled and disappointed

fundamentalist former followers. To Orrin himself, nothing much has changed.

"Love's not new," he says. "Charity's not new. That's what Jesus is all about."

Here are some things that are new, though, in Howard Orrin's televangelical empire:

• The orphanage at his biblical theme park. Called the Land of the Little Children, it is already near its planned capacity of 110.

• A pilot program of six nondenominational day care centers in Newport News and Virginia Beach. These charge fees to those who can afford it and are free to those who can't. The first out-of-state center is scheduled to open this fall in a black area of Washington, D.C.

• Well-baby clinics offering free care to needy mothers three mornings a week at each of the day care centers.

Further down the line, Orrin says, are literacy programs, volunteer-staffed neighborhood centers offering help with government red tape, housing, personal finances, nutrition, and health.

"It won't be tomorrow and it won't be next year, either," the Pastor says, "but someday we're going to have a medical school, too. Our dream is to produce graduates specializing in public health and the medical problems of the poor. Tuberculosis, crack babies, AIDS, addiction, stress and depression, malnutrition, that kind of thing."

All this would sound more natural coming from a Jesse Jackson or a William Sloane Coffin than from a televangelist with a history of fundamentalism, family values, and wildly successful fund-raising. Orrin's previous crusades, after all, have involved militant and occasionally violent opposition to abortion, pornography, homosexuality, and the theory of evolution. In fact, these were the themes of his promising bid for the U.S. Senate.

Why did he give up that bid?

"Same reason I do everything," the Pastor says. "Because the Bible tells me so. And one night during the campaign I was praying, and the Lord made it known to me whilst I was sitting in the quiet of my study that I should open my Bible and it fell open to that very passage in St. Matthew where Jesus tells us to render therefore unto Caesar the things which are Caesar's and unto God the things that are God's. And all at once God opened my eyes and I saw that I was trying to render my whole self unto Caesar instead of unto God. The very next day I got out of the politics business and rededicated my ministry to God's business."

What about the antiabortion crusade, and pornography, and Creationism, and all the rest of it? Are they Caesar's business or God's?

"They're God's business," Orrin says. "Were, are, and always will be. I'm not ashamed for a minute of my role in all those battles. But in my Father's house are many mansions. I have been called to change the emphasis of my ministry, not its principles."

Not everyone agrees. "He's reversed course entirely," says Harriette Dorsen, professor of sociology at the University of Pennsylvania and author of *The Electric Christians*, a study of televangelism. "It'll be interesting to see if he can pull it off."

For Professor Dorsen, principles are precisely the thing Howard Orrin *has* changed. "Remember what Attorney General John Mitchell told us about the Nixon administration?" she says. "John Mitchell said to watch what we do, not what we say. Actions *are* principles."

The history of Protestantism in America, according to Dorsen, begins with the country's rejection of the Calvinist doctrine of predestination as antidemocratic. That doctrine held that only a few persons, known as the elect, were destined from birth for heaven. The rest were doomed.

Increasingly, American Protestants opted for churches that gave a larger measure of individual control over who went where. One result was the rise of denominations emphasizing that being saved was in large measure a result of the individual's establishing a one-on-one relationship with Jesus, often without the intervention of church or clergy. Once you accepted Christ as your personal savior you were reborn, so it no longer mattered if you had been predestined for hell before.

"To simplify greatly," Professor Dorsen says, "millions of Americans now believe that all you have to do is love Jesus really hard, and he'll love you right back no matter what kind of a life you've led. For people who believe this, faith becomes much more important than good works."

This is what gives such importance, Dorsen believes, to the "change of emphasis" in Howard Orrin's Church of Our Redeemer Risen. Orrin, almost alone among the religious right, has signaled that works are at least as important as faith in getting into heaven.

The fastest-growing Protestant sects have been strikingly successful in creating a sense of caring and community among their members. But they have not, typically, expanded their services—their "good works,"—very far beyond that membership, except as a recruiting tool.

"That's what I find so striking about Howard Orrin's new initiatives," Dorsen says. "The people he's helping aren't expected to sing for their supper, so to speak."

The Pastor agrees. "If a mother takes advantage of our day care facilities and wants to come to our church on Sunday, we're delighted to have her. But I don't care if she's a Christian or a Jew or even an atheist, if she needs a place to leave the kids off during the day, they're welcome. The only criterion is need."

So far that has been the only criterion used at the new orphanage, too. "A good orphanage is one that's always trying to put itself out of business," says Orrin. "Our policy is to place babies with the best adoptive parents we can find, without regard to the religion of that household.

"We've taken criticism for that, but we feel that the best possible parents are what a child needs, not the best possible parents that happen to agree in every little respect with our own religious views."

Of all the Pastor's "changes in emphasis," this one is particularly upsetting to some of his former followers. "I can't condemn it too strongly," says Harold Grindell, once a top aide in Orrin's organization and now pastor of his own church in Rocky Mount, North Carolina. "Think of it from the point of view of the innocent babe condemned to be raised by unbelievers. By concentrating on this life instead of the next one, Orrin is depriving that babe of life everlasting. I can't think of a more un-Christian thing to do."

Orrin refuses to fire back. "Brother Grindell is entirely right to focus on eternity," the Pastor says. "I hope to meet him there. I just feel like this world is where we qualify for the next one."

This is more than a departure from the Reverend Howard Orrin's typical style of dealing with those who disagree with him. It is a total reversal. This is the man, remember, who once called the national leadership of the prochoice movement "a bunch of she-male deviates who have gone beyond hating men to murdering mankind."

Who once said of the false rumors that Michael Dukakis had been hospitalized for a mental breakdown: "I don't know if it's true, but if it's not then some doctor up there in Massachusetts is guilty of malpractice."

Who on another occasion said that the late Robert Mapplethorpe's photographs of naked blacks engaging in homosexual acts "make a strong case for castration."

What happened?

Many people say that Wanda Vollmer happened. Vollmer, a forty-one-year-old woman with an indomitable Bay State accent, is an unlikely addition to the hierarchy of the fundamentalist Protestant movement. Raised a Catholic, she was most recently employed as manager of a massage parlor in Cambridge.

But little more than a year after she walked through the door of Orrin's campaign headquarters and volunteered her services, she has become his head bookkeeper and day-to-day administrator of the Church of Our Redeemer Risen. She's also a member of the board of directors of CORR, Inc., the nonprofit corporation that governs Orrin's whole broadcasting and business empire.

"That woman was the cause of it all," says the Reverend Grindell, who resigned from the board two months ago. "She poisoned the mind of the Pastor against some of his wisest and most trusted advisers and forced them off the board. She took a fine, upstanding Christian institution and turned it into an I-don't-know-what. Well, I do know what, but I won't say it, thank you very much."

What Vollmer turned it into was an organization that takes in nearly as much money as it did before, but gives a great deal more out. "We'd look at the phone banks before and all we'd see was revenue stream," Vollmer says. "I sat in one day, and it was an education fielding those calls. Half the people phoning in pledges needed help themselves. So we started organizing that, trying to get that help to them."

A part of each of Orrin's programs is now devoted to appeals for help, in the form of volunteers to provide medical services, companionship, food, and even just money for those callers who need it. A newsletter goes to the entire million-name mailing list, in an effort to match those who can give help to those who need it.

"We call ourselves communicators for Christ," Orrin says. "Our goal is to build a caring community through use of modern direct mail technology. You know how the lawyers say, 'including but not limited to'? Well, that's our ministry. We're not limited to supporters or even those who accept the ministry of Jesus, and we include everybody. Jesus didn't ask those multitudes in the desert whether they believed in him before he would perform the miracle of the loaves and the fishes. All he needed to know was that they were hungry."

Orrin agrees with his former colleague, Grindell, on at least one thing: Wanda Vollmer has become a major force in his organization. "What opened my own heart up toward a wider ministry was Sister Wanda," he says. "She's as different from most of the women I'm used to as night and day. She's a lapsed Catholic and a reformed sinner who's been places and seen things I don't even like to imagine. But she's got more of the real spirit of Christ in her than anybody I believe I've ever met."

"She's right behind him whispering in his ear all

day long," says Harold Grindell. "He won't do a thing till that woman tells him it's okay."

"I've learned to trust Sister Wanda's advice," Orrin agrees amiably. "She's trained in accounting and bookkeeping, and she has a solid knowledge of the Bible, so she can pull both ends of the operation together. Make the Lord's trains run on time, you might say. And within budget."

One thing that keeps the operation within budget is a drastic cut in salaries and perks at the top. "Sister Wanda reminded me of what our Lord Jesus said about rich men and camels," Orrin says. "I won't say what my own salary was before, but I'll tell you it's a lot less now."

Sister Wanda isn't so shy. "The Pastor's whole package was pretty close to a half million dollars a year," she says. "It's in the hundred-thousand-dollar range now. Practically all executive salaries have gone down, including honoraria for board members. Practically everybody else's salaries have gone up."

Perks have followed the same pattern, with limos at the top being replaced by private autos and mileage allowances. Lower down on the ladder, there's now free day care for the children of clerical staff, as well as a staff physician and nurse. There's even a small gym with a sauna and aerobics classes, open to all employees.

One faithful participant is Howard Orrin himself. "That aerobics is as tough as anything I ever did," the Pastor says. "Diane's worse than a marine drill instructor. But I'm fifteen pounds lighter for it, and I feel at least ten years younger . . ."

The story went on for a little while longer, but it didn't answer quite all my questions. "Where you going so fast?" Joey Neary said when I set his money out on the counter for him and folded my paper.

"I got to make a call."

"What's that thing hanging on the wall there, numbnuts?"

"This is kind of a special call, Joey. This is long-distance."

"Wow, *long-distance*! Hear that, guys? No wonder he's going home. Our phone ain't got a long enough wire. Lucky if we can reach Allston on the fucker, and Dorchester is completely out of the question."

Back home I put the unread parts of the paper in easy reach beside my La-Z-Boy recliner, opened the magazine section to the Orrin story, and dialed Newport News.

"Sister Wanda," I said when she answered, "this is Brother Tom. I was calling because I wanted my heart opened up toward a wider ministry."

"You could use it, Bethany. Definitely."

"Actually, it wasn't that. It was serious business. Wanda, I want to know something. This Diane that you hired to do the aerobics, would this be a certain Diane Ackerly from the Boston area that you mentioned to me once or twice as being your sweet mama?"

"Same name, but it's just a coincidence."

"Other thing I'm wondering is why you told the papers how much Orrin makes and just let it go at that."

"Instead of what?"

"For instance, how much do you make?"

"Seventy-five. Very reasonable for a right-hand woman like me."

"Plus whatever you can carry home, right?"

"No, just the seventy-five. It's funny, Bethany. I'm starting to believe this shit. It's kind of fun. I'm just working out a deal now, we pick a bunch of high school kids with good brains and bad attitudes, you see what I mean? The kind of kids that don't want to be investment bankers or plastic surgeons to the stars. We help them through college and then medical school, and they run our clinics. What do you think?"

"Go for it."

"I got the first kid already in the program. Guess who. Roy Shipley."

"Goddamn, you *are* having fun."

"It's like a weird machine, this business. You should come down, Bethany. I could show you around. At one end the money comes in, not so much now that we've pissed off a lot of the real hardcore peckerwoods. But Lordland is holding steady, and we're picking up a new element of members that we didn't have before. What you might call your nonidiot element.

"So in comes the money, and then at the other end, out it goes again, only naturally you hold something back for operating, upkeep, capital improvements. Six million bucks for that fucking orphanage, I couldn't believe it. And I rode the ass of those contractors day and night, too."

"I can believe it, if you got it built in less than a year."

"Well, that was part of it, what made it cost so much. Performance bonuses. I bet those goddamned Japs don't pay performance bonuses. Probably in Japan you got to kill yourself if you don't meet your schedule. Try that shit here and we'd be up to our ass in dead contractors."

"Jesus, Wanda, a year in the corner office and you've already turned into Lee Iacocca."

"Hey, once I got the old guard cleared out and my own people in, it turns out it's not so different from running my little joint in Cambridge. Same kind of problems, except there's more zeros on the end of the numbers here."

"How's piggy coming along? Did he mind it when you cleaned house?"

"Not a problem. You were right, the fucker's empty inside."

"Of course you got him by the balls, too."

"I understand that. But suppose you're a Communist all your life and suddenly somebody comes along with a gun and says, Okay, now you got to be John D. Rockefeller. Well, guys like you and me might go along, but inside we'd still know we were really Communists. Orrin, if you tell the guy he can't be a Communist anymore, a minute later he's forgotten he ever was one. Whatever he's got to be, he's happy with it."

"I told you he was an empty suit, Wanda. Just like George Bush. Whatever you stuff inside, it doesn't matter to the suit."

"Well, to me it's amazing that a person can change overnight like that. It's like if a judge sentenced me to five years of being straight and right away I started to get wet panties during Tom Cruise movies. You know?"

Tom Cruise was too much of a stretch for me. But I knew.

"Probably you don't even have to get out the riding crop anymore," I said.

"I never even did that at the beginning. Back then I hated the asshole so much I did something worse."

"What was that?"

"Nothing."

"I don't get it."

"Don't you know the old joke? How the worst sadist of all is a guy who won't beat a masochist?"

"Wait a minute here. You kept him happy by *not* beating him?"

"Yeah. He'd beg me but I wouldn't do it."

"A no-show job, so to speak?"

"For a long time, yeah."

"You mean now you're beating him again?"

"Well, yeah, maybe once in a while I do."

"Why?"

"Well, we work together a lot, and he always does what I say without complaining, and he's actually pretty damned smart. Plus he's a hard-working son of a bitch, and he's terrific on the tube."

"Why does that mean you've got to beat him sometimes?"

"How can I help it, Bethany? I'm beginning to like the guy."

JEROME DOOLITTLE

HALF NELSON

A TOM <u>BETHANY</u> MYSTERY

Coming in Hardcover mid-October from

POCKET BOOKS